PRAISE FOR THE CAIT MORGAN MYSTERIES

"In the finest tradition of Agatha Christie . . . Ace brings us the closed-room drama, with a dollop of romantic suspense and historical intrigue." —*Library Journal*

"Touches of Christie or Marsh but with a bouquet of Kinsey Millhone." —*Globe and Mail*

"A sparkling, well-plotted, and quite devious mystery in the cozy tradition." —*Hamilton Spectator*

"Perfect comfort reading. You could call it Agatha Christie set in the modern world, with great dollops of lovingly described food and drink." —CrimeFictionLover.com

"A delight for fans of the classic mystery . . . Cait Morgan . . . and her husband, make a pair of believable and very real sleuths."
—Vicky Delany, national bestselling author of the Lighthouse Library mystery series

THE Corpse WITH THE Garnet Face

CATHY ACE

Cover image: AleksandarGeorgiev, istockphoto.com
Cover design by Pete Kohut
Interior design by Pete Kohut
Editing by Frances Thorsen
Copy editing by Renée Layberry

LIBRARY AND ARCHIVES CANADA CATALOGUING IN PUBLICATION
Ace, Cathy, 1960–, author
The corpse with the garnet face / Cathy Ace.
(A Cait Morgan mystery)

Issued in print and electronic formats.
ISBN 978-1-77151-165-0 (paperback)

I. Title. II. Series: Ace, Cathy, 1960– . Cait Morgan mystery.

PS8601.C41C657 2016 C813'.6 C2015-907632-3

We acknowledge the financial support of the Government of Canada through the Canada Book Fund and the Canada Council for the Arts, and of the province of British Columbia through the British Columbia Arts Council and the Book Publishing Tax Credit.

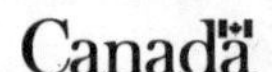

Canada Council for the Arts
Conseil des Arts du Canada

The interior pages of this book have been printed on 100% post-consumer recycled paper, processed chlorine free, and printed with vegetable-based inks.

Printed in Canada at Friesens

16 17 18 19 20 5 4 3 2 1

For the man who put a ring on my finger in Amsterdam

Woman on a Telephone

I WAS HAPPILY NIBBLING ON the lemon and poppy seed muffin that had become my usual weekend breakfast treat when the phone rang. I didn't need to look at the number displayed on the handset to know it would be Bud's mom, Ebba Anderson. As mothers-in-law go, I'm sure she's better than most. Recently married at the age of forty-eight and a half, I have to admit I don't have much mother-in-law experience, and her early Saturday morning phone calls have become as much of a staple as muffins. This time, she sounded distraught when I answered; it's not a state with which she's unfamiliar.

In her gently swooping Swedish accent, she wailed, "He's dead! Jonas is dead!"

I knew better than to respond with more than, "Oh dear, that's terrible news, Ebba. I'm so sorry to hear it. Hang on, let me get Bud for you." I turned to my husband and said, "It's your mom, Bud. She's upset."

Bud didn't look surprised.

"Just a moment, Ebba," I said, and handed the phone to Bud, hissing, "Sounds serious. Good luck."

Bud listened for a moment, then said, "Who on earth is Uncle Jonas, Mom?" He shrugged his shoulders in a dramatic fashion and rolled his eyes. I knew only too well how telephone calls with his mother could run on, so I poured myself another coffee to help wash down the muffin. As I took my mug out onto the back deck, I heard him say, "But you're an only child, Mom. At least, that's what you always said. So he's *who,* exactly?"

The warmth of the late-July morning's sunlight won out over

my curiosity, which is saying a lot. Usually I can't help but want to know exactly what's going on, in every detail, but I was feeling a bit shell-shocked after a particularly brutal month at the University of Vancouver, where reorganization at the school of criminology had led to professors merrily stabbing each other in the back. To my horror, I'd discovered quite a few of the metaphorical knives had been out for me. A vision had been set out for the school with a significant shift in priorities, and my future seemed to hold the challenge of more teaching hours, exponentially more grading, and much less time for research. I needed more than a muffin to make that prospect seem sunny, so I closed my eyes, and allowed our loving black Lab Marty to lick my ankle. Eventually he nudged me into offering him a crumb or two.

"Well, what do you think about that?" asked Bud as he marched out onto the deck, coffee sloshing about in his mug. Marty seemed to think the question was directed at him, and his vigorously wagging tail told us he thought it was splendid, whatever it might be.

"What news, Husband?"

Bud plopped onto a chair beside me and wiped the bottom of his mug with his sleeve. I didn't comment. "Mom's got a brother. Well, she *had* one. He died a couple of months ago. And she never, *ever*, mentioned him. I mean—how can a person do that? Not mention a sibling."

He slurped at his coffee, handed Marty a bit of his muffin, and was off again. "Apparently, her older brother Jonas disappeared from the family home in Malmö in 1946, and nobody heard from him after that. Mom says she always thought he was dead. She says her parents forbade any mention of Jonas after he left because he stole what little the family had of value and snuck off in the night like the thief he was. They figured he had probably come to a sticky end."

I sipped, working at being patient while I waited for him to continue.

"What I can't understand is why she's so upset. I had to talk to Dad in the end—she couldn't stop crying. I . . . um . . . I said we'd pop over sometime later today. That's okay with you, right? We didn't have any plans for this afternoon, did we?" Bud's expression spoke volumes. I allowed him to play through the entire gambit. "We could pick up a take-away curry on our way home. Or fish and chips. How about it? Then we wouldn't have to cook at all. We'd probably end up eating at much the same time as usual, and we could open a bottle of wine."

His eyes appealed to me over his mug.

"Of course we can visit your parents," I said, smiling. "It'll be a nice drive over to New Westminster on a day like this, and a pleasure to be out and about with you in the truck. Maybe I'll have time to run around on the mower before we go," I added pointedly, aiming to remind Bud of the list we'd made the night before of all the garden chores we were facing. "If not, there's always tomorrow, I suppose. Unless I have to do some work. You know, emailing and stuff."

Bud put his big, comforting hand on my knee. "Still worrying about school?" he asked gently.

I responded with a wan smile.

"It might not turn out as bad as you think." He was using his reassuring voice, but it wasn't working. Changing the subject, he added lightly, "Look, we could get to their place by about four, then we'd be away in good time to have a long evening together. Before we go, I can do the weed-whacking while you mow. I know we're both a bit overwhelmed at having taken on five acres, but we can do it. You enjoy your time racing about on the mower." Standing up to peer inside to see the clock on the kitchen wall, Bud was positively jovial when he announced, "It's not even ten yet—we've got almost a whole day ahead of us. We could be done in no time at all."

Since moving into our new house just before Christmas, we'd managed to get most of the interior redecorating done. Bud's retirement from law enforcement allowed him to work on various projects through the day, and we'd thoroughly enjoyed transforming the place. New floors had been laid—a job best left to the professionals—then we'd spent most of our weekends happily painting. We'd even selected and installed some major pieces of furniture and artwork. To be fair, we'd done pretty well, and the house was more than livable; it was beginning to feel like our home.

Now it was time to tackle the work needing to be done outside. We'd clambered the steep learning curve that accompanies buying a property that gets its water from a shallow well rather than a pipeline, and the challenges of revitalizing a septic system that had seen better days. Those basics addressed, Bud and I had decided we'd wait to see what plants sprang into life about the place—we understood the previous owners of the home had been avid gardeners, once upon a time, but they'd let things slide a bit. It was going to be an interesting year because, having bought the house in November, we had no idea what plants were where. Indeed, we'd been wondering what most of the skeletal shrubs, leafless trees, and stick-like plant remnants would turn out to be.

The spring had brought bulbs of all sorts popping up in unexpected places; forsythia had delighted us, hostas had been an abundant and pleasant surprise, and the rhododendrons had blossomed their hearts out, despite looking rather bedraggled. With this being my first real garden, it wouldn't be long before I discovered whether my thumb was green—or the brown I'd always suspected it to be.

Marty had also learned a new skill since we'd moved in—digging for moles in the moist soil of the septic field. He'd quickly discovered how to sniff them out, dig them up, and catch them before they managed to burrow down again. Then he'd toss them by their little paws so they flew for quite some way. Me? I'd learned how to rescue a wriggling mole from the maw of an excited Labrador retriever without hurting either creature.

Sitting on the deck, which we'd spent weeks extending, I was in no doubt about why visitors to our province called it *beautiful* British Columbia; looking around me I saw birch and alder trees waving against a periwinkle sky, distant mountains with profiles softened by a blur of evergreens, and a mass of dandelions in our so-called "lawn."

"Right," I said with determination, "if we're going to do this, let's do it now. I'll finish my coffee, then haul out the mower and get going. I should be finished in a couple of hours."

"You love riding around on that thing, don't you?" grinned Bud. "I think it's replaced your little red Miata in your affections."

I shook my head. "Nothing can replace Maddie the Miata in my heart, Husband, and don't you forget it." With Bud having polished off his muffin, Marty returned his attention to me. "Oh, okay Marty—I love you more than the mower or Maddie, and yes you can have my last morsels. Come on." I carried our plates from the deck through the open-plan sitting room to the tiled floor in the kitchen, placing them so Marty could lick them until they sparkled. However, instead of drooling behind me in anticipation of crumb-laden plates, he took off down the steps of the deck to a little copse at the back of the house.

"Marty's gone squirreling," called Bud.

I popped the plates into the dishwasher and cleared around the countertops, wiping down as I went. "I wonder if bouncing about cutting the grass for a couple of hours will work off that muffin," I called to Bud as I began to make my way to change into gardening clothes.

"Absolutely!" called Bud encouragingly. "Whoa! Look out, Marty's back and he's got a gift for you."

I wondered if I was about to be presented with a squirming mole, but, on this occasion, Marty dropped an exceedingly muddy stick onto the sitting room carpet, and wagged his tail so hard his whole body writhed. His black snout was more than a little grubby, and I admonished him with my usual "Outside toy, Marty," to no avail. He smiled up at me, his pink tongue flopping about, the waves of black fur along the ridge of his back gleaming in the sunlight. My heart—as always—melted. I bent to pick up the stick, and realized it was more likely a root. I rubbed my thumb over it, and, as the mud fell away, I realized I was holding an antler. The bed of it told me it had been naturally shed by one of our local deer, though who knew when; the state it was in suggested Marty had found it buried deep somewhere.

Having washed it under running water to clean it off properly, I carried the antler out to Bud. "Look what Marty brought me. Isn't it beautiful?" Bud smiled. "I'm going to put it on display somewhere, then I'm going to change."

"Whatever you say, Wife," called Bud as I gave Marty the tiny amount of encouragement he needed to follow me to the cupboard where the treats were hidden. Finally happy with the spot I'd chosen for the antler—high on a shelf where a doggie nose wouldn't be tempted to sniff it out and think it was a chew-toy—I made my way to the bedroom where I pulled on a T-shirt emblazoned with the University of Vancouver's crest, threatened it with a few sweaty hours of work, and mentally told my less-than-charitable fellow professors what I thought of them. I was going to enjoy decapitating dandelions . . . and would allow myself to see each of them with the face of a colleague.

The Letter

WE DIDN'T TAKE MARTY WITH us when we headed off to Bud's parents' house. Ebba, Bud's mother, had never seen a knickknack she didn't like, making Marty's tail a lethal weapon in the Anderson house, and he wasn't a dog who liked to stay put for terribly long. It was shame, really, because Bud's father, Leo, loved Marty like a grandchild and always brought him a toy when they visited us. The toys usually remained intact for about three minutes, but Leo and Marty were both happy while the fun of destruction lasted, and I pretended I didn't mind the clearing up.

Soon we were all settled down with a plentiful supply of coffee and Ebba's homemade *marziners*—a concoction of pastry I swear must be ninety percent butter, stuffed with almond filling, and topped with tooth-gratingly sweet icing.

As I nibbled, I listened with interest as Bud took the direct approach. "I hope you won't get upset again, Mom," he said, "but you said you had to tell me about Uncle Jonas, and you had a letter for me. So, while I line my arteries with your wonderful pastry, why don't you tell me all about it?"

"Eat," was all Ebba replied, passing a plate to Bud I knew he'd struggle to empty.

I sat quietly, studying Ebba as she mentally prepared herself. It was clear she'd been crying throughout the day, and she looked frailer than I'd ever seen her. At eighty years of age she was wearing well; her short, sturdy body hadn't let her down at all to date. The bluish folds beneath her eyes told of a sleepless night, and I reasoned if she had a letter for Bud she must have received it on Friday, there being no mail delivery on a Saturday.

Ebba sighed and looked at Leo, her husband of almost sixty years, then glanced around the room, seeming to take comfort from the myriad items that cluttered every surface. It seemed she was reassuring herself she was safe.

"Jonas was a bad boy," she began bluntly. "He was four years older than me, which is a good deal when you are small. He was born at just the wrong time—1929. He grew up through the war years. They were not good years for anyone, and certainly not for Sweden, whatever the outside world might have thought. I remember him as an angry boy. Mother insisted he keep going to school, but he hated the Nazis and wanted to run away to fight in the war. Mother and Father would not allow this. When the war ended he was sixteen, and he disappeared shortly afterwards. I was still not a teenager." Ebba snorted—it was something she did quite often, for many reasons, and usually with no warning. "No one called people 'teenagers' in 1945. There were children, and there were people who worked. That was all. I don't remember the specifics of his leaving; he certainly didn't say goodbye to me, or anyone else for that matter. One day, he just wasn't there anymore. I don't know exactly what he took from our family because no one told me that, but it must have been something important, because of the way my parents acted. I recall whispers about family jewelry, though it could not have been of any great value because we were never wealthy. My mother cried for weeks, and begged the police to find him. But they were too busy with other matters. Those were difficult days for Sweden. He'd been gone for the whole winter when my father finally told me I was never to speak of Jonas again because he'd broken my mother's heart."

Ebba drank deeply from her coffee cup. "That is all I know. Then this arrived. Yesterday. From Amsterdam." She held up a large brown envelope. "Inside it were letters for me, and for you, Bud." She pulled some papers from the envelope, among which was a second, smaller envelope, as yet unopened. "The letter from the lawyer says I must give this to you. Here."

As Ebba thrust the unopened envelope at Bud, he placed his coffee cup carefully on the table and reached toward his mother. I noticed that he glanced at his father, who tilted his head almost imperceptibly.

"What did the letter to you say, Mom?" asked Bud.

Ebba looked deep into her husband's eyes as she replied to her son. "It said what it said. It was for me."

"Tell him," said Bud's father quietly. "Be fair to the boy."

I liked the way Leo often referred to Bud, his fifty-five-year-old son, as a boy, and I allowed myself a little internal smile. I suspect a bit of it showed on my face because Leo added, "He'll forever be my boy, Cait, even with all this life behind him."

I knew the Andersons had always been tremendously proud of Bud's career and achievements in law enforcement, and they'd been supportive without being suffocating when his first wife, Jan, had been tragically killed a few years earlier. They were decent, kind people, who'd moved to Canada with Bud as a babe in arms. Leo's lengthy administrative career in local government, and Ebba's eventual role as a sales assistant in a dress store, meant they weren't suffering an uncomfortable retirement. Both in good health, their levels of socializing put Bud and me to shame—they were well known at the Scandinavian Centre in Burnaby, where I understood Ebba's baking was highly regarded.

"Jonas died a couple of months ago. He'd been living in Amsterdam all that time. Had a house there. I suppose, under the circumstances, he made a good life for himself."

"What do you mean 'under the circumstances,' Mom?" pressed Bud.

Ebba straightened her small shoulders. "The mark on your back?" she asked Bud. He shrugged and I knew she meant the small splodge of a red birthmark at the base of his spine. "I have one on my leg, high up. Jonas had one on his face. It was big. It was all of his face when he was a child, but it seemed to get smaller as he got bigger. At least, that's how I remember it." She seemed satisfied she'd provided a full explanation.

"Was his birthmark a problem for him? Is that what you mean?" said Bud gently.

Ebba replied thoughtfully. "It made him bad. He had no real friends. I remember that. Boys would call out at him in the street when Mother made him take me places. And girls laughed at him. Yes, it made him bad."

We all allowed Ebba's words to sink in. "Do you have a photograph of him?" asked Bud.

Ebba handed a couple of stiff, old snaps she plucked from the pile of papers she'd taken from the envelope. "Here."

I leaned over to see the man Jonas, but what I saw was a little boy in a faded, almost sepia-toned photograph who looked as though his face was black with dirt. His birthmark was certainly considerable. The second photograph showed a man I judged to be his fifties, not far off Bud's current age. He had a build similar to Ebba's—short and essentially cylindrical. This photograph was in color, and showed him wearing a tan corduroy pea jacket and peaked cap. He was smiling, his teeth a white gash in a face that was largely purplish. Yes, his birthmark covered slightly less of his face than it had done when he was a small boy, but it was so significant it would have been the first, and possibly the only, thing anyone would have noticed about him.

"That must have been difficult," I said with sympathy.

"It made him bad," repeated Ebba. "The letter from the lawyer says he was a good man, but I don't believe it. Once you're bad, you're bad. He proved that by running off with whatever it was he stole from our family."

Bud tried to laugh it off. “Oh, come on, Mom. I know rates of recidivism are pretty high, but people *can* pull their lives together and make something of them, even when they’ve done some pretty awful things. It might be that your brother suffered because of bullying, and had an even tougher life because of the times in which he grew up—but that’s not to say he couldn’t have made good later on. Did he marry? Have kids?”

Ebba snorted. “You see the picture?”

“Mom, people *can* look past the outside and fall for the person inside.”

“He was bad inside too.”

Bud’s quiet sigh told me he was battling frustration. I decided I’d rescue him. “Open the envelope, Bud. I’m dying to know what’s in it.”

Relieved I’d provided an escape, Bud sounded eager. “You both okay if I open it here, now?”

Ebba and Leo Anderson agreed.

The rip was loud, the contents of the envelope somewhat underwhelming. It contained an old-looking iron, mortise-lock key with a long barrel, and a handwritten letter. Bud scanned the letter in silence before his mother made it clear with a snort he should read it aloud.

> I know you ‘Bud’ Anderson. I have been watching you for many years. I am happy the Internet has made this easier. Your mother was an earnest girl. I expect she is an earnest woman. I hope your father is happy with her. If he is, he must be a patient man, and maybe he is the jolly one. I am very old. Too old, some would say. I will die soon. It is inevitable. I do not fear death, though maybe I fear dying. I have lived most of my life alone, except for the camaraderie of a small group of special friends. I do not think anyone needs more than this. It is enough.

When you read this I will be dead. I hope it was painless. I doubt it. You will know. They will tell you. And now I have a quest for you. Will you take up my challenge? You must, if you love your mother. It will help her understand me. If she is still alive, of course.

Here is a key you will use to find something very important to me. You must come to my home to see all I have left behind. You must decide what to do with everything, because it will be yours. There are some special gifts for my friends. Please take them to their homes; meet them, talk to them about me, and give them their gifts. This too will help you, and your mother, know who I am. Who I *was*.

I cannot tell you who I am. No man can do that of himself. He is only the person he is because of how people know him, and what he has done. It is time for what I have done to be understood.

I do not know when you will read this. None of us can know when we will die, but one of my good friends had a son who is now a lawyer. He has promised he will arrange everything. I trust he will do as he has promised. If you are reading this, he has done his job. His details will be with this letter. If you contact him he will make the arrangements I have requested.

Bud, can I trust you? Come to my home. Do as I ask. You will be glad you did, I think.

If she is still alive, tell your mother Jonas never wanted to leave her, but was driven away by hatred, and pulled toward something he loved. Until you find out more about me, that is all I can say.

I wish I had known you. I hope you come to know me.

—Jonas.

The writing was that of someone whose hand shook a little with age; rounded loops made with a fountain pen scrawled across good-quality writing paper. His signature was rounded too, comfortable-looking. The silence was broken by one of Ebba's alarming snorts.

"Didn't want to leave me? Then he shouldn't have gone."

"It's an intriguing letter," said Leo quietly. Looking at his son with a twinkle in his eye, he added, "You'll go, of course." It wasn't a question. "For your mother's sake."

"I don't want him to go," snapped Ebba. "Just because a bad man writes and says 'go' does not mean my son must go. You do not have to go for me, Bud."

Bud didn't surprise me when he said, "What if I want to go for myself?"

Ebba rose, snatched Bud's plate from the table beside him, and said, "Then go. I will not stop you. But remember I warned you he was always bad."

"I won't forget, Mom," replied Bud quietly. "Cait and I will go together. There's a lot of upheaval at work for her right now, and there's nothing she can do about any of it. We'll go to Amsterdam for a couple of weeks. It'll do us good."

"It will be expensive, and full of tourists," said Ebba dismissively.

"You know I can afford it, Mom. With my pension, and the compensation I got after Jan's death, I can more than manage. We've each been to Amsterdam before, but never together."

It was news to me that Bud had been to Amsterdam, but I decided to hold my tongue until we were back in the truck, which I hoped wouldn't be long. I was beginning to get a headache from all the sugar and coffee I'd stuffed into myself, but it seemed I'd have to wait a while yet.

"Is there nothing else you can tell me about your brother, Mom? Anything at all?"

Ebba sighed and plopped herself back down into her armchair. "He was good at drawing. He used to draw horses for me." Her tone told me she begrudged admitting this fact. "I might have some of his drawings upstairs, in my dresser. They won't tell you anything other than what I just said—he could draw. He had lots of books he liked, full of paintings. He loved them more than he loved real people."

"What else?" asked Bud. I'd seen him interrogate suspects during cases we'd worked on together when I'd acted as his victim-profiling consultant, but this was a different Bud—tender, encouraging.

"His singing voice wasn't bad when he was a boy. I don't know what happened after his voice broke because he didn't sing after that. He used to sing to me at night in our bedroom, when I was small. I liked it. He would sing me to sleep. Old Swedish lullabies." Ebba's eyes were looking into her distant past and they filmed over with tears. "I wish he hadn't gone away like that. It was never the same after he went. There was a big hole, and I wasn't allowed to ask about him, not even to mention his name." She looked up at her husband. "It was hard for me, Leo. I was still just a little girl."

Leo Anderson slowly pushed himself out of his seat and moved to hold his wife. "Cry, Ebba, out with it. It'll be good for you."

Ebba's little shoulders began to shudder beneath her husband's bony hands. "He's dead, Leo. Now I'll never see him. Never know him. The hole will never be filled." She dissolved into tears.

Bud stood. "I'll go to Amsterdam, Mom—*we'll* go. I promise we'll do our best to find out what we can about Jonas, and we'll come home and tell you all about your brother."

We felt it best to leave, and did so after a good deal of hugging. I wasn't sorry to get away; I felt useless. I hate feeling useless—it's so frustrating. One of my weaknesses is that I always want to fix everything for everyone. And I can't. Life can't always be fixed.

The drive home was pretty quiet for a while. Eventually I said, "When are you going?"

Bud revved the engine unnecessarily. "*We* could get everything sorted in a week or so. I'll check flights when we get home. I'll call this lawyer guy on Monday morning, and we'll take it from there. You know you won't achieve anything by hanging around in your office arguing about these changes, don't you?"

I sighed. "Yes, I know. I'll have to get the all-clear to be away. I can't keep swanning off at the drop of a hat."

"Family bereavement," said Bud. "You married me, you married my family. Jonas is your family too."

I swatted Bud's arm as we sat at the traffic lights. "You know that's not what either of us thinks, about marrying the other's family, but I suppose I could use it to our advantage. Just this once."

"Good. So—fish and chips, or curry?"

"You know how to spoil me, Husband."

"You deserve to be spoiled, Wife."

"I hope he wasn't really a bad man, Bud. It would be nice if we could tell your mom he made a good life for himself."

"We'll see," replied Bud. "Now come on, make a decision, I need to turn right if it's fish and chips."

"Turn left. We'll have a curry, and a nice beer or two, no wine," I said.

"Whatever you say."

Interior of a Law Office, Amsterdam

"HE WAS GOOD MAN," SAID Menno van der Hoeven as he ushered us into his office. "I'm glad you were able to make the trip here to Amsterdam to fulfill Jonas's wishes. I hope you had a pleasant journey. Coffee?" He offered us a seat.

Jonas's lawyer had the tall, slim frame of an athlete and he towered over us. His springy, curly hair was thinning and yellowish gray. Dark pants and an open-necked shirt gave him an air of casual professionalism, though his glow suggested he'd been exercising strenuously just before our arrival. Bicycle clips on the corner of his desk weren't a surprise, nor was the fact that they were neon yellow.

I sniffed the coffee before I drank it. Bud said, "We appreciated you sending a car to collect us at the airport, and the hotel you recommended is just fine. Thanks."

"The Plein Hotel near the museums is an excellent location. You will find it very easy to get about," said Menno, curling long fingers around his cup. Menno spoke English well, with a soft accent that caressed the sibilant sounds and massaged the *v*'s to sound like *f*'s. "It was my pleasure to make the arrangements." He smiled warmly. "Anything for Jonas's family. He and my father were great friends, you know. It is for this reason I want to make everything as easy as possible for you. Now—shall we get to business?"

Menno van der Hoeven sprang effortlessly from his seat as though uncoiling to strike, but all he did was move to his desk, pick up a yellow folder, and return to the chair next to the coffee table.

Opening the folder, he looked at Bud and began, "Your uncle was, I now understand, born in Sweden. I have known him my whole life and believed him to be Dutch. Jonas de Smet, as I knew him, never told me anything about his early life, though I understand from my mother that my father knew about it. I am an advocate in the laws of the Netherlands, and your uncle had all the correct papers to prove he was Dutch. With a family history between us, I will fulfill his wishes as if he were born a Dutchman. This is best, though it might not be exactly correct. The rules governing inheritance in the Netherlands are complex, being based upon Roman and Napoleonic law, but, since he had the correct papers, I will continue to act as though he was properly Dutch."

Bud and I exchanged a puzzled glance over our coffee cups. Being drawn to Amsterdam in response to an unheard-of aged relative's last wishes was odd enough—now this? "Jonas de Smet" had been passing himself off as Dutch and had somehow managed to get hold of paperwork to prove it? I knew for a fact that Bud's mother's maiden name had been Samuelsson, so I further surmised Jonas had also taken a false name; "de Smet" was the Dutch equivalent of "Smith." Highly inventive.

"The first thing I must tell you is that he left everything to you, Bud. His will is perfectly legal, and is succinct. He wrote it in Dutch and in English. I can let you have a copy. You will see it says exactly what I have told you, with the addition that you must make some bequests. If you wish to sell his house, this law firm has connections with good companies that can do that for you, or with you. If you prefer to keep the house and rent it out, I can also direct you to a good company. There is one tenant in Jonas's home. Hannah Schmidt. She has lived in the bottom part of the house for many years. She is anxious to know your plans and has telephoned my office almost every day. I am sure you will meet her. I also have a letter for you," said Menno, pulling an envelope from the folder.

"He liked letters, it seems," observed Bud wryly as he took the long, cream document from the lawyer's hand. "A generational thing, I guess."

Menno looked resigned. "My mother is the same. No email. At least she now has a mobile phone so she can get hold of me in an emergency. She never turns it on, of course."

The upright lawyer seemed to be trying to connect with us. His office, though sparsely furnished, spoke of a successful practice, which suggested a trustworthy legal practitioner. Blond woods, pale leather upholstery, and clean lines made for a bare-bones aesthetic. Two overgrown spider plants on a shelf across the windowpanes suggested he, or someone else at the practice, liked greenery. The only problem was that, although he was saying all the right words, his tone wasn't utterly convincing.

"Did you bring a laptop with you?" he asked Bud.

"I brought mine," I replied. Bud threw me the same withering glance he'd given when he'd seen me lug the thing to the truck we drove to the airport. "I needed it so I could keep in touch with everyone back at the university," I explained needlessly.

"Ah yes, the University of Vancouver. I understand you work there, Mrs. Anderson."

I felt Bud hold his breath.

"It's Professor Morgan, actually," I said as gently as counting to five would allow me to do. "I kept my own name after Bud and I married."

Menno didn't miss a beat. "This is not unusual in my country also. What do you teach?"

I knew the Dutch were noted for their bluntness, but I found the no-frills way Menno spoke to be somewhat off-putting. "I'm a professor in the school of criminology. I'm a psychologist who specializes in profiling victims."

The lawyer's jawline firmed. "So we are all involved with justice," he noted gravely. "Good. That means you will both do as Jonas asked." Blunt to the point of brusqueness. "I have this for you also," he continued, extending his hand to Bud. It held a computer disk. "I have not seen what is on this, but Jonas told me it was a recording of him speaking to you. You can use a disk with your laptop?" He seemed uncertain.

I smiled wryly. "It's old enough to still have a CD player in it."

"Good. You can watch it later, alone. I believe I know some of what it will say. Jonas told me he wanted you to make certain bequests to his friends. He asked me to keep an up-to-date list of their addresses." Another sheet of paper was passed.

Bud took the paper and cast an eye across it. "When did my uncle make all these arrangements, Mr. van der Hoeven? I don't really understand the situation."

The advocate smiled laconically. "Menno, please. We are almost like old friends." He tried to make his smile brighter. "Yes, it is unusual. Jonas approached me about five months ago. You will see that my mother is on the list. My father died three years ago. A heart attack. It was not unexpected."

I could tell from Bud's body language he'd spotted an opening. "How did Jonas die? I have no details."

"He was discovered at the foot of the stairs leading from his apartment to his front door. The belief is that he had fallen, and lay there for at least two days. The tenant who lives downstairs has a separate entrance, so no one had been into your uncle's apartment for some time. The weather was unusually warm. Eventually his tenant alerted the police when—" he paused, genuinely uncomfortable for the first time, "—there was the aroma, you see." He was quiet for a moment then added, "Jonas was elderly and known to be unsteady on his feet. It was unfortunate."

Bud turned toward me and I shared his look of relief—at least it wasn't a suspicious death.

As if reading our thoughts, Menno added, "There was no suspicion of wrongdoing. With you a retired policeman, and you a professor of criminal psychology, you might think he died of something other than an accident, but the police informed me this was not so. An elderly man fell. I am very sorry about it. My mother misses his friendship. She has few people left from her past."

It was odd to hear about the death of Bud's relative from a man who knew him much better than anyone in Bud's own family had done. I realized Menno was probably more deeply affected by Jonas's passing than either Bud or me—or even Bud's mother, for all her tears.

"And his remains?" asked Bud hesitantly.

"Jonas requested no gathering to mark his passing. No memorial. He was cremated. His remains are at a funeral home. You can collect them whenever you choose."

Bud looked uncomfortable, and I suspected he was grappling with the idea that his uncle's ashes might end up joining those of my mum and dad, which were in two urns on the mantelpiece in our new dining room. We'd finally agreed that was where I could put them, for the time being.

"Did Jonas leave any instructions on that matter?" I asked.

"Not with me," replied Menno. "Maybe it's something he will tell you in the recording."

Spotting Bud's worried expression, I ventured, "You said he was a good man. Did you know him well?"

The lawyer's jaw muscle tightened. "He was my father's friend, you understand, my mother's too. He was one of the group of people with whom they mixed for all my life. Sometimes he was there, sometimes he was not. He was, to me, always an old man, though he truly was only twenty years or so my senior. He would bring me candies when I was small, and gave me a watercolor painting kit for my tenth birthday. I was not a good artist, though he tried to show me how to make the colors work on the paper. He was thoughtful in his gift when I married, and made a portrait of my wife's cat at the time. It was an excellent portrait. We have it still, long after the cat has gone. He was a talented artist, and loved art with the same passion my father had for it. Have you heard of the Group of Seven?"

Bud and I both nodded.

Menno looked pleased. "Maybe it was mentioned in the letters I sent to Canada from him for you. It was Jonas, my father, and five other art lovers. They spent many years as friends. I believe you will meet the five remaining members. That was his plan."

Both Bud and I showed our surprise. "I think we're speaking at cross-purposes," I said. "You don't mean the same Group of Seven *we* mean."

Menno shrugged. "I know only one."

"Bud and I thought you meant the Group of Seven Canadian artists," I said. "Carmichael, Harris, MacDonald, and others. A group of men from Ontario who transformed the way Canadians thought of art from the 1920s onwards."

"Wasn't Emily Carr one of the members of that group?" asked Bud. "She's one of British Columbia's most famous and respected artists," he added by way of explanation to Menno.

"No, never a member," I responded. "It was an all-boys club. They only invited non-Ontario guys to make sure it represented a little bit more of Canada, but no women. Emily Carr was influenced and supported by them, even exhibited with them."

Luckily, Menno didn't allow us to get sidetracked. "The Group of Seven I mean was Jonas, my father and five more. One was a woman. You have their information on the list."

"Is that what he did, then?" asked Bud. "Was he an artist? We know absolutely nothing about him, you see."

A faint smile played around Menno's lips. "An artist? As a hobby. He was good, but not a professional. Over the years he worked at many art galleries and museums around Amsterdam as a guard. He never married, so had only himself to support. He retired when younger people were found for the jobs, then he led walking tours of the city. I believe he did this until he was around eighty years of age. Recently he had returned to his love of art in different ways, I believe. He told me he was writing a book." Menno stopped short. Why, I wondered? "I think it must have been about art history."

Menno's tone became a little more terse. He hardly glanced at his watch, but I noticed it.

"Is there anything else you need to give us, or can tell us, before we leave?" I ventured. "I'm sure you have other appointments."

Menno stood and chewed his lip. "I am late for a meeting downstairs. We have a community session this time every week. It is how we . . . give back. My colleagues will expect me. But I wanted you to be able to come here as late in the afternoon as possible, so you could rest at your hotel for a little time after your arrival."

Bud stood. "Thanks for your consideration, Menno. We'll get out of here and call you if we have any queries. We'll see what Uncle Jonas de Smet has to say for himself, read all this paperwork, and keep you apprised of our plans. If we need help, we'll ask." He held out a set of keys he'd taken from the envelope. "I can see Jonas's address here, and I guess these will get us into his place."

Menno agreed, then led us down the narrow staircase and to the front entrance, where we parted company.

As Bud and I stepped out into the warm August sunshine we were assailed by the sights and sounds of a busy urban thoroughfare where trams clattered along and bicycles whizzed past like silent missiles. All around us, groups of tourists were addressing maps or handheld devices and pointing at things across the canal or on the front of tall, narrow brick buildings.

"It's changed a lot since I was here last," said Bud wistfully.

"And when was that exactly? You weren't particularly clear when we spoke about it before," I said pointedly. "Or will you have to kill me if you tell me more than you have already? Was it one of your CSIS-cleared trips?"

Bud hugged me close as a cyclist sped by with a child sitting in a precarious-looking attachment behind the seat. "I was here to liaise with international law enforcement colleagues. Part of the gangbusters team initiative I was leading just before I retired."

"And you think the place has changed a lot in two or three years?"

Bud looked around and seemed uncertain. "Either it has, or I have."

"More likely you, because these houses have been here since the seventeenth century, this canal hasn't moved at all, and I'm pretty sure they've had trams and bicycles for a lot longer than a few years."

Bud scratched his hand through his silver hair—his tell for stress. "Maybe it *is* me, then, Cait. When I was here last time I had an agenda, a purpose. I was with colleagues sharing a common goal. I filtered out a lot of the local color. Had to. I honestly don't recall it being this noisy, bright, and busy. Then again, it was winter, and the light was different."

"The famous Dutch light—inspiration for generations of artists," I mused as we made our way through the busy streets. "This time of year it's filtered differently than in the winter. Even tulip time is gone. It's the bulb-peeling season when the nights are warm, and the days can be horribly humid."

Bud grinned. "That's unusually poetic for you. Know all about humid nights in Holland, eh?"

"You know very well I spent a whole summer here, peeling tulip bulbs. It was while I was at Cardiff University—and, yes, I was with my boyfriend of the time, and a couple he knew. We made it through ten weeks somehow with two tents, one cooking stove, and no money. I wanted to kill his friends by the end of it."

"I won't ask why, because I suspect it's a long story that somehow revolves around food . . . and drink," said Bud, distracted by a window display of hundreds of cigars. "This is an old store," he said, indicating the sign above the door. "Look—it's been here since 1686. Same company. Selling tobacco and cigars. That's quite something when you think about it."

I laughed. "You'd think you'd never left the New World before, Bud. What's got into you?"

Bud puffed out his cheeks and gave my question some thought. "Cait, it's all so unnerving; I believed Mom was an only child, that my entire family history was known to me, and pretty straightforward. Now it turns out that wasn't the case." He scratched his head again. "I guess I'm rethinking who I am."

"That's quite a big thing."

"It sure is."

"And this from a man who's more than a little familiar with undercover work, so used to lying to get by."

"That's different. That's work, not life."

"Sometimes the lines between the two can blur."

"And sometimes they have to be redrawn."

As we stopped in front of our hotel, I noticed how its modern glass and chrome seemed out of place with so many ancient buildings along the street. "Shall we take a look at the CD your uncle made for you, and read his letter?"

"Yes, and let's order some room service. I'm starving," said Bud, flashing me a broad smile.

"You know the way to my heart so well."

Portrait of an Artist Wearing a Hat

THIN CRÊPES, STUFFED WITH HAM and Gouda cheese, glistening with a béchamel sauce, and topped with almost transparent apple slices, sat beside some sugar-dusted pastries on the serviceable desk in the corner of our far-from-spacious hotel room just half an hour later. Bud and I devoured our meal, and I felt a bit guilty I hadn't savored the food more than I had. Eventually we sat back with a bottle of Heineken beer each, and I set up the laptop so we could view Jonas's message.

The screen was big enough to do the job and the speakers more than adequate, so we managed to each get a good view and hear what was said. It was a strange experience. Jonas de Smet sat so close to the camera that his face, and his jauntily angled tan corduroy peaked cap, filled the entire screen. As he fiddled around setting things up, I studied the man's birthmark. From the middle of his forehead to the middle of his chin, covering most of the whole of the right side of his face, was a purple stain. The skin was lumpy and uneven. One jagged edge of the mark rounded his nose, which was unblemished, and the other descended toward the area of his neck below his ear. For a moment it was all I could see, all I could focus on. Had he been sitting in front of me as a living person, instead of as an image on a screen, I think I would have turned away—but the situation allowed me to study him without his knowing it or my being embarrassed to do so. The left side of his face suggested he might otherwise have been a good-looking man. The oddest thing about seeing him this way, however, was that he looked at me with Bud's eyes; despite the birthmark, the eyes were unmistakable. It was an eerie sight.

Finally, digital Jonas settled and smiled. His perfect teeth, surrounded by unblemished lips, were even, white, and a stark contrast to his skin. When he grinned, the right side of his face puckered, but the left side had lines upon it that suggested he was used to smiling. That was the one other striking aspect of the marked side of his face—it had no wrinkles, whereas his unblemished side was aged, as you'd expect of a man in his eighties. The birthmarked side, though uneven, had withstood the ravages of time. An odd side effect of the condition, I surmised.

Tipping his cap at the camera, Jonas de Smet spoke. He had an extraordinary voice. I don't know what I'd expected, but his deep baritone wasn't it. He had none of Bud's parents' singsong Swedish intonation; it was pure Dutch pronunciation of perfect, yet formal, English. He began with a laugh—deep and throaty, as if he'd just heard a good joke. I got the impression this was a natural state for him. I analyzed his every expression as he spoke, while listening to his words. Bud watched with his mouth open just a little, his eyes transfixed; it was as though he was trying to look through the screen to see the man himself.

"Welcome, welcome to my city," said Jonas. "Isn't she beautiful? Of course she is. Her canals, her architecture, her history, and, of course, her art. That is why I came here—for her art. I don't know what Ebba has told you about me, but whatever it was she was probably wrong. Ebba was always certain she was right, but quite often she was not. It's funny how we humans can be like that. I have been the same. I thought I knew everything when I was sixteen, but what I have seen and felt since then—well, let's say I now know how wrong I was about life, art, and love."

The vision of Bud's uncle disappeared as the man moved beyond of the scope of the camera for a moment then reemerged, a thin trail of blue smoke streaming out of the side of his mouth.

"If everything has happened correctly," he continued, "you are Bud Anderson and Cait Morgan watching this. Bud, you are my nephew, my heir, and my chosen messenger from beyond my grave. You have received a key and a list of contacts, as well as this recording and a letter. I suspect you are puzzled, so let me explain.

"If I tell you, in this form or another, about who I am and what I have done with my life, it will mean nothing. Well, next to nothing. I want you to learn about me for yourself, from my friends, then tell my sister what you have discovered. It will be real. It will be an investigation, and I know you are good at those.

"The delivery of bequests will allow you access to the people I have known my whole life. Since I left Sweden, that is. I never went back. It is my biggest regret, a huge loss for me, but I knew it would be that way when I walked out of my parents' home when I was no more than a boy. Of course, at that time I didn't know how it would make me feel. I did it with a light step because I wanted something I could never have there—I wanted to bathe in the light of the Dutch Masters and feel its luminosity on my skin. I wanted to touch the corn Van Gogh had conjured on canvas, and drink at bars where he drank. I wanted so much, and none of it was in Sweden. So I left.

"My father was a brute. He doted on Ebba, but to me he was harsh. I didn't want to become like him. He hated my disfigurement. It came from his side of the family, and he hated seeing what he had given me. He couldn't look at me, so he hit me. Ebba would not know this, and I would prefer she never knows. But she is your mother, so you will decide."

Jonas took a deep draw on the small cigar he'd been holding outside the frame, then winked at the camera. "I have cut down, but only because . . . it is so expensive now." He aggressively stubbed the cigar into what I assumed was an ashtray beside the camera, leaning forward to do so. As his birthmark approached the camera it was as though we were seeing a close-up of the surface of a purple planet. My reaction was to wince; his blemish looked as though it would be painful.

"I wish we had met. You will go to my house and find what I have left and know what to do. I have chosen you because you are a good, law-abiding man, which means you are unusual. I trust you to follow my wishes and do the right thing. The letter you have been given upon your arrival in Amsterdam should be read while you sit at the window in my bedroom. Only there. Nowhere else. It will not make sense anywhere else. Then you will know what to do. Exactly what to do."

Jonas sighed, and sat back in his seat. The marked side of his face showed almost no micro-expressions, but the unmarked side suggested subtle delight. He was feeling smug, but trying not to show it. To be fair, he did a pretty good job of it.

"You'll enjoy the tasks I've set for you, Bud. Success, *lycka till!* Good luck, my boy."

The digital Jonas reached forward, then he was gone. Bud kept staring at the screen, shaking his head. I waited.

"I cannot imagine what it must have felt like to go through life with a face that's so tough to look at," were Bud's unexpected first words. "What would that do to a person, do you think?"

I gave the matter some thought. Bud deserved a serious answer to a serious question. "So much depends on the person, and the family of the person in question—how they are brought up in their earliest years to be able to cope with the way society will treat them. How to deal with the reactions of others. If, as Jonas said, he had a difficult relationship with his father, it might be that the anger your grandfather displayed was the outward expression of guilt he felt within himself. That could mean your uncle grew up feeling guilt, projected onto him by his father, or both parents. If your mother was the family favorite, that could have further embittered Jonas. It's hard to say.

What I saw on the screen was a man who faced the world as though he were no different from anyone else. That could be because he was facing a camera, not a room full of strangers, but I got the distinct impression he was at peace with his looks. He might have worked hard to rationalize that the responses he saw on the faces of people he met were more their problem than his. Given what Menno told us he'd done for a living—working with the public the whole time, it seems—maybe he'd seen every possible reaction to his condition, and had learned to cope with it."

"Maybe his never marrying, as Menno told us, means Mom was right; perhaps it was too much for any woman to bear?"

I shook my head. "Oh, come on, Bud, you know better than that. If one person can get to know another as a friend, there's every likelihood they'd get past the physical aspects and relate to the *inner* person. Beauty might be in the eye of the beholder, but when there's a physical abnormality involved, there's no reason to think there mightn't have been someone prepared to see past that to the man inside. You can see past all this extra padding I've developed since our wedding, right? Why couldn't someone see past his birthmark?"

Bud grinned and stood up. "It's the padding that keeps me warm at night, Wife—and you know I love you. I don't get all caught up in this weight business. Though I get what you're saying about Jonas. It could just be that he never met the right woman."

I agreed. "It's possible he met too many of the wrong ones and kept himself occupied that way," I added wickedly.

Bud's expression told me he didn't agree, but it set my mind off on a different tangent. "I wonder if he had models for his paintings. He certainly seemed to have a pretty forceful personality in that little video, and he's not been short on giving you, and Menno, instructions. He might have used the fact that people were embarrassed to look him in the face to be able to dominate them. Who knows?"

"Not me, for one," replied Bud.

"And not me, for two," I grinned back. "We can find out. It seems that's what he wanted. Even if he wasn't a victim of foul play, I could profile him as such."

"Want to go to his house to unearth what we can?"

"The words 'Pope' and 'Catholic' come to mind."

The Artist's Home: A Sketch

IN AMSTERDAM, BICYCLES ARE BOTH silent and deadly. Luckily, negotiating the bike lanes in Vancouver had me pretty well-trained for this foray into the land where two wheels reign supreme, but even I had to be on my guard. Far be it from me to suggest the people who ride bicycles are all homicidal maniacs, but I began to get the feeling they were taking aim every time I made my move to cross the cobbled streets. And my word, could they shift!

Jonas's house fronted onto a canal—not so unusual in Amsterdam, of course, but it wasn't what I was expecting; it seemed like a highly desirable spot, and not somewhere a man who had low-paying jobs could have afforded to buy. It was an old house, built in the seventeenth century by the looks of it, with a brown-brick façade decorated with white trim, and one of those delightful gingerbread-style pointed roofs. A large, white-painted wooden arm poked out above the topmost window, where I knew pulleys would be set up to allow for furniture to be hoisted up from the street and through the windows—the internal staircases not allowing for the moving of large pieces. It made me pause for thought. *If Bud and I were to take on the responsibility of clearing Jonas's house,* I wondered, *how much of a logistical nightmare might that be?*

The front door was to the left of the building, and up a couple of steps from the street, but it wasn't one front door, it was two—both alarmingly narrow. As Bud and I mounted the steps, one of the elaborate lace curtains at the window to the right of the right-hand door visibly twitched. I wondered if we were about to be accosted by Jonas's tenant, but we let ourselves in without anyone coming to greet us.

Once the slender door was open we were faced with a staircase that climbed before us; it was almost like a ladder and was no wider. "I guess this is where they found him," said Bud gloomily. "I can see how coming down these would be dangerous. I'm not looking forward to it myself, and you'll have to take real care, right?"

I readily agreed. I'm hopeless with heights, and I could imagine only too well how steep these stairs would look from the top. Of course, we had to get up them first, and that wasn't exactly easy. The inadequate handrail had seen a lot of wear, and I used it to help pull myself up the steep and deep steps. Enclosed by a wall on each side, it felt as though an escalator should have been installed. I was panting by the time I got to the top. I reckoned the apartment downstairs must have been on two floors, with Jonas using the top three-fifths of what I'd counted to be a five-story building.

At the top we walked through a stout wooden door and found ourselves facing an opening. Across it hung a forlorn-looking curtain made of multicolored plastic strips. Peering inside we saw a diminutive kitchen, which filled the whole of the back of the house. It looked clean enough, but smelled musty. The front of the house was behind us, facing the canal, and was just one large, open room, with chairs that had seen better days, a few low tables, a small, round dining table with some rickety seating, and another staircase leading back toward the rear of the house directly above the one we'd just used.

"Keep going?" asked Bud. I replied with a short "Uh-huh," hoping I wouldn't pass out before we made it up.

This time the top of the staircase faced an open door to the bathroom, directly above the kitchen below. It was small, containing only a basin and a bath with a shower attached to the wall—a relatively recent installation if the newness of the chrome fittings was anything to go by. Beside it was another door, which revealed an improbably narrow lavatory cubicle. This time the front of the house was being used as a bedroom; the open space contained a bed, two dark wood wardrobes, a couple of chairs, and a dressing table. I wondered if Jonas had picked up the furniture as a job lot. A glass door led to yet another flight of stairs, which we labored up, emerging into a room set up as an artist's studio; the bare wood floor was covered in a mass of dried paint drops of all shades and hues, looking almost like a piece of abstract art itself. The walls were bare brick, and covered almost entirely from floor to ceiling with various paintings, which were also stacked around the walls, making the floor space smaller. Two empty easels stood in the middle of the room, one facing the windows at the front, the other the windows at the rear. A table between them was littered with tubes of paint and acrylic, pots of dried color—which I assumed had once been water—and brushes of every size and description, plus a comprehensive collection of artist's palette knives. Two large boards had been loaded with piles of paint, and looked to have been in use when Jonas had died. They were now a solid mass. It was a sad sight. Jonas had clearly been a man who produced a lot of work, even if it had only been his hobby.

"Eclectic," said Bud.

"That's one word for it," was all I could manage.

Surveying the artworks made me wonder at Jonas's talent; there were so many different types of pieces it boggled the mind. Perhaps what I was seeing was the result of a decades-long journey through artistic expression, or maybe Jonas had just enjoyed "playing" with art. Here I could see Jonas's distinctive signature on canvases that depicted almost photographic representations of bowls of fruit, vases of flowers, humans, and animals. These pieces jostled for space with other scenes reminiscent of Seurat's pointillist preferences depicted in the style of Dali, and Renoir's outdoor frolics reimagined as Matisse pieces. Some looked for all the world as though they were real priceless works by Van Gogh, Breugel, Titian, Hals, and even Rembrandt. That was until you looked closely and noticed a swirl out of place, or a hat at the wrong angle—and the swaggering brushstrokes of Bud's uncle's name.

"Some of these look . . . well, 'real' I guess is what I mean, but they're not. Are they?" asked Bud with hesitation.

"That one over there of wheat fields, with crows?" Bud followed my pointing finger and nodded. "The real one by Van Gogh is thought to be one of his last, if not his very last, painting. A print of it hung on the wall of one of the corridors of my old school, Llwyn-y-bryn, in Swansea. I saw the piece every day for years, and I loved it." I closed my eyes to recall the print I'd known so well and smiled to myself. "Jonas has depicted the painting almost exactly. Indeed, the closer I get to it, the more I can see it's nearly an exact replica—but more than that, he's captured the intensity of Van Gogh's brushwork. However, this one has fewer crows, and they're in slightly different places."

Bud looked suspicious. "Really? Fewer crows?"

"Trust me."

Bud shrugged. "I trust that photographic memory of yours," he conceded, "so I guess that's what he liked to do—make copies of well-known pieces, and change them up a bit, signing his own name too."

"That would legally allow him to be clear that he wasn't intending to create saleable forgeries," I agreed, "though he's done more than that. Look—he's taken the well-known subjects of a certain artist and mixed it with the technique of another. There—that's Vermeer's *Milkmaid* painted in the style of Van Gogh, here's Hopper's *Nighthawks* done just as though it would have been by Seurat, and that's a Picasso version of the *Mona Lisa*. Can you see it?"

Bud bobbed his head about a bit, but his expression suggested that all he could make out was a jumble of bodily components. "Looks like a mess to me," he said, "but you know the sort of things I like."

I certainly did; Bud and I had finally reached a happy medium when it came to art for our new home. "Maybe we'll have time to pick up some good prints from the Van Gogh Museum and the Rijksmuseum while we're here," I replied. "They'd always be a reminder of this visit. All the best galleries are open again—the Rijksmuseum's been under renovation for the past ten years, and the Van Gogh museum only just reopened in May. It's too good a chance to miss. I wonder if they still use those triangular red boxes for the prints everyone seems to buy."

Bud's expression told me he wasn't focusing on what I was saying. "What on earth are we going to do with all this?" He scratched his head. Hard. "If we're responsible for the lot of it, do we just chuck it all out? Give it away? I mean, who would want it?"

"Some of the furniture looks fit for the dump—though how that system works here in Amsterdam, we'll have to find out. And if you decide you want to rent the place out, even then I think we'd have to clear every floor and replace everything, because I can't imagine they have less-strict rules about the fire-retardant qualities of furnishings in rentals than we do in Canada. I haven't seen anything that could possibly pass that sort of test. The bed looks ancient, but probably not old enough to be worth anything. We could have someone come to look at the place from the rental company Menno mentioned to check it over. They'd know about codes and rules, and the expectations of the marketplace."

Bud looked thoughtful when he replied. "Yeah, that's a good idea. At least then we could work out what we'd have to spend to make the place rentable, and know what income it could bring. Or maybe it'll turn out it's better to just sell the place." He sighed. "It's a lot to sort out. I know we only planned to be here for ten days or so, but I'm wondering if that's realistic. Just clearing this room could take that long. And then there's this business with the bequests."

"Do you want to go to his bedroom and read that letter?"

"Sure," said Bud, sounding defeated. "I can't imagine why the thing has to be read there, but I guess we're doing everything else he asked us to do. Besides, I need to get away from this lot. For a large, bright room, it's pretty claustrophobic up here. Tell you what, let's open a couple of the windows on every floor and get a bit of a through-draft going. It might freshen things up a bit. We'll meet back in the bedroom. I'll let you do this one, and I'll tackle downstairs."

A few minutes later I was perched on a stool designed for someone a good deal taller than me, while Bud was on a low ottoman. We were in Jonas's bedroom and ready to read the letter he'd written for Bud. I was anxious to know what Jonas had saved up for this set of what would undoubtedly end up being instructions.

"In the video he said I was to read this letter next to the window in his bedroom," said Bud. "I'm right beneath the four windows, so I hope the letter will make sense. Here goes."

As Bud carefully opened the envelope I said, "Aloud, please, so we can both be told what to do at the same time."

"Okay."

> For Bud, my heir—my hands, feet, eyes, and ears: I rely upon you from now on. Thank you for doing all you have done so far, and for what you will do. You are now in my home. I hope it looks appealing. Maybe you think I lived a boring life, or maybe you have already seen my studio. This is the only part of my home that will show you the real me. The rest of the house? Just somewhere for my body to be taken care of. In my studio you will see how my spirit lived. If you have done as I have asked, you are in my bedroom, at the windows. Look ahead of you. You see the wall has three paintings on it. They are all portraits of my good friends.

Bud and I looked up. Two of the three portraits in question were about a couple of feet square, but the one in the center was much bigger. All three portraits carried Jonas's clear and distinctive signature, and each showed a well-known portrait but with the face of the subject changed.

Bud stood, I jumped down from my perch, and we both walked the few steps it took to be able to examine the paintings more closely. Bud peered, and I closed my eyes to recall the original works in a sort of snapshot, then looked at Jonas's work.

"He's captured the originals to a T," I said quietly. "He was an extremely talented artist. The styles, the brush strokes, even the rendering of the 'replacement' faces—they're all exquisite."

"As you know, I'm no expert," replied Bud, "but these even look old. Look—they've got the crackly stuff all over them."

"The aged varnish. You're right. I wonder how he managed that. Without the faces you'd think these were the real thing, though of course everyone knows where the real ones are. You know, in galleries and so forth, like the ones upstairs. What else does the letter say?"

> These portraits are gifts for the people in them—or for their families. The names of the people portrayed are on the back of the paintings. They might not care for the frames, but I hope they enjoy the work I put into them. The woman is Greta van Burken, shown as Rembrandt's *Juno*; the man on the right, shown as Van Gogh from his self-portrait, is Pieter van Boxtel; the other is a portrait of my best friend in the Group, Willem Weenix, as Frans Hals' *Laughing Cavalier*. In my studio you will find more portraits. For Dirk van der Hoeven, my lawyer's father, I could not resist making him the sullen *Doctor Gachet*,

> as portrayed by Van Gogh. This piece will now be for his family to remember him by, because he died some years ago. Bernard de Klerk I painted as the courting man in the Vermeer piece *The Glass of Wine*. If I say it myself, I am proud of this work. It took me a great deal of time; Vermeer was a master—I am not. Then there's Johannes Akker; I also used the work of his namesake, Vermeer, for him—he is *The Geographer*. My desire is that each person has their own portrait. You will do this for me. The large portrait will not be easy to transport, but it will be worth it.

"Great," said Bud. "This big one's going to be a nightmare to get down the stairs, let alone anywhere else."

"We'll manage somehow," I said. "Now come on, what else is there?"

> Each person will also have one more painting from my collection. One of my recent works. I have labeled them, on the back of each one. I am sure you will find them. I hope you enjoy the search. When all of this is done, then I ask you to select a piece of my work for my little sister Ebba, and one for her husband, Leo. The rest? That is for you to decide. But do not make that decision until you have done all I have asked of you. I hope you understand, one day, why I say this.

"He does think rather highly of his own opinions," I couldn't resist saying.

"Pot? Kettle?" quipped Bud, then he grinned. "The elderly can be like that, determined to have their own way—even after death, it seems. Nearly done." He continued to read.

> My life has been interesting. I have worked, traveled, loved, hated, and through everything I have painted. If all that is left is that which I have painted, the rest will have to be guessed at. This is my legacy. Do as you wish with my house, but be mindful of Hannah, my tenant. One of my new paintings is for her, and there is a portrait of her also. You will find it easily. She can be surly, but be kind to her; she has lived a difficult life. If you decide to sell my home, be sure of what will happen to Hannah before you do it. Every house has its history, this one more than most. You would do well to be certain you have found out all of its stories before you pass it to someone outside the family. It feels strange for me to write that word; I have never had a family, because I walked away from it, so I made my own—with my friends. I wish I could be walking at your side, but my time is over.

"That's it?" Bud sounded surprised. "It doesn't seem there's much more to do than we originally thought—just a few items to deliver to half a dozen addresses, and we already had those from Menno. If we launch into hunting out the pictures he's labeled up in the studio, we might have everything we need today, and we could just splash out to rent a cab to take us from one place to another tomorrow. Then we could get together with the house-rental guy and come up with a plan. We'd have time for galleries, walks, perhaps even a concert or two."

My spirits lifted. "It's the Concertgebouw's 125th anniversary this year. They might have something good on. We'll have left before they have the Royal Concertgebouw Orchestra performance on the twenty-sixth of August, but I happen to know they have the Australian Youth

Orchestra and Joshua Bell playing the Tchaikovsky Violin Concerto on the thirteenth. That's tomorrow, isn't it?"

Bud checked his wristwatch. "Yep, tomorrow. I'm a bit muddled up myself. But a youth orchestra?" His wrinkled nose told me he didn't think much of the idea.

"Having been in youth theater, and youth choirs singing with a youth orchestra myself, I'm going to leap to their defense. The enthusiasm, the tone, and the dedication can be of the highest level, and if this is representative of Australia's best, they're probably very good."

"Even so, there might be something else. Tell you what, let's crack on with what we have to do, then we can play around with what we want to do. I fancy the idea of the Bimhuis."

I know I tutted aloud, because Bud's face told me he'd heard it. I'd never known him to listen to anything other than classic rock music, hence my puzzlement at his enthusiasm to visit Amsterdam's world-famous jazz venue. "Why there, all of a sudden? I went to the original one back in the eighties, and I'm not sure it's your sort of place. I know it's now housed in a new building, but still . . . you? Jazz? Really?"

"I went there the last time I was here. Great place, out on the waterfront with a big deck, and a good setup inside," was all he said.

"And there was me thinking it had been all business when you were here."

"We needed to get away from the meetings and the intensity of it all. But come on, let's not dawdle—the sooner we start, the sooner we finish. Race you up the stairs to the studio," he said, but I held up my hand to stop him running off.

"I know we need to do stuff up there, but you could do it while I have a good look around Jonas's home and build a bit of a profile of the man—in my own way."

Bud looked thoughtful, then agreed. "That's a good idea. Come up and tell me all about my uncle when you're done?"

I smiled at him. Bud likes to think he has enough control over his eyebrows to make them as effective as mine, but he always looks drunk when he tries to raise just one of them. I allowed him his moment and said, “Very well. I’ll be as efficient as possible.”

The Artist's Home and Studio: A Detailed Study

HAVING SPENT ABOUT FORTY-FIVE MINUTES acquainting myself with Jonas de Smet's belongings and lifestyle, I finally clambered up the steep stairs to join my husband, who'd been clattering about in the attic for the whole time. I was delighted to see he'd made some considerable headway. A collection of canvases was stacked neatly against one wall, which he'd cleared of other paintings.

"Have you found every piece Jonas wrote about?" I asked, then sneezed four times. Bud's efforts had released clouds of dust into the air, and I could tell it was going to affect me for a while.

"All but three," he replied, looking rather pleased with himself. "I'll take the chance to have a bit of a breather while you fill me in on what you've found out about Jonas in your searches, then I'll tackle this last wall. The missing pieces must be hidden in here somewhere—it's the only section I haven't been through yet."

Bud perched himself on the only rickety chair in the space, which sat in front of an empty easel. The fading sunlight streamed through the window at the front of the house and gave his silver hair the look of a halo. His face was in shadow, which made me think of his uncle's birthmark.

"First things first," I said, holding a photograph in a silver frame so Bud could see it. "Any idea who this might be? Seen him in any of the paintings up here?"

Bud took the frame and peered at it, shifting it about to get rid of reflections. He smiled. "I've seen a lot of this guy. His face appears time and time again, from when he was a young man until he was really quite old. But he isn't one of the guys on the list—at least, I don't think he is because I haven't found the paintings of *The Geographer* or *The Glass of Wine* yet, so I guess he could be one of those two guys. Why? Where was this?"

"This, and about ten others of the same person, were all in the drawer of his bedside table. This was the only one in a frame. The others looked as though they'd been handled a great deal. They show the same man at many ages, and always in the same setting; a dark, curtained background. In each of them he's simply looking directly at the camera, smiling. The photos are quite—well, disarming, I suppose. They show the man in an open and honest way, but he's not displaying any real emotion. Is it possible Jonas was gay? Maybe it was a part of his psyche that he couldn't deal with when he was young, a contributing factor to his leaving his family. It's not unusual even nowadays, and back in the forties I dare say it was even more of a challenge for a young man to come to terms with his sexuality. If he had no friends, as your mother said, and his father was already beating him, it's likely he had no one to turn to."

Bud shook his head. "No idea, Cait. That would be more your department. Find anything else that throws light on his life—any part of it?"

"Lots. Where would you like me to begin?"

Bud shrugged. "How about you do it like you used to when you consulted for my homicide team? That usually worked quite well. You choose—general to specific, or vice versa."

"Okay," I replied, sinking onto a shabbily upholstered chaise longue, "if you're comfortably perched then I'll begin."

Bud settled himself more steadily, and I began to tell him what I'd discovered. "Whatever his sexual preferences, he lived alone, that's quite clear, and I don't get the impression he entertained. He has one or two of most eating and drinking requirements, and no stash of glasses or plates to cater for company. There's the possibility people would visit and bring their own supplies, but that seems unlikely. His bed tells me he slept alone, and favored the middle of the bed. It's an old bed with an old mattress, and the indentations make that much clear. He was generally clean and neat; unlike this room, his clothes, accessories, and so forth are all washed, pressed, and neatly hung or folded. He didn't have many clothes—in fact, surprisingly few—but even those covered in remnants of paint are freshly laundered. There's no way for him to have done that here, unless he washed by hand in either the kitchen or bathroom sinks, which seems unlikely. His toiletries speak of a man who shaved, kept his teeth clean, and showered rather than bathed. His towels are old and worn, unmatched, but clean. There are a lot of them, which might suggest he used them only once, or showered often. As I said, he didn't have many clothes, but those he had were well made, and old. Some darning and mending has been done on some items, not terribly well. He liked hats—he had about a dozen—and favored caps made of corduroy. He had almost as many outdoor coats as pairs of pants, which suggests a life spent outside a good deal, even in heavy rain or low temperatures, as signified by the rubberized waterproofs and heavy winter coats. Stout shoes, rubber boots, snow boots, and sandals were his choice of footwear—again, all well made, but worn. I'd say he invested in his clothing—none of it is what you'd call fashionable, but the chap was in his eighties after all, so I'd suggest he'd bought good clothes in his sixties, and had kept them going."

"Sensible way to be," said Bud, who has been known to invent bizarre ailments just to avoid going shopping for clothes.

"Yes, dear," I countered, drawing a smile. "Other than the familial similarity in your attitude toward clothing, there's not much else to suggest anything of a lifestyle that took him away from his love of art. I'd say Menno's summary of his life is borne out by what I have seen here."

"Did you think Menno wasn't telling the truth about Jonas's life?" Bud sounded surprised.

I decided to come clean. "I get it that the Dutch are blunt, but Menno seemed disconnected from emotion when he spoke about Jonas. His micro-expressions suggested he was concealing either facts or at least an emotion he didn't want us to observe. He might have been acting in a culturally normal way, and yet he was still hiding . . . something."

Bud looked thoughtful. "I didn't get that from the guy at all, and even though we have our differences, we're not usually that far apart when we're assessing someone. It could be that I've let my cop senses dissipate a bit since I retired. I wasn't focusing on whether he was telling the truth. Why were you?"

I paused for a millisecond. "I always do, can't help myself. Is that bad?"

Bud smiled warmly. "Not bad, but a bit sad, Cait. Sometimes I wish you could just relax and swim with the current. Like all that stuff going on back at home. You need to let go and wait to find out what the real plans are for your department."

"Not now, Bud. Let's focus on this, please?"

"Okay, agreed. So, you think Menno van der Hoeven was hiding something, and you don't trust him, right?"

I shrugged. "Afraid so."

"Leaving that aside for a moment, did you spot anything here that might suggest there's more to Uncle Jonas than Menno told us?"

"Menno mentioned that Jonas said he was writing a book. There's no computer here, and I can't find anything that looks like a handwritten manuscript, which is odd, if Menno was telling the truth."

"What if Jonas wasn't telling Menno the truth?"

"Fair enough. However, there should be a computer, surely? In the letter from Jonas we read in Canada, he mentioned using the Internet had made it easier for him to follow news about you. So where is his computer? All I found was half a charger cable."

"Half?"

"You know, they come in two pieces—one part has the transformer on it and hooks into the computer, the other part goes to the power outlet. All I found was half a cable, under his dining table, coming out of the power outlet. It suggests to me that someone removed a computer and part of the cable, not realizing that another part of the cable remained in the wall."

"Find anything that looks as though it might be opened by our mystery key?" Bud stood up and arched his back like a cat—I suspected he'd been bending for some time.

"Nothing. No boxes, cupboards, not even a locked drawer. Did you bring it with you?" I asked.

Bud thrust his hand deep into the pocket of his khaki pants and pulled out the key. Once again I was struck by how small the turning end and opening end were when compared with the length of the barrel. I took the key from Bud and rolled it in my hand.

"It had to be designed to fit into a lock deeply set within something," I said.

"We already agreed on that back in Canada, before we left," replied Bud, now stretching his arms above his head. "It doesn't mean we're any closer to finding out what it opens. Have you checked the locks on all the doors here?"

"Yes. There either aren't any, or they are the wrong type or size. I hoped that just by looking at it again, something would come to mind."

Bud waved his arms around the studio space. "It's not for anything up here. There's nothing but walls and windows, and all these pieces Jonas painted. Speaking of which, how about you help me find the last ones. Just try to find anything with a note on the back—he wrote people's names in fat pencil on the one's I've found so far."

"Okay, I'll start at this end, and you at the other."

It took us only another ten minutes or so to find all the remaining pieces. Soon we were able to assess the nature of our tasks. One thing was clear: the oversized portrait of *The Laughing Cavalier* was by far the largest piece, which was a relief.

"I'm going to suggest he bought canvases to stretch onto frames here. The supplies in that corner suggest he made them himself. And look at all this paint and acrylic. He must have been an art supplier's dream customer," I observed.

"One of his Group of Seven is just such a dealer—look," said Bud, holding the list Menno had given to him so I could see it.

"Well, that's a bonus," I replied, "and it's the guy who's in the massive piece, Willem Weenix. According to my handy-dandy tourist map, it looks like his shop isn't more than a ten- or fifteen-minute walk from here." As I pointed out the street Bud looked relieved. "We won't need a vehicle for that delivery, at least; we can just wrap it up and carry it ourselves. Of course, we'd have to be pretty careful, given how many people are on the streets."

"It might as well be a giant pane of glass," said Bud glumly. "You're right, though. I wonder if there's any packing paper here. Seen anything like that?"

I shook my head. "He has a lot of old sheets, and I found some string. We could use those."

"Good idea, but let's do that tomorrow. I suggest we go back to our hotel room so I can wash all this dust off me, and get rid of the smell of old paint." Looking at his watch, Bud added, "It's getting on, Cait, and I don't think we should stay here too much longer. Let's make sure everything is secure, then head back to the hotel, get cleaned up, and start phoning people to make arrangements for our deliveries.

Fancy dinner out somewhere, or should we just fall back on room service again?"

"Bud, Amsterdam has great food, and it's not a culture that shuts its doors at nine o'clock at night. We've got time to do everything we need to do, and go out to eat. I have a hankering for Indonesian food—how about you? Okay with that?"

"Indonesian? Here?"

"They have some fantastic Indonesian restaurants in Amsterdam. Don't forget, Indonesia was a Dutch colony up until the end of World War II; they arrived in the archipelago in the late 1500s and stayed. In fact, as I recall, Amsterdam is one of the best places to eat *nasi goreng*, which has all but become a Dutch national dish. There's something called *rijsttafel* too, with lots of different dishes all served at once, covering the table. When I was here decades ago it was a great treat for the four of us. With the years of training I've put in since then, I bet just the two of us could manage a smaller version. It would be tasty, and there are such fun places to eat—let's not just hide away while we're here, Bud."

"Agreed, but nothing too spicy for me. You can look online to find somewhere while I shower. Maybe that laptop of yours will prove useful after all. Now, come on, help me shut up the place. I'll go down the stairs ahead of you, just so you have a soft landing if you stumble."

Still Life: Exotic Foods

THE FRANTIC PACE OF TOURISTS pounding the streets of the museum district surrounding our hotel hadn't slowed at all. Bud and I hurried along, avoiding pedestrians and cyclists alike, arriving at Sama Sebo at 9:28 PM precisely. There had been a last-minute cancellation at the restaurant. We didn't stop to take in much of the exterior, but when the door opened, the aroma of spices and the cacophony of dozens of diners overwhelmed us. The woman who welcomed us requested that we have a drink at the bar while the wait-staff prepared our table, which we were happy to do; it gave us a chance to soak up the atmosphere. Weaving our way across the room, Bud and I agreed the quirky mix of Indonesian artefacts comprising carved wooden figures and richly decorated fabrics worked well with what otherwise looked like a slightly quaint Dutch restaurant. Squeezing in at the bar, Bud ordered a cold Heineken for each of us; I was just taking my first sip when I felt a hand on my shoulder. I turned to see Menno van der Hoeven beside me, beaming what seemed to be a genuine smile.

"You found this place, and you got a table?" He sounded amazed.

"A cancellation," I replied.

"You were lucky. It is always completely full." Menno cast his gaze around the packed restaurant.

"I don't think they could fit another table in if they tried," replied Bud.

Waiters were holding trays of food above their heads as they wriggled between the tightly packed seats. I suspected that being slim might be a job requirement at the place.

"I am here with clients. I would ask you to join us but I cannot. You understand, of course." Menno's tone was matter-of-fact.

"Wouldn't dream of it," beamed Bud, then his arm was tapped by a waiter who apparently wanted to seat us as quickly as possible. "Have a great evening."

"Did you find anything interesting at your uncle's house? I came across to find out. You have been there, of course," said Menno as Bud and I began to move away.

"Everything will be sorted," shouted Bud over the noisy patrons, and a moment later we were seated at a table that, thankfully, was close enough that I'd only had to ask two diners to move their seats so I could pass.

"He's surprisingly eager to know what we've been up to," I observed as I picked up the menu.

"Cait, stop it. He was just being pleasant," replied Bud while I hunted about for my reading cheats. The lighting wasn't overly bright, so I spent some time contemplating what to have. My mouth watered even as I read through the list of dishes and ingredients.

"Fancy the *rijsttafel*?" I said eventually.

Bud looked alarmed. "It says it's twenty-three dishes. *Twenty-three.* That's a lot of food, Cait. I'm not sure I could manage it."

"They're all tiny," I said, smiling sweetly. "Not much more than a mouthful for each of us, really. Look, they're having it over there."

Bud followed my glance and said, "The entire table is covered with food. What if it's all spicy?"

"It won't be. This is a tourist area, Bud. For all that they give the place an authentic Indonesian air, I can't imagine they want to scare off their main source of income. I'm sure it'll be fine. Come on, let's risk it."

It took no longer than ten minutes for the plates and bowls to arrive, and, when it was all laid out, our table looked like an ocean of food.

Bud looked less than enthusiastic as the waiter explained the dishes, and I could see him taking note whenever the word "spicy" was mentioned. But I couldn't wait to dive in.

An hour later I admitted defeat; I'd managed to clear most of the little bowls of their luscious, glistening, steaming contents of meat and fish, but it was the rice that did for me. Bud had stopped grazing long before I did, and I watched him as he studied Menno and his companions across the busy restaurant.

"Not much of a talker, considering he's supposed to be entertaining clients," observed Bud. "I see what you mean about his manner. Even I can tell from here he doesn't seem to have much of a sense of humor about him. He doesn't really engage, does he? Is that a Dutch thing?" he looked around. "I'm not sure it can be—there are a lot of animated conversations going on in here, and I can't believe everyone is from another country."

"I still reckon he's hiding something. I hope his mother will be more open when we meet her tomorrow," I added. "Great job lining up all our appointments, Husband—even though we've had to spread them across a couple of days. I hadn't realized two people were so far out of town until we saw their locations on that map."

"We'll be busy," replied Bud, "but I think it's right to start with the art supply store, where we need to deliver the biggest piece. Once that's gone we can collect everything else from the studio for tomorrow and put it all into a cab."

"Or cabs," I managed as I munched. "We're not going to want to be just in and out of the homes of these people, Bud. The whole point of this exercise is to take the time to get to know about Jonas, not just to dump the paintings and run."

"I know." Bud looked pensive. "I wonder if this is the sort of place he came to, or if it's too touristy. Cait, are you sure I'm not going to have to roll you back to the hotel—you're looking a bit hot and bothered, you know."

"I'm still just about okay, but I'm glad I stopped eating when I did."

"Here comes Menno," said Bud, giving me a gentle kick under the table. He raised his hand to shake the lawyer's. "Good meal?" he asked.

Menno's expression hardly changed. "It is too much food for four, but I made some effort. My guests did the hard work. As you did, I see."

"It's delicious," I said, wiping my mouth after a swig of beer. "We loved the variety of dishes, but you're right, it's a lot." Menno's slim frame suggested he didn't eat much of anything at all, and I felt myself blush. "Do you eat here often?"

"Only with clients." He seemed to be implying the place was only good for out-of-towners and I felt quite cross.

"Not the sort of place for locals then?" I added grumpily, fielding a burp.

"No." One word, speaking volumes. I bit.

"Luckily we're tourists here," I snapped, "so no one will condemn us, I'm sure. We're all sorted for tomorrow, by the way. We're off to see Willem Weenix at his shop first thing, then we'll be seeing your mother." I had no real reason to be so annoyed with Menno, but I was.

"Please say hello to her from me," was the lawyer's strange reply.

"You don't see her often?" I couldn't resist.

"We disagree on many things," said Menno.

"But she's still your mother," I retorted.

"This is true. Now I must go, my guests are waiting. Goodnight," and with a little bow of his head the man took his leave of us.

"He's weird." I had to say it.

Bud's face creased into a little smile. "You're right. Cold. Or perhaps just truthful."

"That remains to be seen."

Bud rolled his eyes. "Maybe his mother's even worse."

"I hope not."

The Art Supplier's Shop: A Family Scene

WE WERE STANDING OUTSIDE JONAS'S house, ready to face a busy day. It took us another half-hour to wrap the uncooperatively large painting and get it down the narrow staircase to the front door. As we finally emerged onto the street, the enormousness of our task became immediately clear—we had to wait quite a few minutes before we could even get the huge canvas out onto the street itself, let alone turn it, arrange it between us, and set off. As we shuffled along, apologizing every five seconds or so, I wished we were both about two feet taller, which would have made carrying a five-foot-tall painting a lot easier. I envied the tall Dutch their genes. After what seemed like an age working through an assault course, we eventually reached our destination, and we placed the piece of art gently on the blue and white tiles at the front of the beautifully presented store so Bud could open the glass door, which announced WEENIX ART SUPPLIES: ESTABLISHED 1962. As he began to do so, a woman in her twenties ran toward us and opened it on our behalf.

"We don't buy," were her first words, "and we don't do valuations. We sell supplies. That is all."

Bud was the one who'd made our appointment so he took the lead. "Hello, I'm Bud Anderson, from Canada. This is my wife, Cait Morgan. Are you Els? I believe we spoke last evening."

"No. She is inside. I am Ebba. Do you have an appointment?"

Bud smiled. "What a coincidence—my mother's name is Ebba too. Are you Swedish by any chance?"

The young woman with blonde hair, tipped with red spikes, snapped, "No. Dutch. My grandmother was from Sweden. Come in."

At least she held the door open so we could lift our package over the threshold and into the store. Once inside, the young, angular girl called, "Els. For you. People." She allowed the door to clang closed, the bell above it almost rattling off its bouncing hook.

I sighed, and Bud shot me a warning glance, then smiled again as another woman approached us. This one returned Bud's smile and held out her hand in greeting to each of us in turn. "You must be Bud and Cait. It is good to meet you. My father is in the back of the shop. It is his hiding-hole. He was excited to know you would be here today. You can lean that against the counter here. We are not busy."

The man who sat at the back of the store in a small, slightly more private alcove area was a far cry from the beaming, ruddy-faced person I'd been expecting to see. Willem Weenix was much older than he'd been portrayed in the portrait, and was wizened almost beyond recognition. Claw-hands rested in the lap of a man whose clothes hung in loose folds, as did his skin. The only resemblance was the eyes, which still managed to glitter with mischief. He gave us a gummy grin as we approached, and tried to lift his stick-like arms in greeting. He didn't even attempt to rise.

"Of course, you are Jonas's blood," he said to Bud in a tremulous voice. His accent was strong, and his voice reedy. "You look just like him." I wondered about the man's eyesight. Milky lenses spoke of cataracts, while slightly yellowed whites suggested some sort of issues connected with a compromised liver. Willem Weenix was not a well man, and he looked to be failing. I suspected we'd made it to him just in time.

"It's a pleasure to meet you, Mr. Weenix," said Bud gently, shaking the man's partially extended hand. "I understand you and my uncle were great friends for many years. You must miss him. I am sorry for your loss, but, as your daughter may have told you, my wife and I have some remembrances of Jonas he asked us to deliver to you."

"The doctor has told him to rest," Els said to me. "He had a stroke a couple of months ago. He must not always be moving. We live upstairs, but he insists on coming down to the store every day. He says he will wither if he does not." I saw tenderness and worry on her face as she spoke. "My daughter has gone to prepare coffee for us all."

"Ebba is your daughter?" I asked, putting two and two together. Els nodded. "So your mother was Swedish?" again, she nodded. "Your daughter has the same name as Bud's mother, Jonas's sister."

A smile crept across Els's face. "I did not know this," she said quietly. "A coincidence. Names are fashionable, then old. My daughter does not like hers. Maybe her late father and I should have given her a proper Dutch name, but my mother was already dead when she was born, and I wanted to recall her with my own daughter."

Bud had taken a seat beside the old man; the two were deep in conversation, it seemed. Bud stood and said, "Of course," then motioned to me to follow him.

"I said we'd bring the portrait in here, for Willem to see it," said Bud, so, for the last time, we struggled with the huge piece and finally set it against the wall, then removed the two bed sheets we'd tied around it at the studio earlier in the day.

As the linens fell away, Els gasped. "It's magnificent, Father. He has shown you exactly as you once were." I spotted her quivering chin, and she turned her head from her father so he couldn't see her tears.

There wasn't much Willem Weenix missed, it seemed. "Don't cry, my child. I am not young anymore, but I am not dead yet. Time for tears when I die. Now, help me up to see it properly, Bud."

They tottered across the room until he was able to focus on the portrait in its entirety, then Bud supported him again as he moved closer to study the painting of his own face. He nodded the whole time, or maybe it was a less controlled movement of his head—it was difficult to tell. One thing was clear when he turned to look toward me and his daughter—his eyes were alight with something. I suspected it was memories of the days when he'd been as vigorous as the man on the canvas before him.

"He was an excellent artist," was all he said, then motioned to be returned to his seat. We were rejoined by his granddaughter, who carefully placed a tray of coffee cups and saucers on a little table beside her grandfather. Each saucer held one biscuit.

Looking at the painting for the first time, she moved toward it, then back again, then approached it until her nose touched the canvas. Finally, she stepped back.

"My clever, talented girl has trained in art for many years, and in portraiture also," said her mother proudly. "She is now an expert restorer. I wonder what she thinks of this portrait of her grandfather."

Ebba looked at her mother, then her grandfather, and finally scowled at Bud and me. "You are making fun of us, I think. Who painted this? Han van Meegeren?"

"No, it is not one of his. My very best friend in the whole world painted it, Jonas de Smet," said Willem sharply. "Why? Don't you think it's good? I think it looks very much like me, forty years ago."

It surprised me when the girl pulled a magnifying glass out of her trouser pocket. She returned to the painting, examining it closely.

Eventually she said, "Extraordinary. I've never seen anything like it."

Willem let out a little, "Ha! Good?"

Plopping the magnifying glass onto the table, the young woman who'd selected a career that involved the study of the minutiae of great works of art said, "If it wasn't for the size, which is all wrong, and the fact that it's your face, Grandfather—and that it is signed 'Jonas,' of course—I would say this is the best version of this painting I've ever seen. I've seen several. And a few very good fakes too. We studied some in class. The reproduction of the clothing is perfect. Even the facial hair is just like the original. You told me you liked Van Meegeren,

Grandfather. Did your friend Jonas share your enthusiasm? Is that why he shows you as *The Laughing Cavalier*? That piece was Van Meegeren's most famous fake. Lost forever, it seems."

I was puzzled. "Why would anyone fake *The Laughing Cavalier*? Doesn't everyone know it's on display in London? No one could ever possibly think they were buying the original, surely?"

"There are many copies, some from the late 1800s; most are more recent," replied Ebba. "Van Meegeren sold one, they say. Do you know him?" Bud and I both said we didn't. The young girl smiled. "He died of a heart attack before he could be jailed for forgery, in 1947."

"How did they catch him?" I asked.

Clapping her hands, the girl replied, "They didn't. He confessed. He had to, or he'd have been tried for treason."

I was at sea. Already annoyed that I'd never heard of the person she was talking about, I wanted the full story. "Treason?" It seemed a bit extreme.

Willem butted in, a thoughtful smile on his face, "In the war, the Nazis took everything they could. A lot of people got Van Meegeren to paint fakes of their precious pieces, so that's what ended up being ripped from their walls. One of his fakes, a Vermeer, was found in Hermann Goering's hands, and Van Meegeren was about to be charged with having sold a Dutch national treasure to the Nazis. Arrested him as a collaborator, they did. He had to paint a fake in front of a panel of experts so they'd believe he could do it, and they found him guilty of the lesser charge. It was a very big story at the time."

It was a fascinating tale, and I suspected there'd be a good deal more to it. I told myself I'd do some Internet digging into the chap's life when I had a chance; I hate not having the full picture.

As Willem had been talking, slowly, I had watched Ebba as she examined the painting. "This is the best rendering of the costume

I have seen. The lighting on the subject's face—your face—is also excellent. Did your friend paint for a living, Grandfather?"

The old man smiled and nodded. "No." *So, he nods for yes and no.*

Walking toward the staircase, his granddaughter asked, "Is this for you now?"

Willem's head bobbed.

"May I study it?"

"Certainly. Will you copy it?"

"You know I am not that good, Grandfather," she replied, then made her way upstairs. "Call me if you need me. I am reading some papers for a class tomorrow."

"She teaches restoration as well as practicing it," said the proud mother, by way of an explanation. "Much of what she does with her students is practical, but she has a summer school class to teach that is all about theory. A lot of it is chemistry, not art." The bell on the shop door drew her attention, and she rushed to greet a customer.

"Jonas said I would learn about him from his friends," said Bud, sensing his chance to glean something. "My mother never really knew him, so I know she'd be grateful to hear anything you could tell me about her brother."

The more I watched him, the more I was convinced Willem's head-bobbing was an involuntary motion. It became more pronounced as he gave Bud's question some thought.

"We knew each other for—" he paused, and I could see his curled fingers working, "—almost seventy years. That is a long time. There is too much to tell, so what *really* matters? He was a talented artist. He loved art—all art—though he favored the work of some artists above others. Van Gogh, Vermeer, Rembrandt, Hals. These were his idols. They were the reason he came to the Netherlands, and why he stayed. He found this country through art, and made it his home. He was not afraid to study hard to learn, and he knew there were no shortcuts in life. He worked at his art, and at his art history. He laughed easily, loved recklessly, drank foolishly, and never took a friendship for granted. I loved him."

Impressed by Willem's ability to distill seventy years of companionship into such a meaningful description of Jonas, I ventured, "Did you meet him here, in Amsterdam?"

"In 1948, I moved from the north of Holland to Amsterdam for work. It was hard after the war. Reconstruction here meant more jobs. I was in my prime. Older than Jonas by five years. These hands did good work. I was strong, tall, with big arms, like a windmill. Jonas and I met at a bar. He was sketching the barmaid. It was a good sketch. She gave him two drinks in return for the sketch. I congratulated him. He sketched me, but I had nothing to give him in return for the sketch, so he made me promise to meet him for a drink at another bar the next night. I did, and, again, he made a drawing of the barmaid. This time we had one drink each, and a good conversation. We talked about Van Gogh, and how he would try to exchange sketches for food and drink. Jonas thought it amazing that it was easier for him to do this than it had been for his idol. He could not understand how people didn't see the genius of his hero. He worshipped Van Gogh. When I met him, Jonas was already a guard at the Stedelijk Museum. They had Van Goghs there. He said it was his dream come true. Of course he had almost no money. I had a little more. He lived on the floor of my bedroom for two years, so we both saved some money. He taught me about art. I loved him even more for that."

I noticed a tear roll down Willem's folded cheek. It disappeared into a deep crease. He wiped at it with his knuckles and sighed heavily. Neither Bud nor I spoke, but his daughter returned from the storefront and announced, "Jonas was a talented man. This is a beautiful painting. We will display it in the shop, no?"

"That is good," said Willem simply. "I do not know when he made this painting, but it is of me when I was happy. I think he loved me too. This portrait tells me so."

"There's something else for you," said Bud, pulling the much smaller piece Jonas had bequeathed to his friend out of the pillow-case in which we'd packed it. He handed it to Willem. "It's not another portrait, but he indicated it was to be given to you."

The old man's hands curled around the edges of the piece; he showed surprise at seeing a representation of Vermeer's *Girl with a Pearl Earring* in the manner of Edvard Munch, of *The Scream* fame. His fingers moved across the uneven surface of the thickly painted piece lying in his lap, then he picked it up to peer at it more closely. He smiled. "This explains a good deal, right Els?"

The elderly man's daughter moved to take a closer look at the piece and mirrored her father's grin. "Indeed. It explains why he became one of our best customers. He bought more supplies of acrylic than I could imagine anyone could use. Most people come to a place like ours because they adhere to the traditional materials. But Jonas? He became a devotee of acrylics in the past few years. Now I see why. It was a part of his sense of humor. He's been making fun of the masters. Good for him."

She turned the piece to examine the back. Bud and I had noted how the canvas had been drawn around a wooden box-like structure to allow the acrylic paste to be applied all around the edges of the "two-artist" pieces Jonas had been making. The picture itself wrapped right around the edges of the structure, meaning they would be impossible to frame, unless you wanted to lose a part of the image.

"The artist's dilemma," said Willem, sounding suddenly tired.

"Pardon?" said Bud.

"Jonas and I talked about this a great deal. The artist paints without a frame. The artist can rarely afford one. Frames are chosen by people with money but with no aesthetic investment in the piece. Most artists hate the way their work is framed, but have no choice in the matter—by then it is sold. They need the money for supplies to paint the next piece. Jonas admired the painting by Van Gogh where he used an old frame for his work and painted the frame so it was a part of the picture—all one piece. It was a great pity they damaged this piece when it was stolen once, but they repaired it, and it looks good now, I understand. I think this is Jonas's joke. No frame, just the work. I love how it feels. It feels like life—full of unexpected highs and lows, turns and paths. Jonas made me love art so much that in the fifties I stopped being a laborer and began to be a supplier of paints and brushes to students taking art lessons here in Amsterdam. In those days I had a great love of the work of Munch, who only died in 1944. I am happy Jonas remembered that, and gave me this gift, so I can feel the work as well as look at it. Ah yes, it was good of him; he was the best of us."

"The best of the Group of Seven?" asked Bud, but Willem had fallen asleep, his eyelids fluttering, his breathing heavy.

Els placed the two-artist piece on the table and ushered us into the shop. "He is tired. He will sleep for a few hours, then I will help him walk upstairs, where he will eat, then take another nap. That is the way of it for him now." A shadow of sadness moved across her face as she looked from her father's heaving bosom to the glittering eyes of the smiling portrait. "Father was right; he was always a strong man. He built this business from nothing, and earned much respect from Amsterdam's artists, and those who visited. He was not an artist himself, but he has helped to create much that is beautiful in this city, and around the world."

"Was Jonas the leader of the Group of Seven? Or was Willem?" I ventured.

The woman smiled. "No, the Group had no leader, but I do not know a great deal more. The person who would tell you most is Bernard de Klerk. He was the youngest in the Group. I think the last to 'join,' if you can call it that. He and Greta van Burken, the only woman in the Group, would probably know more than I do. You will see every living member of the Group, correct?"

Bud answered brightly. "That's the hope. Jonas left each person a portrait, and another piece. We're to give them to the living relatives if the original member is deceased."

Els frowned. "Deceased? You speak like the police." Her tone was suddenly guarded.

"I was the police, for many years, in Canada," explained Bud.

"It is good that my father did not know that. He does not trust the police."

I saw Bud straighten his shoulders a little. I knew what was coming. Quietly, but firmly, he said, "All we do is keep the peace, and make sure justice is served. Society needs policing, to allow the honest to live the best lives they can."

Willem's daughter's expression softened. "I apologize. My father is an old man. His experience with the police has not always been happy—accused of unfair things in his life—and it disrupted our family many times."

Curious, I had to ask, "What happened?"

"We live in a city of art where many robberies have taken place over the years," replied Els with a shrug, "often with the art being recovered right away because the thieves are so stupid. There have also been many dishonest artists living and working here. They paint bad fakes, then try to sell them to unsuspecting tourists. You see it in the flea markets all the time. It's foolish, but they do it. People can be so greedy—they want to believe they have found a great bargain, bought an Old Master for a song. They only have themselves to blame. These dishonest artists needed supplies, and my father sold supplies. You cannot interrogate everyone who wants a few tubes of ochre and umber. The police did not, and still do not, see things this way."

The business manager in her awakening, Els spotted a couple in plaid shorts and brilliantly white running shoes peering into the front window. I could tell by her body language she sensed potential customers, probably for the prints that hung above the art supplies on display. "Do you need to leave now?" she asked rather pointedly.

Bud took the hint. "Yes, we should. We have a busy day ahead of us. But before we go, briefly, do you recognize this man, by any chance?" I picked up on what he meant and thrust one of the photographs of the unknown man I'd brought from Jonas's house in front of her.

Weenix's daughter gave the photo a moment's attention then shook her head. "I might say he could look familiar. Possibly a customer, once? It's not someone I know. Is it important?"

"Probably not." I could tell she was getting anxious about allowing potential customers to escape her sales pitch.

Bud seemed to sense the same thing and chimed in with, "Please say goodbye to your father for us. It was a pleasure to meet my late uncle's best friend. We wish him and your family good health, right, Cait?"

"Absolutely," I said mechanically as I observed the couple beyond the window having a serious discussion about a large, unframed print on canvas of the original Vermeer's *Girl with a Pearl Earring*. "Thanks so much. I hope you share your father's passion for art. This seems to be a successful business you have here."

"It is, and I hope it will continue. The Americans are coming back to Europe now, and we have all the museums open again. Business is getting better." Els walked toward the door and opened it to allow us through. "Thank you for bringing the pieces. They mean a great deal to my father," she said, smiling at us; then, with exactly the same smile, she turned her attention to the couple outside and said smoothly, "It's an excellent price for a superior print. We can ship to anywhere in the world, if you like." Bud and I walked out onto the street glad to be free of our burdens, and left her to work on her marks.

"Back to Jonas's house to pick up the next lot, right?" said Bud, striding out as best he could. "It's getting pretty warm already. Could be a long, hot day."

I wished I'd packed a water bottle in my handbag, then thought better of that idea and said, "Quick beer at the bar at the end of Jonas's street before we get going?"

Bud looked at his watch. "It's already almost eleven." I adopted my cute, smiley face. He relented. "I guess a quick one wouldn't hurt. Maybe they'll have air conditioning. That store was so stuffy; I don't think I could cope with the smell of the oil paint around me all the time. It must get into every fiber of your clothes."

"Of your being, I'd have thought," I replied, then we picked up the pace heading for the hostelry I'd suggested, which I happened to know was called Koenig's Bar. I visualized an ice-cold bottle in my hand and felt less sweaty by the minute, though the reality was a little different.

The Solitary Drinker

THE BAR WAS DIMLY LIT. I suspected it was for the best, because the wooden backs of the seats felt greasy to the touch, and the place smelled stale. The barman looked about twelve years old, and showed no interest in us at all when we walked in. We perched on the sticky stools and waited until he decided to acknowledge our presence.

"Two Amstels, please," said Bud, smiling. Nudging me, he added, "See? I changed it up."

The youthful server dragged two bottles from a chiller behind him, snapping off the tops with an experienced hand and placing them in front of us with one deft motion. He might not have looked old enough to drink, but he'd clearly opened his fair share of beer bottles. Rather than speaking, he picked up a glass rather half-heartedly, and gestured toward me with it. I shook my head, grabbed my bottle and took a deep swig. It was the best-tasting beer ever. The bottle was half empty before I realized it. I put it down and waited while Bud caught up with me.

"Hey! Hey you," a woman's gravelly voice called from the shadows. "You're them, in't ya?"

I peered into the corner, but all I could make out was a slightly darker patch within the dimness. It stood and moved toward us, becoming a woman with broad features and hips and, surprisingly, a thick Irish brogue. "You were at Jonas's house. I'm right, aren't I?" The woman was making a statement, not asking a question.

My mind whirred. "Are you Jonas's tenant, Hannah?"

Alarmingly, the woman spat on her hand, wiped it on her hip, then extended it toward me. "Aye. Hannah Schmidt, that's me. And you're who, exactly?"

Realizing she was the curtain-twitcher I'd spotted the previous day—Menno had mentioned only one tenant—I explained who we were.

"Aye. Looked right at me yesterday, you did. So—are you going to sell?"

She went right to it, and—for some reason—she asked me, not Bud. "I don't think Bud's decided yet, have you?" I said, being as noncommittal as possible.

"Haven't made up my mind," he confirmed, eyeing the woman up and down.

She reminded me of one of Van Gogh's *Potato Eaters*: rough, gnarled features, crumpled, sack-like clothing in beiges and browns tied tightly around her middle, and a scarf knotted at her throat. Her voice could have etched glass. In his letter, Jonas had said she'd lived a difficult life. I wondered how much of that was of her own choosing, because I judged her to be a woman who lived life very much on her own terms.

"I found him, you know," Hannah leaned in as though confiding in us. "Terrible shock it was for me. Feared for my own heart, but I got the cops and so forth to come to look after him. Been under the same roof as a dead body for days, I had. No one even took me pulse."

"Would you at least let us buy you a drink so you can tell us all about it?" I asked.

Her face lit up. "That'd be grand, t'anks." I jumped when she called across the bar in a shout that was all but a cackle, "Large Jameson's, straight," then began to move back to the table where she'd been sitting upon our arrival.

I picked up my bottle, then told Bud with my eyes that he should bring the other drinks and join us at the table. I was hopeful Hannah might be ready to talk—and I wasn't wrong.

Raising her drink to the ceiling, she pronounced, "To Jonas: may he rest in peace," then gleefully glugged about half the dark amber liquid, and proceeded to nurse the heavy bottomed glass in stubby-fingered hands. They were so red, raw, and chapped, they looked painful.

"He was a good man. A bit weird, though, don't you know. All them artist types are the same, I suppose. A bit off-kilter. Always out and about at night, he was. Did you know he did walking tours and what-not for the last ten years or so? Kept himself going just grand, he did."

Bud and I nodded. "Menno van der Hoeven, my uncle's lawyer, told us," replied Bud.

Hannah rolled her eyes. "And he's an odd duck too, to be sure. Poking about in Jonas's place at all hours he was, after the poor man left us."

I felt I had to be sure what she meant. "You mean Menno has visited the house since Jonas died?"

"Isn't that what I just said?" snapped Hannah. "Came over three—no, four times, he did. Didn't talk to me at all, did he? No. Ignoring me, he is. He's one of them miserable Dutch, not one of the happy ones."

"You think there are different types of Dutch people?" I asked.

Hannah leaned in again. "Right enough. Tall ones and short ones, of course—only the Good Lord knows why he planned it that way—and then there's the miserable, bossy, nit-picking ones, and the happy-go-lucky, laughing-all-the-time ones. Like I say, the Lord must have had a plan for them all, but it's not for us to know."

I couldn't work out why Menno hadn't mentioned to us that he'd been to Jonas's place.

"And here's another t'ing, now. Why was Jonas all a-twitter just before he went and fell down them stairs?" said Hannah, sipping her whiskey.

"What do you mean?" I asked.

"Cleared out a lot of stuff from his place, he did. Up and down them stairs at all hours for months, he was. Always carrying big lumps of things. Not paintings—I'd seen him do that often enough. Big lumpy sacks they usually was. Then a couple of old chairs. Don't know how he managed it. Stupidest things in the world, Dutch stairs. Too steep and narrow for anyone to cope. I'm glad I only have the one lot in my place. And as for where it all went? Who knows? Never even had a bike, your uncle. He was a walker."

"Have you been in Amsterdam long? I notice your accent," said Bud, sipping his drink.

"Not going to lose it, am I? Like you, right?" She jutted her chin toward me. "Welsh?"

"Swansea, originally. Do you know it?"

"Sure I do. They have the ferry from there to Ireland. When d'you leave?"

"I moved to Canada over a decade ago and I've been there ever since. Menno suggested you'd lived in Jonas's house for many years, is that right?"

"Fifty years, near enough. Came here as no more than a girl in 1964, and moved in the next year. I was eighteen when I came to Amsterdam. Pretty as a picture back then. But a rebel. Always was. Met a boy back home, got meself pregnant, ran away. I wasn't going to be locked up in one of them God-awful places full of bitter old nuns and have them take me child away from me. Amsterdam was a place for rebels back then. Full of them. Even the Beatles came here that year. Oh, loved that Paul, I did. Don't you t'ink he's aged well?"

Desperate to get Hannah back on track, I said, "How did you find Jonas's body? Do you have a key for the front door to his home? We've seen how you and Jonas each had a separate entrance to the place."

Hannah shook her head. "No key for his part. He was the landlord, I'm the tenant. But I knew something was up, and I was right there when the police came. I saw him first."

"How did you know something was amiss, Hannah?" asked Bud.

The woman gave the matter some thought. "It was the noise. There wasn't any. Jonas wasn't light on his feet, and the noise comes through to my bedroom from his living room. He was up and about at all hours. Told him about it, I did, too many times to count over the years. Of course he worked shifts for most of his life, so he was always 'irregular' in that sense. Then, when he was painting, not working, he said it was for the light. Pain in the proverbial for me, him clomping about up there at all hours. Then it was quiet for a few days and I knew he hadn't gone away. Always told me when he went away. Not normal, so it weren't. That's when I knocked and knocked, but got no answer. When I was knocking at his door I noticed the smell. Terrible bad, it was, so I phoned the police. Not what I wanted, having them around the place, but I couldn't break the door down meself, could I?"

We all allowed a few moments of silence to pass.

In an effort to find out more about the woman, I finally said, "I see you married." I gestured toward her wedding ring.

Smiling down at the narrow band of gold, she let out a mighty, joyous laugh that echoed in the still-empty bar. "For five minutes," she said, then winked. "Never could pick the good 'uns, me. I'd lost the baby, decided to go back to the Old Country, then fell for one of Jonas's friends, Bernard de Klerk." She stared back across the years. "Good-looking boy. Even more rebellious than me, though. We gave it a go, but it didn't work out. We weren't married in church after the civil ceremony, so I didn't mind gettin' divorced. I know they say once a Cat'lic, always a Cat'lic, but a girl's got to be sensible about this stuff. I never took this off, though. I t'ink of him still. Sometimes."

"Bernard remarried, I understand," said Bud gently. Hannah shrugged. "I spoke to his wife on the telephone last evening. We're visiting him tomorrow. Jonas left some items for him, and for all his friends. There's an offer for you to come into his studio and pick out whatever you'd like from his collection of works, and there's a portrait of you too, for you to keep. He was a gifted artist—there are some lovely pieces."

I wondered if Bud had Hannah pegged for a "vase of flowers" type, as I did. Still life studies didn't seem to have been something Jonas had tackled often, though I'd spotted a couple of canvases in the early Dutch style featuring fruit, glassware, and even insects that I suspected might appeal to the woman.

She shook her head. "He was always too figurative for my taste. I prefer abstract." My surprise must have shown, because she added, "Love me some Jackson Pollock, I do," and grinned wickedly.

"In that case, you might not be keen on your portrait, which is in the style of Van Gogh, but you might like some of his other pieces," said Bud.

The woman didn't look convinced as she sipped her drink thoughtfully.

"Were you close?" I asked. "Fifty years is a long time to share a house."

Hannah contemplated the tiny drop of whisky left in her glass. "We shared nothing, just some nights when we'd talk. He'd come to my door with a bottle, and I'd invite him in. Maybe a few times a year, that's all. August, when it was hot; about this time. November, when it was biting outside, and you'd be afraid your fingers would drop off. End of January when everyone is unhappy."

"My mom's birthday is next week," said Bud. "Perhaps he would drink with you when he thought of his sister?"

"Never talked about family, only art. It was how we met, and how I met Bernard."

Bud and I waited, hoping she'd be more illuminating. When it was clear that she wasn't offering any more insight, I said, "Hey, I've finished my beer. Fancy another drink before we leave?" Hannah's reaction was predictably positive, so Bud left to get another round of drinks. I pressed on with, "So how exactly did you meet Jonas?"

Hannah preened a little—a disquieting sight. "Like I said, I was quite a looker back then, and I did a bit of modeling on the síde. I heard about this group of artists who wanted someone for a series of life studies, and that's when I met them all. The Group of Seven, they was. Funny lot. None of them professionals, like, just painting for fun. Jonas was good. Everyone said he could have made a living at it. All he wanted to do was moon over the stuff in the galleries he worked in. Like a kid, he was. Passionate about the art he loved, but I t'ink he missed a lot of the good stuff because he wore them blinkers. Maybe age made them more transparent and he saw past them to a wider range of works. He never said. Sat for them for months, I did, off and on. Not much money, but good company. I'd fallen for Bernard, so I'd have done the modeling for free, to be with him."

"We just met Willem Weenix," I said. "He seemed like a good, steady type."

Hannah rolled her eyes. "Might look that way now, didn't back then. A chancer, he was. Did he tell you how he got started with that shop of his?" I lied and shook my head. "No, he wouldn't. Not the real story, anyways, though I expect he's got one off pat for the tourists. Stole stuff he did, to order, for all his painter friends. Sweet-talked a girl who could get him into some warehouse outside the city where he could get pretty much anything people wanted. Not easy back in the fifties, I shouldn't think. By the time I turned up he'd got that shop set up, and he's gone from strength to strength ever since, so he has."

"A lot of entrepreneurs got started in a bit of a dodgy way," I said, hoping for more from Hannah.

"To be sure they have, and many a lot worse than lifting a few rolls of canvas and some tubes of oils. All of them Group people were a bit . . . off. Know what I mean?" I shook my head. "Willem had the sticky fingers—and all of them happy to buy what they knew to be stolen goods, of course. Bernard was good-looking, clever, and had a way with him—but he was a user. People, not drugs—though there was sure a lot of them about the place too. By the time I found out, I'd married him and it was too late to do anything about it, except get divorced. I reckon he was glad to be rid of me for what I bet was the next girl what came along. Then another after that. And another, no doubt. Kept out of me way for a good long time, he did. Then I heard he finally settled for one with money and a good family business, which he joined. Became a draftsman at an architects' company, he did. Retired now, if he's lucky. Pieter van Boxtel? An accountant by day, a hard-drinking, lascivious, so-called artist by night." Hannah's face clouded. "I didn't like him. Too wild, even for me. Johannes Akker was nice. Reddish hair, plump, steady. Back then he worked in the . . . what was it? Something to do with transport—anyway, he ended up working on the planning and building of the metro. It opened in '77. Princess Beatrix did it, before she was Queen. Very nice do, it was. We all attended. I suppose Johannes must have been important by then. Did you know she went to school in Canada, did Beatrix, during the war, and that our Princess Margriet was born in your Ottawa?"

I resisted the temptation to tell Hannah I had known those little nuggets of information. Instead I said, "There was one woman in the Group, we understand. Greta van Burken. Were you and she friends?"

Once again Hannah laughed with gusto. "No way. Now there was a woman who walked around looking as though there was always a smell under her nose. May the Good Lord forgive me, but I hated her. Hated her hats, too. I've never known anyone else able to make me hate hats, but she did. She might not even have had a top to her head for all I know. I never, ever saw her without a hat. She bullied them into letting her 'join,' she did. She wasn't ever *really* one of them, I don't think. Money, though, you see. Whole family had pots of the stuff, and they had good contacts with City Hall, too. Because of her, Jonas always worked where he wanted, when he wanted. Knew everyone, she and her family did—the people who ran the city, the museums, the palaces, the police. Probably still does, if she hasn't already been killed off by someone she attacked with her tongue." Hannah grabbed the drink Bud had set on the table in front of her as he retook his seat.

"Greta once told Jonas an orange he'd painted was as bad as a Cezanne orange," confided Hannah, laughing. "Can you imagine? A put-down of Jonas *and* Cezanne, in just a few words. Typical of Greta. Of all of them she was the only one who did her art all day. Never worked a real job in her life. I heard from Jonas she'd married well—though how that could be, I don't know. She and I agreed on one thing: we both thought she was top dog."

"Who else was there?" asked Bud.

"Dirk, Menno's father. A good, solid man. Not good-looking, but tall, straight. I should have fallen for him. Should have chased after him. But no, typical of me! I went for the bright, shiny object, only to be disappointed. Shakespeare was right, 'All that glisters is not gold.' Dirk was a good man, a quiet man. He loved to draw flowers, landscapes, outdoor stuff. Sketched and did watercolors a great deal. Jonas used to try to get him to use more pigment, but Dirk stuck with washes. Maybe that's why I preferred Bernard—nothing wishy-washy about him. Dirk deserved a good, steady woman, but he got Marlene." Hannah's facial contortions suggested that this wasn't a good thing. "Worse than a flibbertigibbet like me. Now, Dirk's career I followed, best as I could. Not a man in the news, but he made his mark. Antiques trade, he was in. Meant he could always be with beautiful old things, and a sharp brain for a deal. Gave up creating art altogether, as far as the outside world was concerned, but I knew his spots, and he'd plant himself out on the canals and set up his easel and have at it. I daresay his boy Menno is a good man too, but he's noisy."

"When he visited Jonas's home after he had died, did Menno make a lot of noise?" Bud sounded eager.

"Sounded like he was movin' the furniture about the place. Scraping and banging. Must have worn clogs doing it, too."

"Do you remember exactly when Menno was there, Hannah?" pressed Bud.

"They took poor Jonas on the T'ursday, and he was there a week later, also on the T'ursday, twice, then again on the Saturday and Sunday. Not after that. I've been on the telephone to him a lot about what's going to happen about me home. I'm a bit old for too much change, you see. Take pity on an old woman, won't ya? Don't be t'rowin' me out on the streets." She maintained a serious, pleading look for a few seconds, then laughed aloud. "Ah, you'll do what you want, I know that much. And why would you two be wanting a house in Amsterdam, so far away from where you live? Makes no sense, it doesn't."

I finally got to ask a question I'd had tickling around my brain for quite a while. "If you've been living at that house for almost fifty years, when on earth did Jonas buy it? As far as we know he arrived here in 1947 when he was only eighteen, and he wasn't exactly flush after that. If you moved in in 1964, when did it become his property?"

Hannah looked pleased with herself. "Ah, now that I do know, because we talked about that. He bought the house, outright, in 1956. I seen the papers wit' me own eyes, I did."

I was amazed. "He was just twenty-seven. That's extraordinary—especially if his only work was as a guard at a museum. That can't pay a great deal. Was there something wrong with the house? Some reason why it might have been sold off cheaply?"

"Well, I t'ink it was from the Jews," said Hannah quietly.

We looked surprised, because we were—and puzzled.

Hannah leaned in and dropped her voice. "After the war there was a lot of places—houses, apartments, shops, you know—that had been taken from the Jews during the time the Nazis occupied the Netherlands. Most of them poor souls never came back from the camps. Whole families wiped out. Every generation, gone. So a lot of places were never claimed. They say a hundred and forty t'ousand Jews or more was taken from Amsterdam. After the war, only about twenty-five t'ousand or so was left alive to come back, and t'rough the fifties and sixties a lot of them left. Can't blame 'em wanting to sell up and get out. Lot of bad blood about the place, even after the Black Tulip thing when the Dutch kicked out the Germans and took everything they owned." Hannah leaned forward. "The Dutch ran the railways what took the Jews away to the camps, you see, even policed the whole t'ing—Nazis didn't have to do it themselves, they did it for them." She sipped her drink.

Bud shifted uncomfortably in his seat. "But there were a lot of Dutch people who left the Netherlands and joined up with the Allied Forces to fight against the Nazis, and the Dutch Resistance was famous. I know for a fact that lots of ordinary Dutch people risked their lives to help the Jewish population," he said quietly. "The whole Anne Frank thing, for example."

Hannah spoke conspiratorially. "They even got her, didn't they? Ever read anything by Mulisch?" Bud shook his head, and I nodded. "You should," she said to Bud. "*The Assault* and *The Discovery of Heaven* challenged, and some would say even changed, the Dutch psyche. He wrote a lot of other stuff, of course, but those two did it. Never understand the Dutch until you've read them books, you won't."

"You said you married Bernard de Klerk, and you're Irish, but you're called Schmidt," I said. "That's because . . . ?" I allowed the question to hang in the warm air.

Hannah delighted me again with her laugh. "I'm Irish, so I hate to make a long story short, but I will, because it should be. All Jonas's fault, of course. When I got divorced from Bernard, I said I'd go back to my maiden name, Delaney, but Jonas said I should take a more European one. So I picked Smith—in German. It confuses the heck out of the Dutch. Like I said, they have a complicated relationship with the Germans, so my fluent Dutch, Irish accent, and German name confound them many a time. It's grand to watch them try to decide if they should ask me about it, or not." She finished her drink. "I'll walk back to the house with ya," she said, standing.

"Before we go," I said, quickly pulling the photograph of the unknown man from my purse, "Did you ever see this man visiting Jonas at all? Or have you seen him anywhere else?"

Hannah took the photo from me and held it close to her face, squinting. "Blurry. Too blurry. Doesn't look like anyone I know. Though . . . maybe someone in the area? Looks like a common type of face for these parts."

I took the photograph from her, and we rushed our beers while I wondered about how on earth she'd been able to just "pick a new name" for herself after her divorce. I suspected it wasn't something one was able to do easily or honestly.

"Later, boy," she called at the young man behind the bar, who didn't look around but waved in our general direction. "Vibrates with personality, that one," she quipped as we blinked in the sunlight and headed toward her home. It was only then I noticed she walked with a pronounced limp and wore one shoe built up in the sole. Making good speed, she turned back toward us and almost shouted, "I t'ank the Good Lord every day that when that police car hit me chasing t'rough the streets in 1986 and took me leg with it, the compensation was enough for me to live here, as I do. I do miss me leg, you know, but it meant I could give up me work and rest a bit."

"What did you do?" I asked.

"Ran a brown café. The Marie Café. Best *gezellig* in town, if I do say so meself. Takes an Irish woman to run a good bar, you know."

"*Gezellig*? Is that a drink?" asked Bud.

"It's like the Irish *craic*," replied Hannah, "you know, spirit, fun, atmosphere."

"That must have been hard work," I observed.

"Couldn't do it properly once I lost me leg," said Hannah sadly. "Doesn't mean I can't go back as a customer t'ough," she added with a wink. "Now, come on, I t'ink you two could work a bit harder to keep up with a one-legged old woman who's had a couple more whiskeys before lunch than she's used to."

Bud and I cantered to do as she'd asked, then, arriving at her front door, she said, "Want to come to mine for a cuppa? Go on wit' ya, you know you do."

"We really should get the pieces we need for our next appointment," said Bud. "How about tomorrow? Around ten? Then you could come up to my uncle's studio and pick out something you like."

"It's a date," replied Hannah. They opened the two front doors at the same moment, and we all trooped inside.

Cityscape: Summer

OUR NEXT TWO VISITS WERE due to be to Menno's mother—Dirk van der Hoeven's widow, Marlene—and to Pieter van Boxtel's home. Bud had taken the advice of our concierge and booked a car with driver, rather than hailing a taxi. According to the concierge, we'd only have ourselves to blame if we risked taking a cab from a taxi rank, where drivers often didn't speak English, or know the city. I'd kept my mouth shut, because I wondered if the concierge was getting a kick back from the company he'd recommended after frightening us half to death. In any case, the price quoted for what we wanted had seemed reasonable. However, now the car was five minutes late and I was beginning to wonder if we'd made a mistake.

Waiting as patiently as possible, I pondered how easily a person could come to love the city. I sat perched on the windowsill of Jonas's sitting room, overlooking the canal and the streets below through an open window. The water was busy with craft of all types and sizes, and was like a living, breathing thing moving through the largely brick- and cobble-built cityscape. It brought the colors of the sky down to the streets, and lightened and brightened the view in myriad ways. Sunlight played on the wakes of the vessels, the reflected light bouncing off windowpanes, while tinkling cycle bells, and the lack of motor noises from cars, all made for a unique visual and aural experience.

"I guess that's him," said Bud leaping to his feet, indicating a sleek, black car that had edged its way along the canal-side road, and stopped in front of the house. "Come on, we'd better be quick. He can't really wait there for long."

"Bud, we rented this vehicle just so we could *not* rush, so let's just take care to get the pieces out and into the car safely." We'd balanced them on the stairs, set against the wall, so all we had to do was take each one and place it in the trunk of the car, then we jumped in ourselves and off we went. I didn't have a chance to pay much attention to the driver himself as he and Bud arranged the artwork in the car, because I was keeping an eye on the open front door to the house. By the time we got going, he was just a neck above a white collar, with a thatch of sandy hair above that, and a pair of sunglasses reflected in the rearview mirror. Because I was sitting directly behind him, it was all I was likely to see until we reached our first destination.

"I am Frans," said the driver, not turning around. "I have driven here for many years—all my life, in fact. I know where you are going and will take you there efficiently. Do you want for me to tell you about our history as we go?"

I threw Bud a look of alarm, which he interpreted correctly. "We'll just sit back and take it all in; thanks, Frans," he replied on our behalf. I squeezed his hand in gratitude. I was glad of a bit of time to mull over everything Hannah and Willem had told us about Jonas and the other members of the Group.

"You want music?" asked Frans.

"No, thanks," we chorused from the back seat.

"Air okay?" asked Frans.

"Just fine, thanks. It's nice and cool back here," I replied, hoping he'd shut up.

"Let me know if you want anything," he concluded, sounding disappointed.

It wasn't long before we were traveling along wide boulevards constructed between modern buildings, designed to accommodate multiple lanes of traffic as well as the trams, which thrummed alongside our car. I noticed Bud checking his watch. "She said to come anytime," he said, "but I wonder if it would be polite to let her know when we'll get there. It's sort of lunchtime."

Without waiting for me to reply, Frans said, "We'll be there in five minutes. Maybe she will make lunch for you."

I rolled my eyes at Bud. "How about a quick call?" He pulled out his cell phone and punched in a number he read off our master list. After the call ended, he said, "She's there and ready for us. I'm not sure she's with it. Sounded a bit vague."

The Waltzing Woman: A Study

A FEW MINUTES LATER WE pulled to a halt outside a building that made me think of a barracks; an unappealing pale brick frontage with too-regular rows of windows piercing the façade loomed up beside us. It filled the whole of one side of the street. Entrances were let into it at militaristically regular intervals and were topped with large metal numbers.

"Here we are," announced the driver. "Apartment 1558 will be through this door." He double-parked on the street. "I cannot stay here. I will drive until I can find a space and wait. Phone me when you need me. You had better both get out on the safe side," he added, quite unnecessarily.

We pulled the correct parcels from the trunk and made our way into the unwelcoming entrance. Inside the glass doors was a sterile, narrow hallway lined with gray marble. One wall was covered with mailboxes and numbered buzzers. Bud pressed 1558. We waited. And waited. He pressed again.

Finally, a clicking, crackling sound became a female voice. "*Laat me met rust!*"

"Hello? Mrs. van der Hoeven, is that you? It's Bud Anderson."

Silence, then an uncertain, "*Goededag. Wat is uw naam?*"

Bud looked puzzled, I stepped up. Hoping I didn't confuse the woman, I decided it was best to say, "*Zijn naam is Bud. Spreekt u Engels?*"

"Of course I speak English. Are you Bud, my son's friend?"

"Yes," replied Bud.

A buzzer sounded and I sprinted for the glass door that popped open ahead of us.

"A bit more than a little confused, I think," said Bud as we worked out how to make the elevator take us to the correct floor. "I think this might be a bit more delicate than we thought. Menno might have warned us."

"He might not see it," I ventured.

The door marked 1558 was opened by a woman I towered over—and I'm only five-three, five-four on a tall day. Beady, rheumy eyes blinked up at us, and her whole face twitched like a bunny's when she wrinkled her nose as though sniffing us.

Straining to look along the corridor toward the elevators, she said, "Where's Menno? Is he with you?" Now face to face, I recognized her accent as French, not Dutch. It came as a surprise.

"We are here alone, Mrs. van der Hoeven," said Bud patiently. "I am Bud Anderson. We just spoke on the telephone."

The lawyer's mother looked unsure as she moved back inside her front door and slammed it shut in our faces. In the uncertain silence that followed, Bud and I exchanged meaningful glances. A few moments later the door opened again and the woman said, "I spoke to my son. He said you are safe. Come in. I am Marlene. Sit."

An armchair and a sofa designed for two slim-hipped people were the only seats available in the tiny sitting room. Bud sat first and I squeezed in beside him. We held the two paintings in front of our knees. I felt nervous; when the elderly begin to swim about in their reality, you can never be sure which current will carry them in what direction, so it can be difficult to keep up. I was suddenly certain it would be a challenging meeting, not helped by the fact that the room was stiflingly hot and stuffed with too much old, dark-wood furniture—some of it beautiful and of good quality—covered and filled with all manner of knickknacks. My mind flew to Bud's mother—she and Marlene van der Hoeven shared an aesthetic when it came to home décor. Marlene's room was made to feel even smaller by the fact that almost every inch of each wall was covered in art. Mainly watercolors, with some large, garish prints, and a few fine oil pieces thrown in for good measure. I judged the watercolors to have been executed by the woman's late husband. I wondered if the prints were examples of her preferred style of art.

"Are those for me?" asked Marlene van der Hoeven, smiling at the paintings.

I wondered where on earth she would hang them "Yes, they are."

"Oh good, I can't wait to see them," she squealed, her face lighting up like a little girl on Christmas morning. Leaping from her seat with a surprising fleetness of foot, she pulled the wrappings off the paintings. The linens we'd used to protect the artwork lay on the carpet in a flash.

"My Dirk!" she cried, hugging the portrait of her husband as Van Gogh's famous *Doctor Gachet* as best she could with her little arms. The second piece—Jonas's two-artist piece marked as being for Dirk and family—she reacted to rather differently, immediately deflated. "That's not pretty at all. Why is that so horrible?"

I looked at the canvas mounted on the same boxy construction as all of Jonas's inventive pieces and considered it carefully. This one was smaller than the portrait of the woman's dead husband and portrayed the well-known scene Seurat had depicted of *Bathers as Asniers* in the style of Klimt, the sky and grass a riot of gold and black, the faces of the bathers shown in almost deathly hues of blue and purple.

"It looks like the light on a hot, sunny day," I said, trying to sound positive about the gold leaf of the sky.

Marlene stared at the piece, then clapped her hands. "You are correct. I will look at it and always see the sunshine. I will remember the days when I was young, and would join the boys to dip my toes in the canals and eat picnics in the parks." She seemed happy to stroke the golden sky. "It's fun," she said, almost wickedly, as though she was doing something forbidden. "I was never allowed to touch anything my husband painted. See? They are all under glass. It makes them look dead. I like art I can touch." She turned her gaze back toward us, a disappointed expression puckering her face. "Is that it? No money? Just these two paintings?"

As far as he was able—given he was pretty firmly wedged between my hips and the wooden arm of the small sofa—Bud wriggled. "These are the only items Jonas asked me to bring to you."

Marlene retook her seat and pouted. "Oh," was all she said. She seemed to have lost all interest in the paintings and waved her little arm toward the wall behind her. "They are all by Dirk. He was a good painter. Not as good as Jonas, but not bad. Menno can't draw a stick, but he can play the piano competently." I suspected that Menno van der Hoeven did everything competently, rather than with passion. I wondered which parent he'd taken after, but my train of thought was broken. Marlene had leapt from her seat and began to waltz around the tiny room. She hummed a tune I knew well—Eric Satie's "Je Te Veux"—and closed her eyes as she went, causing us to pull the paintings at our feet even closer to our bodies. Eventually she began to sing the words of the song, twirling about in the cramped space. Bud and I exchanged a worried look.

The buzzer at her front door gave all three of us a start. Stopping in her tracks and opening her eyes, I could tell Marlene was dizzy, confused, and about to topple. Bud and I rose together—the only way we could—and we lunged for her as she swooned. Both paintings fell flat onto their backs on the carpet, which cushioned them, but my foot caught the corner of the Seurat/Klimt, and a big chunk of the thickly applied gold leaf of the sky at one of the corners flaked off.

We were more concerned about Marlene than the painting. Bud rushed into the reception hallway, shouting he'd find a glass of water, just as the front door of the apartment opened. Menno van der Hoeven walked in. "Mama?" he called. He looked more surprised than worried when he saw me at his seated mother's feet trying to fan her face with my hand, the paintings now filling the floor as Bud tore toward the kitchen.

Bud's cop instincts had kicked in; he was back in a moment with a floral bone china cup full of water, which I held for Marlene to sip.

"Have you been dancing again, Mama?" asked Menno flatly.

"Just a little," replied Marlene, as though nothing had happened. "These nice people brought your father to see me. Has he gone already?"

"Papa is dead, Mama," replied Menno in a matter-of-fact tone.

Finding his comment odd, I stood up, not quite knowing what to say—not a normal state of affairs for me. I waited for Menno to give Bud and me a sign as to how we should react to his mother's confusion.

He continued, "I don't think he's gone, Mama, I think he fell onto the floor." He took the one step necessary for his long legs to get him to the far side of the paintings and he righted the larger piece, the portrait of his father. He turned it to face his mother. "You see? Here he is."

Marlene clapped her hands. "Yes. As good as ever. That hat suits him," she added, smiling.

I looked again at the portrait and marveled at Jonas's talents. It was so like the original, right down to the tonality of the paints, it made me shudder to think how good an artist Bud's uncle could have been if he'd ever developed his own style. Spotting a few photographs of Menno's father wedged in between towering tulip vases, blue and white china, and lots of little figurines of goose-girls sitting atop the cluttered, antique furnishings, I noted, "Jonas captured your father's features very well."

Menno was still holding the portrait at an angle that allowed his mother to see it, but he glanced down and said, "Yes, but I think he overdid the sadness in the eyes—that was more *Gachet* than my father."

I couldn't argue, because I could only see three photographs of the late antiques dealer, and everyone smiles when there's a camera in front of them.

"What else did he send?" he asked.

My tummy tightened. "Jonas had written everyone's name on a piece from his collection, in addition to a portrait. This one was for your father and his family. I'm afraid I accidentally kicked it when your mother became a bit . . . disoriented . . . and I think I've damaged the corner. I'm ever so sorry."

I leaned down to pick up the artwork and realized only a smallish piece of the gold leaf from the topmost corner had come off. "It's not too bad, and your mother didn't seem all that keen on it to start with. There are lots of other pieces that are, shall we say, 'similar.' Bud and I could easily replace this with one that's not damaged."

I pointed the damaged corner toward Menno and he peered at it. "I see. The paint, or whatever it is, goes all the way around the edge. This is unusual." In his blunt manner, he added, "It is definitely damaged. You would prefer one that is not broken, that's right, Mama?"

"I don't like old, broken things," she said quietly.

"Tell you what, Menno," said Bud jovially, "how about we take this away and we'll drop another piece into your office sometime. We'll try to find one just as . . . um . . . golden, or at least sunny-looking, and then you can bring it to your mom whenever it suits you. She obviously loves to have her walls covered with art, and maybe she'll find room for two more pieces."

"Bring a small one, Bud, whatever color it is," said Menno with finality. To be fair, looking around the room, I understood why he said it.

Marlene was not going to be able to tell us much about Uncle Jonas, if she even remembered him at all. We all seemed to reach a silent agreement we should leave.

"Menno, we're so glad you popped by, but perhaps we should move on to our next appointment now," said Bud.

Menno looked relieved. "Good. Mama, stay here. I will say our goodbyes." He waved toward the door.

With the two of us outside in the common hallway, and Menno hanging on to his mother's door, he and Bud put their heads close together and spoke quietly.

"She seems all right now, but she was quite confused and disoriented," said Bud. "I think she was dizzy after waltzing about the room for a few moments. I'm sorry, Menno. I'm so lucky my mom is okay; it must be tough for you. A worry."

Menno looked puzzled. "My mother is very well, thank you. You do not know her. What you see as a problem with her mind is how she has always been. It is not unusual."

Marlene appeared behind her son at the door. "Did they kill Jonas to get his pretty pictures, *zoon*? Your father said they would. They killed your father, you know, and now Jonas, I think."

Menno sighed. "She talks in an unusual way sometimes. She means nothing. Now, if you please." He didn't slam the door in our faces, but he pushed it shut firmly, removing the chance to ask him about his visits to Jonas's house.

"We need to talk," I said.

Bud replied with, "I'll phone Frans first and we can talk while we wait for him."

I took the damaged painting from him, wrapped the sheets we'd picked up off the floor around it, and tucked it under my arm.

Standing outside on the street in the shade cast by Marlene's building, I knew exactly where I wanted to start the conversation. "What do you think she meant by that comment about Menno's father being killed for Jonas's paintings, and Jonas himself being a victim too?"

Bud shook his head. "I knew you'd go there," he said, almost smiling. “Cait, I don’t care what Menno might have said about her actions not being unusual, the poor woman’s losing it. There’s no question in my mind. Forget what she said. It meant nothing.”

I had to decide how to play things. “I could be wrong . . .”

Bud chuckled. “You’ve never once said that and meant it,” he said—lovingly, of course.

I gave him my sweetest smile. “I could be—there’s always a first time, you know. But I don’t think I am. I think there’s a chance someone killed Jonas to be able to get their hands on his paintings. But, if so, why? They’re good, but not *that* good.”

Putting his arm on my shoulder, he said, “Uncle Jonas fell down the stairs. He was old, infirm. If he’d been able to sell his stuff for large amounts of money, his home would be full of valuables, but he wasn’t living high on the hog. He was getting by. Sure, he was gifted, but art was his hobby. These two-artist pieces are a case in point. He was clearly having a great deal of fun with them.”

“Come on now, Bud, you and I both know a lot of criminals who’ve made a fortune from their illegal enterprises who don’t look as though they are enjoying living the high life, but they have the money hidden away somewhere. What if that’s what the mystery key is for? Some sort of lock-up where he’s stashed the loot?”

“Why are you talking like a character from a Humphrey Bogart movie all of a sudden? Listen, none of this in the car. That Frans has ears like a bat.” As the car pulled up in front of us, I agreed, and we returned the damaged painting to the rear of the car.

“Good meeting?” asked Frans as we slid ourselves into the back seat and buckled up.

“Fine, thanks,” said Bud. “About how long until we get to the next place?”

Frans tapped his GPS system. “With this traffic, about eighty to ninety minutes.”

"Okay, thanks, I'll call ahead," said Bud, pulling out his cell phone.

It was going to be a long hour and a half, so I decided to do a bit of thinking. I wriggled into the corner and pressed my forehead against the cool window, focusing on the glass itself, not the scenes flashing past. Sometimes concentrating on what's in the foreground can help us better understand what's in the background, and I had the distinct impression that was what I needed to do.

Where the City Meets the Countryside: Landscape

PIETER VAN BOXTEL'S HOME WAS in Hoofddorp, where the grids of streets met waterways, and the suburban landscape frayed into the brown fields, now empty of their world-famous bulbs. As we neared the town, industrial buildings loomed on the flat horizon. Neat houses lined the roads, and everything looked clean, fresh, and newly painted under the summer sun. We pulled up in front of an unprepossessing brick-fronted house that suggested recent construction and an interest in sustainability, its roof being covered with solar panels. The postage stamp of a front garden was neatly arranged with borders of shrubs and flowers that signaled welcome. At the front door we rang the bell, holding two rectangular paintings, one much larger than the other. I couldn't help but wonder how much the real Pieter would look like Jonas's portrayal of him as Vincent van Gogh.

The woman who opened the door was tall, rail-thin, and wrapped in a floral dress that didn't quite reach her knees, showing bare legs. She looked to be about fifty, based on her skin tone rather than the color of her hair, which was dyed blue-black and knotted on top of her head.

She eyed Bud suspiciously, but her gaze softened when she looked at me. Our sheet-wrapped parcels drew most of her attention.

"Bud Anderson and Cait Morgan for Mr. Pieter van Boxtel," announced Bud in his most professional tone.

The woman looked uncertain. "Mr. van Boxtel did not say he had visitors coming."

"I spoke with him on the telephone about an hour ago," replied Bud.

"I'll see," the woman replied, then shut the door in our faces.

"Do we look suspicious?" I asked Bud in astonishment. "That's twice in one day."

"It could be these," he said, nodding at the paintings.

She opened the door again. "Come. Shoes, please."

The pile of shoes just inside the front door, and the fact that she herself was wearing house slippers, was a clear enough indication of what she meant. The blond wood floors and cream throw rugs added more weight to her request. The house was spotless; indeed, it gleamed. Expecting a traditional interior to match the brick frontage, I was surprised that the hallway led through a house that, other than the front wall and half of the roof, was made almost entirely of glass and metal. It was a symphony of starkly modern architectural design—almost shockingly so. The opposite of Marlene van der Hoeven's claustrophobic apartment, this was bright and airy, and had almost no adornment on any surface, horizontal or vertical. The light on the white walls was the only decoration, the angles and planes of the walls creating shadows that would certainly shift as the sun moved.

"Come," she repeated, and shuffled along the hallway. She seemed to be polishing the wood as she walked.

"She's the cleaner?" I whispered to Bud as we followed. He shrugged. "She can come and do our place next," I added.

Lounging on a chaise made of white leather with a chrome frame, set in the middle of the wide-open space that comprised a cooking, eating, and sitting area, was a long, thin man with thick, white hair slicked back and curling on his collar. He was dressed entirely in shades of soft green. He got up with an efficiency of motion I found surprising in someone who must have been in his mid-seventies. He was across the cavernous room in what seemed like no more than three long strides, his hand outstretched, his pale blue eyes glittering beneath hoods of lightly tanned skin.

He greeted us like long lost family members, "Ah Bud, Cait, how good of you to come; I have been looking forward to your arrival. Helga, some tea for my guests, please. Or would you prefer something else? A cold beer? It is a warm day after all."

I was suddenly aware I hadn't eaten since the mammoth *rijsttafel* the night before, and realized that another beer might not be such a good idea. Then I reasoned it would be better than a cup of tea, which I really didn't fancy.

Sensing my hesitation, Pieter added, "A pastry with tea, or some ham and cheese with the beer?"

Before Bud could answer, I said, "Savory sounds good, thank you, with a cold beer for me."

"That'll be good for me as well," said Bud.

"Thank you, Helga," said Pieter, then turned his attention to our parcels. "Would you like to put those down over here?"

We leaned them against the side of the chaise and turned to admire Pieter's garden, which was what he'd been looking at when we'd arrived. With nothing but glass at the back of the house, the outside really did seem to come right into his home; the sparkling-clean glass doors were wide open, and a dozen or more pots overflowing with greenery and floral displays spilled into the living space from the patio area beyond. Outside was a riot of color—where each plant was growing into, or at least in front of or behind, another. It appeared that while Pieter van Boxtel preferred clean lines and no decoration inside his home, in his garden he favored the impressionist style of landscaping; not one shrub or plant had been cut to shape. It made for a pleasant effect, and one I mentally banked as something we could aim for in our own place when we finally began to make planting decisions.

"It is my heart's joy," said Pieter, looking around, his face suffused with a glow of pride.

Given the presence of Helga, I wondered if he had help outside as well as inside, and thought it as good an opening gambit as anything. "It must be a lot of work," I said. "Is gardening something you and your wife have turned to in your retirement?"

Pieter gave me a look I judged to be a veiled dose of disdain. "I am divorced. For many years. I have two men to do all this. My back—it does not allow for bending."

He'd risen from the chaise fast enough and pretty easily. "I'm sorry you're not as agile as you'd like to be," was what I thought best to say.

I'd taken an instant dislike to Pieter, and wondered if it was because of Hannah's description of him as "an accountant by day, a hard-drinking, lascivious, so-called artist by night." I fought the instinct to give Hannah's opinions weight, and focused on making up my own mind about the man.

Helga put an ice bucket full of bottles of Heineken and Grolsch beers on the high, white quartz counter at which were placed four white leather and chrome stools, which looked as though they'd been spaced with mathematical precision. Six glasses sparkled next to the bucket—three were printed with Heineken logos, three with Grolsch. The correct glasses for beers? At home? Telling.

Beside them sat a wedge of hard, butter-colored cheese on a plate. Another platter was covered with thickly cut home-cooked ham. Grapes and figs sat in two bowls. Snowy porcelain plates topped with white linen napkins were laid out in a straight line. Helga had done all this silently as we'd been admiring the garden. She vanished from the room at a nod from Pieter.

"Sit," he said, waving at the chairs. "Enjoy." His tone made the invitations sound like an order, but, despite this, we did as he asked. Soon I was feeling the unreasonable thrill I get when I use my two thumbs to pop the little metal device that holds the top on a bottle of Grolsch.

As Pieter helped himself to cheese, drawing the little slit in the triangular slicer along the top of the wedge, making curls, Bud poured his own Heineken, and I pulled apart the thick chunk of ham on my plate with my fingers; Helga had provided no cutlery, so I inferred this approach was expected. Pieter's beaming smile as we all tucked in confirmed this to be the case. Appreciative sounds of "mmm" and "yum" followed. The cheese was sharp and strong, the ham succulent and sweet, and the dried figs complemented them both. I didn't touch the grapes. Too healthy, I thought.

Pieter took three curls of cheese and most of the grapes, then, nibbling, asked lazily, "These are the pieces Jonas left to me?" Bud and I nodded, both chewing. "Good," added Pieter. He strode across the room and pulled the wrappings off each piece. The sheets puddled on the floor.

He stood in front of the pieces with his back to us. I was annoyed that I couldn't see his face. He wrapped one arm around his middle and balanced his elbow on it, stroking his chin. He turned to address us. "I like the acrylic piece. Marc Chagall's *Lovers by Moonlight* in the style of Rembrandt? Very amusing. But the portrait? Not my . . . cup of tea."

I looked again at how Jonas had depicted Pieter, and was astonished by how he had captured the essence of the man, while remaining within the creative parameters of Van Gogh's self-portrait. The original artist had portrayed himself clean-shaven, wearing a blue jacket buttoned to the throat. I knew it to be the last self-portrait Van Gogh had painted, one of three he'd created in September 1889 while a voluntary patient at the sanatorium of Saint-Paul-de-Mausole at Saint-Rémy. This rendition showed the left two-thirds profile of Pieter von Boxtel, which didn't flatter him. Jonas had shown him as gaunt, with dark hair swept back; the man's hairstyle hadn't changed, though its color had, and it was the style Van Gogh had sported at the time of the painting. The tragic Vincent had hidden his damaged right ear from the eyes of the viewer. Involuntarily I looked at the right-hand side of Pieter's face and spotted a scar; faint and a little jagged, it ran along his jaw. I wondered how long he'd had it, and how he'd got it.

"It's very much like you," I said. "At what age do you think Jonas chose to capture you?"

Pieter shrugged, half turning to look at the portrait. "In my forties, maybe."

"You didn't have that scar on your face then?" I wondered how he would react.

His right hand touched his jawline. "This? Yes, I've had it since I was young."

"I wonder if Jonas chose this portrait to hide your injured face," I mused. "Did you come to know Jonas before you'd been scarred?"

Pieter van Boxtel straightened his back. "Jonas himself cut me. In anger. He had a bad temper, that man." His tone was not charged with any emotion.

Bud stepped up. "What happened? Why would my uncle have attacked you? I thought you were friends. I thought all of the members of the Group of Seven were close."

Pieter sighed. His shoulders sagged a little. "We were, but we were also young, headstrong, and—I will be honest—we sometimes drank too much."

"What was the cause of the argument?" I pressed.

"It is too long ago; I do not remember."

"I think you'd remember what gave rise to you being marked for life."

Pieter threw a baleful glance in my direction then strode back to the counter, picked up his beer glass, and drained it. He placed the glass down with the utmost care. As he turned toward me, I saw an unmistakable flash of hatred in his eyes before he lowered his eyelids and contemplated his perfectly manicured hands. "He was your uncle, so I will tell you," he said; he didn't look at Bud. "It was because of a woman. Of course." I spotted a half-smile. "Jonas thought I had been unfair to a young woman and I disagreed. Sometimes Jonas thought he ran our Group. He did not. There was no leader, there were no rules. Jonas thought he could say how I should live my life." He finally looked up. "This was before I married, of course."

Bud looked puzzled. "A fight between two young men over a girl isn't so unusual, but how did you come to be so badly injured?"

Once again Pieter stroked his jaw. "It was a bottle, a glass—something jagged. There were punches, then this. There was a lot of blood. Jonas panicked and ran off. Willem took me to the hospital. There is not much flesh here. It took a long time to mend. Longer to heal than the affair with the girl had lasted." A wry smile played around his lips. I suspected that this was a man capable of cruelty. "I will always remember her because of this. I have forgotten most of the others." I was beginning to believe that Hannah might have summed up this man correctly.

"Of course I'm sorry my uncle injured you like that," said Bud quietly, "but I assume you two made up? As friends, you know?"

Pieter smiled coldly. "This was nothing compared to what bound us together."

"You mean your shared love of art?" I knew I sounded disbelieving.

"Yes, that," replied Pieter coldly.

"More than a shared love of art, what did you all have in common?" I asked.

Pieter seemed not to notice Bud's glare at me, and answered evenly, "I would say art was the glue that held us together, to begin with. After much shared time and experiences, we became close. Eventually we all did different things with our lives. Things some of us had not imagined. Through it all, our interest in art was always there for us."

I looked around the empty walls. "You don't live with art around you?"

Pieter replied quietly, "Art does not need to be merely paintings hung on walls. I choose to see the artistry of nature out there, and the interplay between light and planes in here. I do have some pieces in other parts of my home, where only I see them."

"How terribly mysterious," I said, as whimsically as possible.

"I was hoping to learn about my uncle from you," said Bud, changing the topic. "My mother never knew him, you see. So far we've met Willem Weenix, who gave us some insights, and Dirk van der Hoeven's widow, Marlene. She wasn't really able to help much."

"Marlene?" grinned Pieter, stroking his chin thoughtfully. "She never so much as knew or cared what day of the week it was. It astonished us all when Dirk said he was marrying her—then Menno came along soon afterwards. We all understood. By then Dirk was highly respectable, and it was difficult for him to take Marlene to public events. She was always . . . unpredictable. A beautiful woman in her way, but like a child. Is she well? I have not seen her since Dirk's funeral. They had a large house in Bennebroek. Does she live there still?"

Bud shook his head. "No. We visited her at a small apartment in central Amsterdam. It looked as though she'd lived there for some time. She was fully installed."

"Was she wearing a sari? She did for quite a number of years, I recall," asked Pieter.

"No, just regular clothes," said Bud gently. "Did you know Marlene well—before she married Dirk?"

Pieter shook his head. "Not . . . well."

"And my uncle?" pressed Bud. "What can you tell me about him? Anything I might be able to tell my mom?" He spoke with as light a tone as I suspected he was able; it was annoying that we hadn't been able to find out much about Jonas so far.

Pieter offered us another beer, which both Bud and I declined. I suspected he was playing for time. Time to consider his answer—or was it to avoid answering at all, I wondered.

Eventually he sipped his second beer, then said, "Jonas wasn't our leader, but I have to agree that he was the person who held the Group together. He was our center, and certainly our most talented member when it came to making art. I might not care for this portrait, but it is well executed. I like the freedom and inventiveness he has expressed in this other work. However, overall, I think Jonas's main shortcoming was that he never took time to develop his own 'voice' in art. He doted on several artists and traveled a great deal to visit places where Van Gogh, especially, had lived and painted, for example. Like this portrait, he aped great works. That is why I am pleased and surprised to see the acrylic piece. It seems he found his own style in the evening of his life. He chose to rage against the dying light, it seems, by amusing himself with this mixture of subject and style."

I found it curious that a Dutch man would speak about my Canadian husband's Swedish uncle by referring to the work of a poet from my own home city of Swansea. I couldn't let it pass. "You like Dylan Thomas's work?" I asked.

A sly smile crossed Pieter's lips. "Yes, I like many Welsh things." My skin crawled. "Dylan Thomas wrote in a way that is fun to read aloud. I practiced my English by speaking aloud these words by a Welsh man. I thought—and still think—highly of Dylan Thomas. He was a particular hero to me. Your accent is Welsh, I am correct?"

"Yes, I'm from Swansea too."

Given what Hannah had said about Pieter van Boxtel's habits, I wondered if he'd modeled his life after the hard-drinking, womanizing Thomas, with amateur artistic attempts taking the place of breathtaking poetry. I further wondered if Pieter's wife had to put up with what Caitlin Thomas, my namesake and Dylan's wife, had faced. Looking again at the portrait of Pieter, I said quietly, "Dylan Thomas died at St. Vincent's Hospital in New York. Another link to Vincent, and you?"

Pieter shrugged. "A coincidence. I certainly didn't worship Thomas so much that I retraced his footsteps around the world, as Jonas did for his favorite artist."

"When did he do that?" asked Bud.

"Over decades," replied Pieter. "Van Gogh traveled to, and stayed in, many places in his short life. Your uncle did his best to visit every place his idol did, here in the Netherlands, in Belgium, London, Paris, and the south of France—Arles, Saint-Rémy-de-Provence, and Auvers-sur-Oise, that I know of. Whenever he had been somewhere he would return with sketches and paintings he had made, and photographs he had taken, his eyes full of fire. Especially when he returned from France. Jonas went there many times. He told me once he met a woman who claimed to be Van Gogh's daughter. Her mother had been a dancer at a bar, I think. Or maybe a prostitute—that is more likely. Van Gogh had relationships with more than one, I understand. Jonas wanted to believe she was Vincent's daughter. He carried a photograph of her for some time. That was in the sixties. She was an old woman when he met her."

"Was he just as obsessive about his other favorite artists?" I asked. "I understand Hals, Vermeer, and Rembrandt were on his list too, and the range of work we found at his home suggests he at least managed to capture the techniques of many painters, even if he didn't revere them."

"No, he was not as obsessive about any others as he was about Van Gogh. He loved the work of great artists and did whatever he could to be close to it and, as you can see here, to emulate it. He worked in many galleries and museums over the years, taking night shifts when he could. He did not care for the people who came to see the art—his birthmark, you know—but he cared for the pieces themselves. He enjoyed being alone with them. He called it his 'special time,' when he could touch the works."

"Surely those places are all locked down at night," said Bud.

"Automation means everything is on camera, right? And they can't ever have been keen on anyone fondling the paintings."

Pieter shrugged. "Maybe today, but forty or fifty years ago that wasn't the case. Doors and windows had locks, and there were men with flashlights—Jonas being one of them. That was it. Yes, art was attached to the walls, but not with any great care. Much of it was simply hung, and people were trusted to come within inches of it. A velvet swag was put in place to keep people a little distance away, but that was all. It is strange, but true."

"A loop or two of rope keeping the honest honest?" observed Bud wryly. "Maybe you're right, then. Jonas might have become intimately connected with the works of the artists he admired. His ability to reproduce the different styles we've seen in his portraits was extraordinary, and must have required close inspection of the originals."

"You are correct," said Pieter with gravitas as he looked back at the two pieces we'd brought with us. "I will place the portrait of me . . . somewhere, of course. The Chagall/Rembrandt will hang in here. I like it. It makes me smile."

"You had a career as an accountant, I understand," I said to Pieter, calling him back from his thoughts.

"Indeed." He blinked slowly. "It was a good career."

"You live well off it in your retirement," I added casually.

Pieter's face crumpled into a crooked smile. "People are happy to pay someone to do small but important accounting jobs for them. I have retired, but still have some private clients. It helps me afford the gardeners, and Helga." The way he said the woman's name made me wonder if her role extended beyond keeping his house clean.

"Do you think my uncle had a good, happy life, Pieter?" asked Bud, sensing, like me, our interview was coming to a natural conclusion.

Pieter gave the question some thought, then said, "Happy, for the most part. Good? What is 'good?' Fun? Productive? Influential?

Who knows? I think Jonas lived his life for himself and not for anyone else. Though he did allow our Group to benefit from his . . . passion. That is all I can say."

Pulling the unknown man's photo from my purse, I hopped down from my stool to pass it to Pieter. "Do you recognize this man? We aren't sure if he was one of your Group—or maybe you know him from somewhere else?"

For the first time since we'd arrived I noted what I judged to be an entirely open display of inner thoughts and feelings by Pieter. He frowned as he looked at the photo, then shook his head. "Not someone I know." He paused. "Is this recent—I mean, is he this age now? It's not a good shot. Not sharp. Might it be an old photograph?"

"I think most pictures printed like this, on photographic paper from, presumably, a real film, are more than a decade old now. There were some showing him older, so maybe this is about thirty years old."

Pieter shook his head slowly. "Not one of the Group, certainly, not even anyone from our regular groups of friends, or anyone I know personally. He could be from another part of Jonas's life."

Sensing Pieter was hoping we'd leave, I tucked the photo away again and said, "There's just one more thing—and then we'll let you get back to your day, Pieter. When we were leaving Marlene van der Hoeven's home today, she said something to her son that suggested she thought her husband Dirk had been killed by someone trying to get at Jonas's paintings, and that the same people had killed Jonas too. What do you think she was talking about?"

I watched intently as Pieter listened to me, and thought about how to respond. His facial muscles gave away almost nothing; the throbbing vein in his neck told a different tale.

"She said this?" he snapped. "Dirk died a few years ago. He was a healthy-looking but sick man. He always seemed to be in control, but he held his emotions inside him. It ate away at him. In the end his heart could take it no longer. They say she found him in the garden, dead among the roses. That would have been difficult for anyone to accept, most of all Marlene. Poor Marlene. As for Jonas? I heard from Willem he fell at home. It was an accident. Is this not correct?"

"That's what Menno told us," I said, choosing my words with great care.

"And the police told this to Menno, I understand," retorted Pieter. I agreed. He relaxed a little, though the vein in his neck continued to throb. A couple of quick licks of his lips told the rest of the story—Pieter van Boxtel was suddenly worried that Jonas de Smet had not died of natural, or at least accidental, causes. I found his reaction interesting.

It was clear that our host wanted us to leave. I suspected he'd phone Willem Weenix as soon as we were out of the front door, which took us about two minutes, even allowing for putting on our shoes. His farewells were cheerful enough, but I could tell something dark was bubbling inside Pieter van Boxtel.

As we walked along the neatly bordered path toward our vehicle, I said to Bud, "I know we can't talk in the car, but I would like us to go right back to Jonas's house for a *serious* chat."

"Why there?" asked Bud conspiratorially.

"For one thing, we can take the damaged painting back and dump it off, and for another, I want to hunt through the place again. I think we've missed something."

Bud sighed as he allowed the attentive Frans to open the car door for us. "Sadly, I think you're right," he said. His response set my mind racing as we made our way back to the canals of Amsterdam from the canals of Hoofddorp.

Candlelit Interior

AS WE STOOD ON THE step of Jonas's house, Hannah pulled open her door and stomped out. "Hope all your meetings went well today. Didn't one of them want what Jonas sent 'em?" she gestured toward the sheet-covered painting we'd brought back from Marlene's.

"It's been damaged," I said, deciding not to explain how. "We'll replace it. There are a lot to choose from." I hoped she'd let us get on, but it wasn't to be.

"Want to come in for a cuppa?" she said, beaming. "I know you do." She stood back and opened the door as wide as it would go. "Come on wit' ya."

Bud's voice was firm when he answered, "We'd like to Hannah, but we still have a lot to get done today, so we'll have one with you tomorrow, as we said. Do you know if anyone else had a key to Jonas's place?"

"If I'd known someone I'd have called them instead of the police. Anything to keep that lot away."

I decided to ask. "Why don't you like the police, Hannah?"

The woman paused, looked at Bud, and said, "You was one, right?" He nodded. "Well, they ain't all bad, but some is. And I've met a fair few of them in me time. Not only the ones I had dealin's wit' over this thing." She tapped her prosthetic leg. "Believe me, when you run a brown café, you know all the people who run the other ones, and they talk. Sometimes they talk about the folk who drink at their places, and sometimes them's the police. Word gets around. Not everyone with a badge deserves to have one. And a lot of 'em live way beyond their incomes. You know what I mean?"

Instead of following up on Hannah's hints about police corruption, Bud said, "If you'll forgive us, Hannah, we need to get going. Good to talk, as always. See you in the morning." He began to climb the stairs to Jonas's apartment, leaving me to follow behind.

The stairs up to Jonas's sitting room seemed even steeper than I recalled; I reckoned that was because jet lag was kicking in, and I was hungry. The ham and cheese at Pieter's house had been welcome, but had only served to sharpen my appetite.

Plonking the damaged painting against the wall in Jonas's sitting room, both Bud and I flopped into armchairs. Our faces told the tale; we were pooped.

"So, here we are, Wife. What's the plan?" asked Bud.

"I've been thinking," I began.

"Brain the size of a planet, genius IQ, photographic memory—you're always thinking," said Bud with a chuckle. "What about, and what conclusions have you drawn . . . based upon what facts and observations? Full report required."

I sat up a little. "I haven't had a chance to write up any lists, and you know I like them, so you'll have to make do with one from my head. However, before we talk, I need to go upstairs. Want to come? There are chairs in Jonas's bedroom in any case, and I want to check something—after I've used the facilities."

Bud pushed himself out of the creaking chair. "You go on ahead; I'll bring the painting. I'll pop it back up to the attic."

As Bud picked up the piece of artwork the sheet fell away from the corner I'd kicked, and I gave myself a moment to examine the naked corner of the canvas where all the gold leaf had dropped off. I'd expected plain white canvas, but what I saw was a thick, milky coating on top of what seemed to be dark splodges of color. "That's odd," I said. "I wonder what that stuff is?"

Bud peered more closely, then switched on a standard lamp and held the piece close to the source of light. "Maybe he recycled an old canvas from an earlier effort. I've read artists do that a lot. Always have, apparently. Don't know what the white stuff is, though. Some sort of primer? You know, to allow the gold leaf to stick. Some type of glue?"

"I'll take another look later. Got to go—now!" and I clambered up the stairs as fast as I could.

Minutes later, we were sitting beside the windows in Jonas's bedroom; the dying light streaming in highlighted the two spots on the wall opposite us where, until that morning, the portraits of Willem Weenix and Pieter van Boxtel had hung. The whole room seemed unbalanced because of their absence; the largest portrait, of Willem, had been in the center, flanked by the two smaller depictions of Pieter and Greta. Greta's picture was hung to the far left, closest to the wall of the room that abutted the house next door, and now our focus naturally went in that direction.

"They've been there a long time, those paintings," I noted. "Look at the patches on the wallpaper. The places where they hung are much more vivid—the sun hasn't bleached the pattern." I noticed an anomaly and stood. I examined the wallpaper more carefully. "Look, something was pinned here. And for some time, though certainly not as long as the paintings. It's gone now."

Bud made groaning noises as he pushed himself out of his chair. He joined me beside the wall and bobbed his head about. "I see," he said. "You're right. Maybe a tiny picture?"

I shook my head. "There's no hole for a nail or hook, just a pinhole. Besides, I don't recall any of the paintings upstairs being as small as the size of this other mark."

"You'd remember that because you never forget anything," he said with a smile. My eidetic memory is something I don't like people to know about, but Bud and I have relied upon it on many occasions when I've been able to recall details that have helped us in cases we've tackled together.

"No need to take my word for it; you can go up and measure them all if you like."

"It might not have been a picture at all, I guess," mused Bud. "What about one of those photographs of the mystery guy? You said there were lots."

"None of them had a pinhole. In any case, there's something I wanted to check up on the top floor anyway, so shall we go?"

"You go first and I'll bring up the rear."

Bud set me on my way with a playful pat on my bottom, then we both used the handrail to help pull our tired bodies up to Jonas's attic. "He must have been pretty fit, going up and down these stairs all the time," I noted. I hit the light switch as I got to the open space at the top of the stairs, but nothing happened. Flicking it back and forth—because that always works!—I said, "Probably a bulb is out; I'll check. Be careful here. Hey! Why'd you dump that damaged piece right here? I've kicked the blessed thing again!" I stumbled forward and stopped myself from falling by waving my arms. Bud was at my back in a few seconds, and helped me regain my balance.

"I can't leave you alone for two minutes, can I?" he said. "Sorry, you're right, I shouldn't have left it where I did, but I didn't think you'd walk into it."

"I wouldn't have done if the lights had come on," I replied. "Now I think I might have done even more damage. Did I break the frame?"

"Priorities, Cait. Let's sort out some illumination first. There are some candles here. Got a light?"

"Old smokers' habits die hard," I said, handing him a book of matches from the depths of my shoulder bag.

Bud lit five large candles, each at a different stage of use, which sat on a tin lid that had obviously served as a drip tray for many candles over a decent period of time. The flames flickered around the room, bathing it in a soft light that blended with the dying rays of the sun. It was magical, prompting a thought.

"I wonder if Jonas ever painted by candlelight?" I said. "He might have tried to reproduce the original setting in which certain artists worked."

"Good point. That could have been part of his experimentation with technique."

I laughed loudly, the sound ringing around the brick walls of the attic. "Swallow an art book recently, Husband?"

"I'm not a complete Philistine," smiled Bud. "I browse pretty widely, you know. And now that I have full access to all your books too, I find myself thumbing through them on occasion. While you were at work putting out departmental political fires last week, I decided to mug up on Amsterdam. You've got a lot of books about artists. More than I realized."

"A year of art history at Cardiff Uni before I specialized in psychology means I covered a lot of ground. I bought a few when I was here that first time, back in the eighties. The people I'd been peeling bulbs with thought I was mad to spend money I really couldn't afford on books, rather than beer. But there you go—I still get pleasure from those books, whereas the beers would be long gone."

Bud patted his tummy and chuckled. "Beers take longer to get rid of than you might think. We've had a few today, and not much to eat. Would you think I'm a complete wimp if I said I feel done in? Back in the day I could have taken the long-haul flight and the rushing about we've done in my stride. I hate to say it, Cait, but it seems 'the hill' everyone talks about is fifty-five, and I find I'm slowing down a bit since I crested it."

"Wow," I mugged, "you'll be fifty-six next month. An old man. Starting to act your age at last?"

"I'm more than middle-aged," said Bud quietly. "Makes you think, doesn't it?"

I wasn't going to stand for that. "Your mom and dad are both hale and hearty in their eighties—your uncle, too. Who knows how long he'd have gone on if he hadn't fallen? You've every chance of a having good few decades ahead of you. Ahead of *us*. So stop it now. You're just jet-lagged and hungry. Come on, let's call it a day and get ourselves back to the hotel. A reviving shower and an hour or two with our feet up and we'll be ready for another lovely dinner out somewhere."

"Not something as big as last night, I beg you," pleaded Bud.

"Japanese? That's light, and there are some great sushi places here."

"Sushi? Here? When we live on the west coast of Canada? Are you nuts? It can't be better than we have at home. I was thinking of something that's actually Dutch."

I was puzzled. Bud doesn't normally care what he eats. Maybe we'd eaten too many sauces and flavors for his palate the night before. "You know it's not really the sort of weather to be eating lots of stews or cheesy dishes. What about trying to find a fish restaurant? They have good fish here, beyond the sushi variety."

"Okay, let's try to do that. But, even if not fish, something light. Now—back to our hotel. I'll clean up and you can do restaurant research. Do you think the fact that it's Friday night will mean it'll be tough to find a fish place?" said Bud as he began to blow out the candles.

"Hang on a minute!" I shouted louder than I'd meant to.

"What?" Bud sounded startled.

"There, on the wall. See? There are a few bricks sticking out in the shape of an 'X.' The light from the candles is casting a shadow we wouldn't have seen in daylight. I wonder what it is." I strode over to feel the lumpen outcrop. The bricks were loose. "They move," I said, feeling a thrill in my bones.

"Don't pull them out, Cait. The whole wall might fall down," said

Bud, relighting the two candles he'd already extinguished, but he was too late to stop me.

Once I had all five bricks on the floor, and was sure I hadn't caused a major structural catastrophe, I peered into the hole. "Candle please." Bud obliged and I poked about with my hand, then the whole of my forearm. "It goes back a long way," I noted.

"You're probably waggling your fingers in next door's attic," said Bud.

"No, I can't be. The roof is angled. This is in some sort of cavity between the wall and the roof structure. Remember, when we looked up from the street, this window at the front was in the peaked, tiled roof part of the house. This doesn't connect with next door. Hang on, there's something here."

When I pulled my hand out, my fingers were gripping a long wooden box. It had a patina suggesting great age, and the letter *s* was carved into its top.

"Bud, where's that key?" Bud handed it to me, but it didn't look as though it would fit. "Too big. Shame."

"Is it even locked?"

"Good question." I tried the lid. It opened easily. The box was empty. We both made little noises of disappointment. I happened to look down at where I'd placed the bricks. "Play the candlelight down there, Bud." Wax dropped onto the floor as Bud tried to do as I'd asked. It congealed on the little flecks of rosy brick dust I'd created when I'd pulled the bricks loose. "Now isn't that interesting," I observed.

"Very." Beside the mess we'd just made was a similar pattern of dust and wax. "I wonder who did that."

"It could have been Jonas, but it could have been someone else." I closed my eyes for a moment, recollecting the room as it had appeared when we first arrived. "Thinking about it, there was a bit of a gap in the overall chaos, right here, when we first arrived—before you started moving stuff about. That's curious in itself, don't you think?"

Bud sagged. "Today's been a very curious day. Let's take the box, get out of here, and talk about all of this when I don't feel as though one of those bricks just hit the side of my head. I can't cope. This isn't what I thought would happen when we came here. I need to think, and I just can't."

"Come on, let's get you sorted, old man."

The Leidseplein at Night

BY NINE-THIRTY WE'D REFRESHED OURSELVES, found a place to eat, and were grazing on some delicious, if small, succulent steak wraps accompanied by crispy fries and various dips—including mayonnaise. We treated ourselves to a bottle of prosecco, both agreeing more beer wasn't the way to go, that it was too warm for red wine, and that we didn't have a good reason to splurge on champagne. It was fun to sit beneath the stars and the neon, watching the world go by. As the night wore on I began to feel ancient, as the people swirling around and past us seemed to get younger by the hour. We decided to head back to the hotel before we fell asleep at the restaurant.

"The wine's gone straight to my head," I admitted as we weaved our way through what seemed to be even busier streets than when we'd gone out. "And I know I promised not to bring up any difficult topics tonight . . ."

"Thanks for that," replied Bud, "but I know it won't last, so go for it. You have until my head hits the pillow. After that I'm making no promises."

I gave him a playful thump on the arm, and did what he knew I was going to do. "I think we need a plan of action for the morning. First thing, can you get hold of some of your old buddies from Interpol or the secret squirrel squad or whatever, and find out the exact details of your uncle's death? I hope this isn't a bad precedent to set, but if you have useful contacts, maybe now's a good time to use them. I don't feel comfortable having only Menno's scant explanation. He might not be lying, but he might be hiding something. If Hannah's right about him looting your uncle's place after his death, he might have been removing evidence of something suspicious. Possibly a laptop, too. I also want to spend some time getting some stuff down on paper. I know I can recall what I wish at will, but I need some time to lay out my thoughts. We should have coffee with Hannah and meet Greta at the Café Americain for lunch as planned, then go to Bernard's and Johannes's homes in the car you've booked. Once we've seen them all, I'll have a better grip on this, I reckon."

"You don't think Jonas fell down his stairs, do you?" said Bud, sounding glum.

"I don't know about his falling, but I think there's something fishy going on."

"Not every death is murder or manslaughter, Cait. People do die of natural causes or accidents, you know."

"I know, but even if his death *was* just an accident I have the distinct impression there's something going on behind a veil of secrets. This Group of Seven? Very odd. Your uncle's letters and innuendos? Even more odd. I feel there's something just beyond my grasp—and it's annoying me. I'll grant you he was old, and the stairs at his place are a deathtrap, but . . ." I trailed off, not able to find the words to adequately express what I was feeling. "Look, the fact of the matter is that this isn't about me or my instincts; it's about your mother. She's gone through her entire life feeling the loss of her brother. The fact that she never mentioned him to you suggests a deep-seated sense of that loss. A type of grief with no possible outlet. No resolution. We have a chance to give her that at least. She's a lovely woman, Bud—despite her quirks—and she's been incredibly kind and loving toward me. I feel the need to do this to help her very keenly. She deserves some real information and insight. We owe her that."

"I owe her a great deal more, Cait, and you have great instincts," said Bud as we arrived outside our hotel, "so you don't need to prove anything to me. I know your gut reactions aren't that at all—you've usually sensed something you lock away in your hot little brain, and when you pull it out again it makes sense. We're both grappling with the effects of an extremely long travel day, just a couple of days ago. We're still out of sorts. Be kind to yourself, and me, and let's sleep on it. You know you do some of your best thinking when you're asleep."

"Hey! Just because I've been known to drop off while I'm using my wakeful dreaming technique doesn't mean I use dream analysis to help solve cases. Not always, anyway. But I know if I tried my special method right now I'd be in the Land of Nod before five minutes had passed. So, you're right, let's sleep on it."

For about three hours after I snuggled into the comfort of the sheets and my husband's arms, I slept as though I were a corpse myself, without recalling a single dream. When I awoke I immediately knew I wasn't going to get back to sleep in a hurry, especially given Bud's rhythmic snoring. I lay still for quite a few minutes, then decided to give in to my bladder and my need for quiet thinking time. I judged the little lamp on the desk wouldn't bother my comatose husband, and I was right. For the next couple of hours I made lists, struck through items on them, then made new ones. Everything was jumbled. It was a frustrating process.

Jonas's different styles of artistic endeavor, his travels to visit places connected with Van Gogh, his work as a guard, then a walking guide, his attachment to a group of people who—so far—all seemed a little less than likeable. These were all real facts as far as I could determine, but what did they tell me? Did I feel I knew Jonas better now than a couple of days earlier? Not really. And that was annoying. No one seemed to be adding to the picture of the man—there just seemed to be more to back up what little we knew: he was talented and obsessed.

I admitted to myself that my personal dislike of Menno possibly had something to do with the fact that he was unpleasantly brusque, rail thin, and, if Hannah was to be believed, he'd been economical with the truth about visiting Jonas's house.

As for Hannah herself? She was a conundrum. She'd appeared to be open and honest with us, and her assessment of Pieter had seemed to be spot on. But beyond that? A teenage pregnancy, a failed marriage, a lost limb? There are some people in this world to whom tragic or bad things seem to happen with greater frequency than to the rest of the population. There appears to be no explanation for it, but, when you dig deeper, you can often see a pattern of poor choices, of genes leading to ill health, or of styles of upbringing that lead people down certain ill-advised paths. It's usually about the choices—whatever conditioning they might be based upon. Hannah seemed to take responsibility for her bad decisions, and I knew that was why I had warmed to her. But she'd still made them. Maybe her perception of people and their actions should therefore be viewed with caution too. Then again, she'd seemed to hit the nail on the head with her assessment of Pieter.

Willem Weenix, Jonas's best friend, had a questionable start to a successful business career, and that wasn't unusual. His family situation suggested a fair level of normalcy. However, there were his run-ins with the police to consider—and not just in decades gone by.

I couldn't assess Dirk van der Hoeven, but thought about his widow; if Marlene's grasp on reality had always been tenuous, could her rants about someone killing her husband and now Jonas be seen as just that—the ravings of a woman lost in her own world? I made a note to check if Bud would ask his contacts if they could look into Dirk's death too, so we'd have more than what Pieter had told us to go on.

Pieter van Boxtel had made my skin crawl. I spent quite some time trying to work out exactly why that was, and all I could come up with was his manner, which reeked of the lascivious nature Hannah had suggested. Maybe the presence of the brooding Helga had made more of an impression upon me than I'd first thought. Upon reflection, I wondered if a cleaning lady should have smelled so strongly of cheap scent. That was what had set me off, I knew it.

I felt excited to meet the remaining members of Jonas's Group in just a few hours. Then I looked at the bed and clambered back into it. The clock told me it was 5:17 AM, but my body wasn't even sure what day it was. All I knew was I had to sleep.

Morning in Amsterdam

AS I NIBBLED ON BREAKFAST pastries, and sipped strong, dark coffee, I told Bud about the thinking I'd been doing the night before. He agreed with me on all counts, and added his own ideas.

"Since I put out all those calls earlier on that you asked me to make, I've been thinking: I had a slew of briefings on drug trafficking when I was here," he said in a low voice. "That's why I came. Rotterdam is a major gateway for drugs and other contraband into and out of Europe. It's not a new problem, and it will never go away; technological developments help, but it all comes down to people in the end. And people can be bought—which is why smuggling is a problem that will never be solved. I know the patterns we would look for—the types of groupings of people who would come together to allow for efficient trafficking, and it makes me look at the Group of Seven in a different way than you are likely doing."

"How so?"

"Money man? Pieter the accountant; you need one to move, hide, and launder the money. Transport man? Johannes, who worked on the metro project; worth their weight in gold, a good logistics guy. Means of getting stuff into the country, then distributing it? Dirk with his antiques store, and Willem with his art supplies; their setups would allow for import, export, and local distribution. Government connections to allow for cover-ups, and getting to the people whose palms need to be greased? Greta van Burken. See?"

I was taken aback. "What about Bernard—a draftsman? And Jonas himself—an art-obsessed night watchman? What roles did they play in all this? Did they plan it all? Make the connections?"

Bud shook his head. "That's where my theory falls apart a bit—I don't know. *Yet.* Jonas traveled a lot, so he could have been sourcing drugs, or making sales pitches. I don't know about Bernard, but it's a pattern."

He seemed keen for my support, so I gave it. "You could be right, of course. Drug trafficking rings aren't my thing; they're yours, so I bow to your expertise in the field. And you're right, I think what I'm grasping for is an elusive pattern in all this. When I found those loose bricks last night, and then the box, I thought we might have found a physical clue that could help us navigate a path through all this mush, which is what it is right now. I can't believe the box was empty, but I'm *sure* someone else did what we did with those bricks—though it might have been Jonas himself, I suppose. The puzzle is, why hide an empty box?"

"A puzzling box? You love it, don't you," grinned Bud.

I shot to my feet. "How stupid of me. A 'puzzling' box? A 'puzzle' box, that's it! It might not be empty, just hiding its contents."

"Sit down, Cait," said Bud, glancing around. "Finish your breakfast. And that coffee—it's very good this morning, better than yesterday."

I nodded my agreement—I'd blamed my taste buds the day before, but maybe the coffee really hadn't been that good after all. I shoveled my food into my face, making Bud stare, glugged to the bottom of my cup, and said, "Ready?"

"Just like Marty when he goes squirreling," said Bud, rising. "Can't wait to get back to that box now, can you?"

The elevator took forever to arrive, then seemed to stop to disgorge passengers at every single floor, until finally we were back at our room. I pulled the long, wooden box from the drawer where we'd placed it the night before and opened it again. The wood had faded over the years and was a pretty even tone of mid-brown; the varnish was aged and a little worn, but the interior base was definitely a different texture, and seemed too shallow for the overall dimensions of the box.

"I think it's got a false bottom," I said gleefully, "but we'll have to work out how to access it. I bet there's a secret compartment." I suspected Bud's smile was more indulgent than enthusiastic, but he let me fiddle with the box, my reading cheats perched on my nose, my patience running out as the moments passed. There wasn't a single mark or indentation I could see on the entire box, inside or out, except the *s* on the lid, and I'd run my fingernails along that a dozen times. "I'm usually pretty good at this sort of thing," I bleated, then Bud reached for the box, and I conceded defeat.

Resorting to his own pair of cheats, Bud turned the box much more slowly than I had. Eventually he said, "We established last night that the key Jonas sent to us in Canada didn't fit this lock, right?" I agreed. "The end of the key was too big, right?" Again, I agreed. "Tell you what," he continued, pulling the key from his pocket, "Let's see what happens if we do this." He placed the end of the key in direct alignment with the too-small keyhole and pushed against the entire metal fitting. The whole of the keyhole device disappeared deep into the box, and there was a satisfying clicking noise.

"My hero!" I shouted, seeing that the base had popped up. "What's inside?" I suspected that I sounded like a five-year-old.

Bud pulled out a long envelope. "Looks like a letter," he said.

"Another one? Is there a name on it?"

"Nope."

"Open it!"

Bud ripped open the end of the long envelope, and pulled out a many-times-folded concertina of stiff-looking paper. I saw Bud's eyes dart back and forth as he began to read. They grew wide. His eyebrows rose and his mouth made a little "O" shape. It was frustrating to not know what he was seeing, so I leapt up and peered over his shoulder.

The material looked like real parchment, and I suspected that was what it was. It was certainly impressive, as was the handwriting. In the letter we'd seen back in British Columbia, Jonas's cursive handwriting had been rounded, and sort of friendly-looking. This was a letter created in copperplate script, which ebbed and flowed in a stately pattern across the surface of the dried animal skin, the rough, wide strokes of some of the letters suggesting it had been written with a malleable but sharp writing instrument. A quill? And with what? Was that red ink, or . . . ?

"Is that blood?" I said aloud.

Bud sighed. "I have a horrible feeling it might be. Look, where it's wider you can see a brownish tint, like rust. I don't think red ink does that." We exchanged the sort of look that wouldn't be expected of two people who'd seen more than their fair share of cadavers. There was something so creepy about the ancient-looking document that Bud removed all but the essential number of his fingers from it.

Writing materials aside, the thing was a work of art; it was difficult to focus on what it said because of how wonderful it looked. I knew it made no sense, but to my inexperienced eyes it seemed as though it could have been created hundreds of years earlier. I turned my attention to the meaning of the words, rather than their form, and read.

> You who are reading this: I have chosen you because you are of strong moral fiber and an upright person. You have a task ahead that will require you to exercise your judgment and your sense of right and wrong. I no longer possess this ability. I lost myself many years ago in this respect. I have made decisions that were maybe foolish, but I believe I made them for the right reasons.
>
> Art is the embodiment of culture, history, mankind's societal and moral memories. To destroy it is a sin, if

sin exists. I no longer even know that. There is beauty in all art. We must look hard to see it, but it is there. Who are we to judge what is good and what is bad? We can respond to art with our hearts or our heads. I choose to respond with my heart. I have chosen, and I have acted. This has been my life's work. I will be judged by those left behind when I am gone.

But you? I charge you with making decisions that mean you will be judged now, while you live. I am sorry I was too weak to do that myself. The journey will be long and will forever change your life. Take care about the paths you choose.

—Jonas de Smet

We were both quiet for a moment. "It's a bit melodramatic," I said eventually. "Especially if that is blood."

"I was thinking 'ominous,' but 'melodramatic' works too. Hang on a minute, though—how did Jonas even expect us to find this? I know he sent me the key, but he didn't give us any clues about the location of the box. Let's be honest: it was pure chance we were in his studio at night, and you spotted the protruding bricks in the candlelight. It was a fluke. With all the meticulous planning he did, and with all the detailed instructions he sent via Menno, you'd have thought he'd have given us that one additional piece of information, wouldn't you?"

My mind was racing. "Maybe he did, but Menno didn't pass it on? It's possible that Menno was searching Jonas's house for this very box, and he could have even found its hiding place. What if he's the one who left the mess on the floor in the attic? But, without the key, to him it was just an empty box, so he put it back where he found it."

"Why would he put it back?"

"So we could find it."

"If he had information about its location, why didn't he pass that on to be sure we *would* find it?"

I paused. "I don't know," I replied honestly.

"I don't like that he didn't tell us he'd been to Jonas's after the poor man died," added Bud, sounding exasperated.

"Me neither. All we can do is ask him about it. If we tell him we found the box, and just show him the empty version, not this letter, he might tell us something. We can at least confront him with what Hannah told us about him being there. By the way, we should head out if we're going to get to Hannah's in time to present her with her portrait, have coffee, invite her up to select a painting, *and* get to the Café Americain in time to meet Greta. It's all going to be a bit of a rush, so arriving at Jonas's early would be a good idea. We have to wrap up the paintings for Greta too. Thank goodness the two for her are both relatively small."

"You're right," said Bud, checking his phone for messages.

I knew what he was hoping for. "I can't imagine medical records are going to be that easily accessible. You only made those calls an hour ago, and it is Saturday, after all. Though maybe the sort of contacts you have—which I can only imagine are quite high up and probably with all sorts of security clearances—can make the impossible happen."

Bud shook his head slowly as he said, "Okay, stop digging. I only managed to reach one guy. He's pretty well-connected; his name is John, and that's all you need to know."

I smiled sweetly, rather than triumphantly. "Well, possibly not even *he* would be able to conjure up autopsies on Jonas and Dirk van der Hoeven this quickly. Let's get going, and make sure you're on the alert for a vibration in your pocket."

Bud mock-saluted me and said, "I'm going to put this letter, and the box and key, in the room's safe before we leave. I don't think we can be too careful with all this stuff. We still can't be sure what it means."

My insides were squirming, because I was pretty excited that we were going to be working to find out what it all meant, but I tried to hide it from Bud, as I still couldn't fathom his uncle's role in . . . well, whatever was going on.

Woman with Loose Hair

HANNAH MUST HAVE MISSED OUR arrival at Jonas's house, because no curtains twitched at her window as we entered. By the time we knocked at her door, we'd already bundled up the paintings destined for the others and had placed them on the stairs ready to go, and we were carrying Hannah's portrait.

It only took a moment for her beaming face to appear after we knocked, and she beckoned us in with warmth and grace. We entered directly into her living area, which was narrower than Jonas's because of the extra width taken by the stairs leading to his upper rooms plus the set leading to hers. In fact, her living room was tiny; as landlord, Jonas had retained the larger quarters for himself.

The décor was unexpected; much like the woman herself, the exterior belied the interior. Her apartment was seventeenth-century brick on the outside, but sixties chic on the inside. Her love of eye-boggling patterned wallpaper, abstract art, monolithic lamps, primary colors, velvet throws, and shag carpets was beyond question, and the number of records that lined one wall further marked her as an avid collector of vinyl LPs. It was like taking a step back in time to the swinging sixties, in all their groovy glory. I tried not to think of miniskirts and Twiggy, but failed; then I took one look at Hannah and realized she was no Jean Shrimpton . . . though she might have been comparable in her day, if the photographs on the sideboard were anything to go by.

I pounced. "Are these of you?" I asked. Hannah smiled proudly. "Beautiful," I said.

"No more than a girl back then. I was seventeen in that one." She smiled coquettishly. "T'ought I knew it all, didn't I? What an eegit I was. No wonder they were able to take advantage."

"You mean men?" I asked.

"Anyone who wanted to. Mind you, it was looking like that what got me my job, and then I turned it into a career."

"You must have picked up the Dutch language incredibly quickly to be able to work in a brown café," I observed.

"Turned out I have an ear for languages," said Hannah, sounding delighted. "Easiest t'ing in the world to listen and learn. I didn't speak the lingo at all when I got here, but I was pretty good six months later. It's a funny old language, Dutch, but the rhythms and patterns are pretty close to English. Many people spoke English even back then—the well-educated ones, in any case. Not that we had a lot of that type at our place."

"The bar you ran was traditional?" I pressed.

Hannah beamed. "Proper wood fittings, good stained glass, and always full of a cloud of smoke it was back then. Not allowed now, of course."

I'd noticed the aroma of cigars when we'd entered, and wasn't surprised to see ashtrays all about the room. I wondered if she'd light up while we were there—I hoped not; having managed to kick the habit myself I was always grateful that back in Canada it was easy to avoid smokers, but I knew my willpower was still pretty poor whenever I caught a whiff of tobacco smoke on the air.

"I've brewed up fresh-ground coffee, but I bought the pastries. Don't bake. Never did. Leave it to them who's good at it, I say. Give me two minutes. Make yourselves comfy. Don't get a lot of visitors anymore, but I cleared a couple of chairs for ya."

Hannah bustled off to the minute kitchen; there being no door to separate the two areas, I sneaked a peek inside her tiny workspace, which, despite the fact that you couldn't have swung a mouse in there let alone a cat, managed to house a full-sized cooker, as well as a washing machine and a small refrigerator. Bud and I didn't chat, but I let my eyes take stock of the rest of our surroundings. I judged most of the furnishings and décor to be original to the sixties; I couldn't help but wonder what it might all be worth, given the desire for "mid-century modern" that had become apparent as Bud and I had hunted down inexpensive furniture for our new home.

Placing a battered old tray bearing a pot of coffee, mismatched mugs, and plates on a low table in front of us—which looked as though it had been extruded from one piece of vivid orange plastic—Hannah announced, "Lemon tarts. Me favorite. Hope you like 'em. Help yourself to coffee and so forth. My serving days is behind me."

She sat in a slightly ragged, mustard-upholstered armchair and immediately lit a small cigar, which sent blue smoke wreathing upwards. "If you've got 'em, light 'em," she said, then proceeded to munch her way through a tart while taking puffs on her cigar between mouthfuls. It seemed she wasn't going to compromise her habits just because she had guests. Wiping her mouth after the tart, and stubbing out her cigar, she turned her attention to the painting we'd brought. It had been propped up against her collection of vinyl, facing us, the whole time. She'd completely ignored it. Finally, she seemed ready to comment.

"So that's how he saw me?" We all looked. "Not very flattering."

To be fair to Hannah, she was right. Jonas had used as his base the portrait of a woman with her hair falling loose about her face, which Van Gogh had painted in 1885. The woman in the original had been not dissimilar to Hannah herself, which made for a weird feeling—Jonas had captured Hannah with Van Gogh's technique so exactly that it almost outdid the original, because I could look up and see the real person. In the portrait, Hannah looked to be in her thirties. It was apparent that the soft, open, innocent features of the seventeen-year-old girl had hardened by that time, and, since then, she'd broadened somewhat.

Hannah sloshed coffee into a mug from the pot and drank it down. "Not so bad, I suppose," she added, still addressing the portrait. "I wore my hair like that when I was that age. In me prime, I s'pose you could say. Boss of me own place, no men to answer to."

"I bet you made a pretty penny when you sold it. If you sold it. Did you? You know, when you lost your leg?" I realized I could have phrased my questions more gently, but Hannah didn't seem to mind.

She smiled and looked at me. "Sold it to some eegit who t'ought it would be a money machine. He paid too much, but I wasn't going to tell him. At least he kept me staff on for a year or so, which I made him promise."

"How did you ever manage to buy the bar in the first place? That can't ever have been a cheap thing to do here. Brown cafés are all situated in old, well-established buildings, aren't they? Antique wood fittings, years of smoke making them a deep, rich brown . . . that's where they got their name, isn't it?"

Hannah sounded passionate when she answered. "Old, yes. Mine was built in the late 1600s. Jonas loaned me the money, so he did, in 1970. Charged me no interest. I paid him back as fast as I could. Lived here for free while I did it."

Thinking of Bud's theory about drug trafficking, I said, "Did you get a lot of tourists turning up and expecting you to sell marijuana at your place? Muddling up brown cafés with coffee shops?"

Slapping her good thigh and laughing heartily, Hannah rolled her eyes and said, "Oh, you have no idea." She grinned. "We had a big dish set out on the bar covered with one of them giant glass domes, you know?" We both looked impressed as she mimed the size of the dome. "When the innocent eegits would come in looking for dope, I'd sell them one of the chocolate brownies or cookies we kept there. I never said there was nothing in them, and all they saw was a sign that said 'Special treats' with a price. It was my little joke."

"Did many of them walk away thinking they were high?" asked Bud.

"And acting it," she giggled. "All they'd had was a glass of beer and a chocolate biscuit—but they were having fun, and I dare say they dined out on the tale when they got back to their homes. Best money I made was on those little extras."

As I looked at Hannah, I wondered if she might have been part of an international drug-smuggling ring. It seemed unlikely, but I told myself she hadn't always been old, one-legged, and a bit too thick around the middle to make getting up out of a chair an easy task; the photographs proved she'd been lithe and vivacious, and her ownership of a bar and restaurant meant she'd have had an ideal outlet for distribution.

"So you sold up when?" I asked, as lightly as possible.

"1991. It was time. I'd kept it all ticking over after the accident, in 1986, but I eventually had to admit to meself I couldn't do it anymore. You can only rely on good people for so long, then they want to move on. As it turned out, it was a good time to sell. The perfect time. Just before everyone went running about moaning and wailing that the end of the world was nigh. Of course, it all bounced back. But now? They say this year, 2013, has been the worst year ever for the economy in the Netherlands. Still they spend. It frightens me. Seen it all before. Banks? Robbers, all of 'em. Not as bad as 1637, of course, but not good."

Bud shot Hannah, and me, a puzzled glance, "1637?"

"The great tulip market crash of 1637," I said. Hannah smiled knowingly, and Bud's eyes widened. "Could it be that your boning up on Dutch history didn't catch that nugget of information?" I said, smiling. "In 1637 there was a huge slump in the price of tulips and tulip bulbs. The Dutch had become tremendously enamored of tulips after their introduction to the country in the mid-1500s by the Ottomans, and by the beginning of the 1600s—the mid-1500s to the mid-1600s being the Golden Age in Holland—tulip bulbs were in high demand among the status-conscious nouveau riche. I think I'm correct in saying the whole thing went ballistic in about 1634, when merchants trading in tulips began mortgaging and even selling their homes to be able to buy bulbs, then sell them on fast at hugely inflated prices."

"You mean like people who flip houses?" asked Bud, amazed.

I leaned back as I answered. "Sort of, but without all the sweat or investment people put into houses they flip—they just sold them on. Prices reached dizzying heights, and people made fortunes on bulb sales. Then, almost overnight, it all went pop. Families were ruined, homes were lost, inheritances were wiped out. The first, and original, bubble to burst."

"Tulip bulbs?" said Bud. He was struggling with the concept. He shook his head, bemused.

"It'll all go pear-shaped here before you know it," said Hannah bleakly. "If you're going to sell this place you'd best be quick, or be prepared to wait for years. All these austerity measures are bound to hit home pretty soon. That's when we'll see what the Dutch are really made of. It's another thing that colors their relationship with the Germans, them being the best-off folks in the whole of Europe. Many people hereabouts whisper they might have lost the war, but they've ended up winning the peace."

"Is that how you feel?" I wondered aloud.

Hannah shook her head. "There's problems enough to go around, many of them of people's own making. You can't keep borrowing with no way to pay it off and expect things to turn out all right. My old mother might not have taught me much about life, God rest her soul, but she taught me that at least. When I borrowed cash from Jonas it was against my better judgment. He insisted. I was pretty confident I could make the profits to pay it back fast. Only time in my life I ever borrowed money from anyone, and it all worked out all right. I never needed to do it again, thank the Good Lord." She crossed herself, looking serious. She noticed my gaze and added, "Just me little ways—not a churchgoer anymore. So, do you want me to come up wit' you now to pick out another little something from Jonas I won't mind havin' on me walls, or should we do it another time?" She had noticed Bud looking at his watch.

"We're supposed to meet someone for lunch," said Bud apologetically. "We'll be back again tomorrow. How about then? Will you be at home?"

Hannah smiled a comfortable smile at Bud. "I don't get out much these days. Same time tomorrow?"

It was agreed. "We'll have time for you to browse all the pieces he created and pick out something you really like," said Bud brightly as we took our leave.

Outside on the street, having collected the pieces for Greta van Burken, Bud began to hustle me along. "Come on, we can't be late and I'm not sure exactly how long it'll take us to walk there."

The picture I was carrying wasn't terribly big, but the frame on it was heavy, so I was struggling a bit. My hyacinth linen outfit looked crumpled, and I was on the downside of a sugar high from the lemon tartlets. I sweated so much I had to keep stopping to shove my sunglasses back up my nose, and we hurried along at such a speed we didn't have time to talk. All the time I was working on fitting Hannah into Bud's suggested drug-ring setup. Sadly, she fit too well.

The Café Americain: Interior

I ADMIRE ART NOUVEAU, AND reckon art deco is just about perfect—it's the symmetry of it I love—but one of my favorite periods is the time when elements of both were used together by architects and interior designers. I adore it when each aesthetic rubs shoulders with the other. All of which meant the Café Americain was an absolute joy to behold. It had been way beyond my budget when I'd been in Amsterdam as a student, so I was happy to know I'd be able to lunch there.

Dark wood floors, bentwood chairs, chandeliers that looked like collections of Japanese parasols, and stained glass to die for all nestled within a cozy setting of arched ceiling vaults. Upon our arrival I noted the long tables set up for newspaper reading. They were busy, and most of the other tables were full of people enjoying various types of refreshment. Bottles of wine and beer, pots of coffee, pastries, and platters of meats were all in evidence. We scanned the room for someone who could be Greta van Burken. She wasn't hard to spot; she was the only elderly lady wearing a hat in the place. She was sitting close to a beautiful old grand piano, beside the window, at a table surrounded by four large wingback chairs. She looked imperious, which was fitting, as the portrait Jonas had created of her showed her as Rembrandt's *Juno*. The woman's demeanor upon our arrival at her table suggested she'd be delighted that he'd portrayed her as the queen of the Roman gods whose symbolic animal was a peacock, because her hat was held on with a giant hat pin that sported a peacock feather, of all things.

"You are Bud and Cait?" she asked in a heavy Dutch accent. For the first time since we'd arrived in the Netherlands, I was concerned about possibly having to communicate with someone whose English wasn't fluent, or at least proficient. I'd tried to put some time into learning the Dutch language in the week before we'd left Canada, but I'd been too busy at work to really get into it. I hadn't even swotted up on it on the airplane, as I'd said I would. I hoped my few hours of study would get us through the interview.

"Sit," she said. "They will bring the menu. You have gifts for me from Jonas?"

The arrival of the waiter, our swift perusal of the menu, and the ordering of risotto, blackened chicken salad, and a couple of beers held things up a for a few minutes, but then we got to the matter at hand: presenting Greta van Burken with her pictures.

As we removed the coverings, I felt a bit like a purveyor of art, trying to convince a potential buyer to invest. With her slight frame sitting perfectly erect in the large chair, Greta stared at her portrait impassively. During the moments of silence that followed the unveiling, I took the chance to study her clothing, which was expensive, classic, and timeless. I also noted her features, which were expertly made up, refined, and surprisingly un-saggy for her age—which I judged to be around the mid-seventies. Her micro-expressions told me she liked what she saw but wasn't about to admit it.

Finally she spoke. "Not bad, but I was never that fat."

I thought it was an incredible piece, and I didn't think the portrayal was of anything but a normal-sized woman. I decided to bite my tongue.

She gave her attention to the piece Bud was presenting. It was a representation of Caravaggio's *Salome with the Head of St. John the Baptist* in the style of Botticelli. It was stunning.

"Must I take this one?" she asked. She looked at it as though it were a pile of rotting herring, going so far as to wrinkle her nose in disgust.

"I'm sure my uncle would not have wanted to force you to accept anything you didn't want," said Bud in his professional tone. I could tell he was annoyed. "I'll take it back to his studio, if you would prefer."

"I would."

"Very well, then." Bud threw the sheet over the piece again and tucked it beside his chair. I did the same with the portrait she was going to deign to accept, just to make sure it was safe until we all left. I worried about how on earth we were going to winkle information about Jonas out of her over lunch, and began to wonder how quickly Bud and I would be able to eat.

The arrival of two icy beers came just in time to prevent us from having to make small talk immediately. Greta took tea. We all drank, and comments about the restaurant, the hotel, and the surrounding area ensued at a leisurely pace. As she spoke, I could tell her English was excellent, but she used it in a slow and pedantic manner. She struck me as being sufficiently well-educated to have learned it as a child, but rude enough, in the normal run of things, to rarely stoop to use it. Her entire persona screamed "haughty."

I was grateful that the service was efficient, and was thrilled that my risotto was just the right side of *al dente* for me—overcooked in most people's books—and the Parmesan it contained was plentiful and sharp. I ate happily, and Bud seemed content to munch on his salad, because it meant less time to spend either in an awkward silence or just jabbering on about nothing in particular. As for me, well, I'm pretty hopeless at small talk. With less than half my meal left, I finally decided to take the reins and launched into a series of questions I knew I wanted to ask, no matter how things might go downhill once I began.

"When exactly did you meet Jonas, Greta?"

"It was 1955. We ran into each other at a gallery and got to know each other quite well, quite quickly. I joined the Group almost immediately, and we became Seven. It was my joining that allowed the name to come into being." She looked proud at her "achievement."

I was puzzled. "I thought Bernard was the last to join the Group, so surely that honor goes to him?"

Greta regarded me with an icy stare, but didn't respond.

I decided to try a different approach. "I understand you were the only female member of the Group of Seven. That must have been interesting."

"It was, and it wasn't," she replied.

"In what way was it interesting?"

"Oh, this and that," she said enigmatically.

"Were you and Jonas lovers? Is that why you were invited in?" I was playing a hunch. Bud glared at me.

She smiled coldly. "Not for long."

"And what about the other members? Did you work your way through them too?" Bud crunched on his crisp lettuce so loudly I was worried he might shatter his teeth.

"Not quite all."

"I understand you took your art seriously. Jonas did too. Did you work together?"

"Jonas always worked alone."

Bud finally spoke up, having polished off his meal. "I'm trying to find out all I can about my late uncle, to be able to tell my mother—his sister—about his life here. She's keen to know more about him, which I'm sure you'll agree is understandable. What can you tell me about him?"

"Not much a sister would want to know."

Greta was beginning to annoy me. Bud sensed my rising frustration and said, "But surely there's something. Was he kind or generous? Happy, or not? My mother told me his birthmark affected him badly as a boy—was it something he ever got used to? Maybe as a woman you'd know."

Greta stopped pushing her almost-untouched salad around her plate. She looked at Bud and said, "He had your startling eyes, but otherwise he was utterly unattractive. He had no confidence with women. It was why I took him as a lover. He was eager to please and to learn."

I understood what Hannah had meant when she'd said Greta was able to insert a great deal of venom into a single put-down sentence. I was convinced she'd made her last, cruel statement just to embarrass Bud, and paint his uncle as pathetic. I wanted to throw her salad in her stupid, skinny lap. The fact that she was a senior didn't matter to me at all—she was rude, stuck-up, and thoroughly unpleasant. I saw what Hannah had meant about the way she'd grown to hate Greta's hats, too. I judged she wore them in place of the crown she felt she deserved. I inwardly applauded Jonas's choice of two-artist painting for her; she was exactly the sort of woman who'd coolly demand that a man's head be delivered to her on a platter.

It dawned on me that Jonas de Smet had surrounded himself with unlikeable people, and I wondered why he'd done it. I had to admit to myself that Bud might be onto something with his theory of necessity breeding strange bedfellows when it came to the drug trade. I decided to try to find the woman's weak spot.

"I dare say your family's connections with Dutch governmental institutions meant you mixed in some elevated circles as a matter of course, Greta. Why did you fraternize with the Group of Seven—was it the art, or because you fancied a bit of rough?" I heard Bud clear his throat nervously.

Greta van Burken tilted her head. "I don't know that saying."

Her eyes told me otherwise. I managed a fairly inoffensive, "We'll let it pass then," before I stuffed the last of my risotto into my mouth to shut myself up. We weren't going to get anywhere with Greta. I wanted to leave.

"Have you seen the others?" she asked, as if referring to pond life.

Bud gushed, "Everyone except Johannes and Bernard. We see them both this afternoon."

"Willem is still alive?" she sounded surprised. "Willem is very old now, I think."

"Around ninety. We visited him at his art supply store yesterday morning. His daughter told us he had suffered a stroke a little while ago, but that he is rallying," replied Bud, more politely than I would have done.

"He won't last long. They don't at that age," said Greta harshly. "Six weeks my third husband managed after his stroke. He was much older than me," she added, as if by way of an explanation. "Jonas fell to his death, I hear. Typical. He was always clumsy."

I saw Bud run his hand through his hair. I'd had enough; she wasn't going to do this to him. I caught the attention of our waiter, made the international signal that we wanted our check by pretend-writing in the air, then mouthed "*Snel*," suggesting he bring it quickly. I was already planning our getaway, but, before that—and knowing I'd better take my chance—I was contemplating parting shots.

"We hope you enjoy the portrait Jonas painted of you. It was his special wish that you should have it," I began. "It's a shame you can't give us any insights into his life. He was a talented artist and we understand the Group of Seven thrived because of him."

Greta van Burken sighed. She plopped her napkin on top of her food. "The Group of Seven was an excuse for drinking and debauching, with long, boring discussions about art as a cover. I enjoyed my proper art lessons, and I became a good watercolor painter. Most of the others had no talent, but they pretended to play at art very well."

"Jonas organized lessons, life classes, opportunities for people to develop their skills," I said.

"Opportunities to look at naked woman, then drink until they fell over, or fought."

"You belonged to the Group. You took part in it all."

"Only while it was worth it."

"Worth it in what way?"

Greta paused. "In ways I choose to not explain to you." She looked at Bud. "You were police, no?"

Bud looked proud. "All my life."

She shrugged. "Then that is all I have to say."

The waiter brought the check, which Bud insisted upon paying, and we left, carrying the unwanted painting. Our hurried walk back to Jonas's house gave me time to comfort Bud, try to regain my composure—despite getting sweaty all over again—and think through what Greta had said. Or, rather, what she hadn't said. Another one who didn't like the police?

I was relieved when Bud pulled his cell phone from his pocket, stopped to take the call, and rested the painting against his legs. I could tell it was important news. I waited, standing in the swirling Saturday throngs of locals and tourists, hoping it was good news—which in this case could mean many things.

The Man in the Street

"THANKS," SAID BUD, WINDING UP his call. "I owe you." He put the phone back into his pocket and picked up the painting. I was quivering with anticipation.

"So?" I urged, cantering to keep up with Bud, who was striding off. "What did 'John' say? Was it natural causes as the result of an accidental fall, or what?"

"Not news about Jonas, but about Dirk van der Hoeven," replied Bud. He sounded as disappointed as I was.

"How can that be? Is it easier to get hold of old records than new ones?"

"I guess so. Anyway, he says he should have news about Jonas in a couple of hours. We'll have to wait." He sounded resigned.

"What about Dirk, then? Heart attack in the garden, as Pieter told us?"

"More or less."

"What do you mean? Surely it either was or it wasn't?"

"He suffered a massive cardiac arrest, says the autopsy, but there was some question about where it happened, because the body had been moved. In the filed statements, Menno said his mother called him; he rushed to their home, found her dragging his dead father into the house from the garden, so he finished the job. Medics arrived on the scene and pronounced. They took Dirk's remains for examination. Paperwork says heart. He had a history of high blood pressure and high cholesterol, and he smoked like a chimney, apparently. His doctor wasn't surprised that it had happened, nor his family. Note on the file said Marlene accompanied his body to the hospital and kept telling his corpse that she'd warned him."

Pulling on Bud's arm to get him to pause, I was silent for a moment—largely because I was out of breath and not enjoying the feeling of sweat trickling down my back. Finally, I said, "What had she warned him about, I wonder? His poor lifestyle choices? Or that he shouldn't have done something that made someone want to kill him?"

Bud shook his head and looked at me with sad eyes. "All I wanted to do was fulfill my uncle's wishes, and be able to go back to Mom with some knowledge she could cherish about the guy. Instead, there's all of this . . . I don't know, this *atmosphere* of things not being what they appear to be. I don't like it."

"When we've delivered the last of the pictures we'll still have days of our visit left. We can get to the galleries, be a couple of relaxed tourists enjoying the architecture and history of the place. We can linger over a beer in an open square and talk about history, art, and culture—even tulips—to our hearts' content. Let's just push on through, and we'll come out the other end unscathed, I'm sure. This is all about being able to give your mom something she can cling to other than a sad memory of a missing brother—a hole in her life. We can do that, Bud, if we persevere. Let's hope we turn up some real insights into Jonas that show him to have been a wonderful person. I'm sure we will."

"You are a terrible liar, Cait. Something for which I am grateful. We both know neither of us will rest until we've worked out what's going on in the background. It might well be that Jonas fell to his death and that, for once, we're spared the problem of finding a killer. This goes almost deeper than that for me—this is now about understanding the story of a blood relative's life. Mom is getting on, but you're right: even at this stage in her life she deserves something to hang on to that is more than her childhood memory of a brother who left her behind. I was hoping we'd meet at least one person in whom Jonas had confided about why he did that. Then she might get some closure.

It seems he kept himself to himself, and all we have are some stupidly cryptic comments he's made in letter after letter. It's not enough, Cait."

"You want justice for your mom, don't you?"

"You can call it that if you like. What I really want is to understand why he did what he did. Then I can tell her. I'm beginning to care less about what he made of his life after all. Unless, of course, something comes to light that suggests nefarious activities on the part of one or more of the Group of Seven."

"Greta made it clear she wasn't going to say anything much because she knew of your background as a cop. Who do you think told her that? Menno? Do you think they're all still in touch with each other and are throwing up a smokescreen?"

"To hide what?" snapped Bud.

"I thought your theory about drug trafficking held a good deal of water."

"I'm not so sure now."

"Why?"

"I also asked my buddy to look into all the people who belonged to the Group."

I shouldn't have been surprised. Bud's nothing if not thorough. "And?" was all I said.

"Willem had been a person of interest in several cases, as his daughter told us. Often hauled in when dodgy art showed up around the city. But the others? Clean as the proverbial whistles. I didn't expect Jonas to turn out to be some sort of superhero, but I'd hoped for more than this vision of him. It seems he was an unfulfilled man with a temper, who tramped around the world looking for a connection with dead artists he idolized, ignoring the obvious talent he possessed while living his life in dead-end jobs. It seems such a shame he didn't do more with his art. He was really good, wasn't he? I'm not just saying that because he's a relative—and, of course, I don't know art like you do—but everything we've seen that he painted, it's quite something, right?"

I assured Bud he wasn't exaggerating the quality of his uncle's work. We'd arrived back at Jonas's house, so we'd nipped inside, deposited the piece Greta hadn't wanted, and picked up all four pieces we needed for the two appointments we had ahead of us. Bud checked his watch. "Frans is late again," he observed. We were standing on the front doorstep when the car arrived. This time it was a graphite gray saloon, and the driver wasn't Frans.

The dark-haired driver in his thirties who emerged from the vehicle appeared to be of Middle Eastern descent, if not birth, and he spoke with a distinct English accent. It was a surprise.

"Good afternoon. I am Farhad, your driver," he announced as he opened the car door for me.

"No Frans today?" I asked, wriggling into the leather-scented interior.

"Not today. It's his family day. He looks after his mother, who is not at all well. She might not have long."

I felt a bit guilty that I'd thought of Frans only as a mildly irritating driver. Then I reminded myself that he had, in fact, been a mildly irritating driver, but that we all have our responsibilities in life and I couldn't be expected to guess at everyone's. It helped. A bit. With this in mind I decided to make an effort to be a little more interactive with Farhad and opened with, "Your accent is English. Is that where you're from?"

As we negotiated the cobbles and crowds I could see Farhad smiling—not sitting directly behind him was helpful. "What a delightfully polite way to ask that question," he said. "Many people ask where I'm from and are surprised when I say Norwich, England. They expect something much more exotic, and not in a good way. They want to work out if they can trust me."

"Well, I'm Welsh, so I suppose the answer might be no," I quipped.

"Ah yes, the lingering sleight of being invaded and subjugated by another race almost a millennium ago," said Farhad, with good nature. "I feel that too. My family moved to England from Iran back in the seventies. I was born in Norwich, went to university in Bristol, and now live here."

"When did you come here? And why?" I asked. Bud wriggled uncomfortably in his seat as we gathered speed along the boulevards that would lead us away from Amsterdam and toward the coast, where Bernard de Klerk lived.

"I am a linguist. I worked for several years at the international courts at Den Haag, as a translator. I met a girl there, fell in love, and we moved to Amsterdam for her work. She has a good position as a programmer at the European headquarters of a car manufacturer, quite near the airport. I still pick up a bit of translating work now and again, online mostly, but this driving keeps money coming in on a more regular basis, and they like to use me because they have such an international clientele."

"Speak many languages?"

"Dutch, German, French, Italian, Russian, Hungarian, Swedish, Finnish, Spanish, Cantonese, Mandarin, Japanese, and Greek. As well as, of course, Armenian, Iranian, Arabic, and Hebrew."

"Impressive," chimed in Bud. "Covers pretty much the whole world."

"I'm working on Hindi, Korean, Senegalese, and Thai now," said Farhad proudly. "It's fun."

"Good for you," I said with feeling. "Expanding what you can offer might get you more translation work."

"I doubt it," said Farhad.

"Why not?" I was intrigued.

"My name. Farhad Massoud Nasrin will not inspire great confidence in a world where many are afraid of Middle Eastern connections.

Would you want that name associated with your company's online secrets?"

"I'm sorry," I said, feeling it.

"All I can do is my best. My mum taught me that," said Farhad. "My girlfriend is from a long line of Dutch people. They've welcomed me with open arms. That's the most important thing, and they all support us in what we're trying to do."

"Which is?"

Farhad laughed. "Saving up to get married, put down some real roots, and start a family. Same as most people."

Bud and I exchanged a meaningful glance. Love, family, happiness—common human desires.

"About how long is it likely to take us to get there?" asked Bud. "I'd like to phone ahead to confirm our ETA."

"I'd think about an hour from now. We're already beyond the A10, Amsterdam's ring-road, and once we've passed the A5 intersection things should get quieter. However, I'll warn you now that, because it's a summer Saturday, we might have missed the traffic going out to the coast, but we might hit it coming back in. There's a big family fun holiday center at Zandvoort aan Zee, which is just along the coast from where we're headed—Bloemendaal aan Zee. It's not a day-pass place, but Saturday is when many people head for home, or check in for a stay. However, although we might avoid those rushes, that entire stretch of coast is busy in the summer. People take their bicycles to ride the trails. When we head off to Noordwijkerhout we should be okay, but let's hope everyone stays at the beaches for an evening around a fire pit, and we can beat them back into town."

Bud made the call, and we settled in to enjoy the scenery. Holland is so flat, it's remarkable. Not for the first time, I was glad Bud and I would be returning to our home halfway up a little mountain. The sky looked ominously infinite us as we drove along. I felt it was pressing us down against the brown, unpopulated land, ribboned with gray roads, and dotted with vehicles that glittered in the summer sun. It reminded me of one of Hopper's paintings, rather than any of the Dutch masters. Once we glimpsed the much more appealing glint of the sea on the horizon, I felt my spirits lift.

The traffic slowed as the road narrowed, and I could sense Bud's anticipation rise with my own. We were about to meet Hannah's ex-husband, Bernard de Klerk, the last to join the Group of Seven, and the one Willem Weenix's daughter had told us might be our best source of information about Jonas. I allowed myself to feel hope—sometimes a bad sign.

The Glass of Wine

JONAS'S DECISION TO PORTRAY BERNARD de Klerk as the man offering a glass of wine to the young woman in Vermeer's painting had struck me as interesting; it was the only painting that wasn't a portrait of just one subject. I wondered why he'd done it. I'd given the piece a great deal of examination, noting that Bernard's face was portrayed as being much more vivacious than the original, and I secretly hoped he might not want it, because, of all Jonas's pieces, it had appealed to me the most. His attention to detail when capturing the room in which the scene was set was breathtaking, and I felt it was a piece I could live with at home.

"If it's all right with you I'll leave the car here, outside the house, and I'll walk to the sea in my shirtsleeves. I might even get myself an ice cream," said Farhad with a grin. "I could be back here in moments, when you call my number," he added. "We're just a short way from the beach."

I looked up at the imposing house. It was old, and had seemingly been surrounded by much smaller, more modern dwellings as the area had been developed.

Before we were even halfway up the long path that led to the front door, it was opened by a man in pale blue linen pants, rolled up above his ankles, a white, open-collared linen shirt, and a face that was tanned and smiling. "You must be Bud and Cait. *Welkom.* Come, come," he said. He rushed to take the painting from my arms, then ushered us into his home.

My first impression was of the sea. It seemed the house was built in a spot where a little niche in the bay brought the beach around a corner until it was directly behind the rear of the building. Two sets of French doors across the back of the house gave a view of a strip of vividly green grass, pale sand, and the dazzling blue and white sea. The décor used the same colors, minus the green, so the entire place felt light, airy, open, and welcoming.

A barefoot woman with ash-blonde hair and wearing a white linen shift joined us. "Welkom, welcome," she said. "I am Ana, Bernard's wife. Let me offer you something to drink. It's a warm day."

With the sea breezes flowing through the house I felt refreshed and invigorated. "You have a wonderful home," I said, hoping my voice didn't betray my envy or awe.

"It's just the summer house," said Bernard lightly, "but we like it."

I tried to not roll my eyes. Summer house? I could happily sit and watch the storms, and even thoroughly enjoy the rain, in such a place. It was pretty much as close to a dream house as I could imagine. I tried to stop noticing it and focused my attention on the matter at hand. This was made even more difficult when we all settled at a huge circular scrubbed-wood table beside the open doors, with the sounds of seagulls and the surf to mesmerize me.

Gathering myself, I noticed that Ana seemed to be a good deal younger than Bernard, whom I judged to be in his mid-sixties. She looked to be about my age—late forties—but her skin was tight, her firm throat told me she'd never been overweight, and her hair was lustrous. She wasn't tanned like Bernard, but had a honey glow about her. I tried not to be jealous of my gracious hostess and her house.

While nibbling on cashews, we drank icy beers as she and her husband marveled at Jonas's work. I enjoyed seeing the painting in full sunshine too, and, as I looked, I gasped aloud. I can't help it sometimes.

The de Klerks didn't notice my gasp, but Bud did, and raised his eyebrows in query.

I leaned in and whispered to him, mumbling as Ana and Bernard exchanged admiring remarks about Jonas's talent. "Look at the girl's face in the picture. It's a young Hannah. I didn't notice before." Bud squinted, then his face showed he could see it too.

"Do you like it?" I asked our hosts.

The couple turned to face us. Ana's expression was one of amazement and delight. Bernard looked puzzled and a little concerned. Having spotted Hannah in the picture, I thought I knew why.

"It's so beautiful," said Ana. "It will be like having our own masterpiece."

"It's very . . . Jonas," said Bernard, obviously not wild about having himself and his first wife depicted in a setting that spoke of love, courtship, and the efforts of a young man to get a young woman interested in him—and maybe drunk as well. I wondered if he'd accept the picture, and judged that his wife's reaction would make it difficult for him to do otherwise. Would the second wife recognize the first wife? Indeed, *was* Ana his second wife?

"Is that Loes with you in the painting?" asked Ana. "Loes was Bernard's wife before me," she explained, as if she'd read my mind. "She died," she added. "Bernard and I met some time later. We've only been married for a year."

Eager to find a point of connection, I said, "Bud and I married at the end of last year."

Ana leaned over and flung her arms around as much of me as she could, hugging me. "It's wonderful to be a newlywed, don't you think?" She beamed. I smiled and agreed. "And look at us all, so long in the tooth. To have found love at our ages? We are so lucky. Were you divorced, Bud?"

Bud shook his head. "My wife also died." I didn't think they'd noticed the slight pause before he said "died," and I knew he'd rather not recount the tragic tale of Jan's murder when she was mistaken for him by an idiot gang-banger, so I said nothing.

"I'm sorry for your loss, and I understand it," said Bernard. "Congratulations to you both as well. I think all this calls for something better than Amstel. Ana?"

Ana ran lightly to the giant, restaurant-style refrigerator and pulled out a bottle of champagne plus four chilled glasses. Unless that was their normal, everyday way of life, I decided they'd been planning to celebrate the arrival of the pictures. Or maybe something else?

Popping the cork and pouring, Bernard said, "The other piece is beautiful too. In a different way, of course. Jonas had a wicked sense of humor. I recognize this as *Still Life with a Fish* painted in 1647 by the wonderful Dutch artist Pieter Claesz. They have it at the Rijksmuseum. But look at how Jonas has perfectly used the style of Dali to make the composition a real work of surreal art. How about we keep that one here, Ana, and take the other to the city house? It would suit that place more than this. It would work well on the top landing."

"But we never use that part of the house; we'd hardly ever see it," replied his wife with a playful pout. Was Bernard trying to hide it away?

"It would get great light up there, from the roof windows."

After "*Prost*" and "To Jonas" all round, Ana sipped her drink thoughtfully. "You're right. The light would be good. But the light's good on that wall too. We could keep it here."

She turned to me, her lean, toned, honeyed legs effortlessly curled beneath her on the whitewashed wooden chair, and added, "We come here in the winter too. We like to watch the storms while we snuggle in front of the fire." She glanced toward a massive fireplace with a carved wooden mantel that dominated the sitting-room part of the open area. "We have people to visit here more often than in Amsterdam. It would be fun to let everyone see it, then work out that you're in it. They would all assume it's a print. One of those clever ones on canvas. Then they'd see it for what it really is."

Bernard didn't reply, though his intelligent eyes regarded Bud and me. I suspected he was wondering if we knew about Hannah, or had recognized her. He hadn't offered up the information that she was the woman in the painting, which I found fascinating.

With this omission in mind, I decided it was time to see if I could help Bud in his quest for insights to pass to his mom in a practical way, so I waded in with, "Bud and I have been hoping to learn about his uncle from you and your fellow members of the Group of Seven to pass on to Jonas's sister. She never heard from him after he left his family in 1946. We understand you were the last to join the Group. Was it your joining that allowed the title to arise?" It seemed like an obvious question, Greta's claim to having allowed the name to be coined having puzzled me.

Bernard smiled. "No. I didn't meet up with them until 1963. It had been the Group of Seven before I joined, though they had lost one member some time before I met Jonas."

This was the first we'd heard of a lost member, and I immediately wondered if this might be the man in the photographs and portraits we'd found, so I followed the lead.

"How did they 'lose' a member, exactly?"

"I think he died in a boating accident on one of the canals. He was called . . ." Bernard looked toward the plaster-decorated ceiling for inspiration, ". . . that's it—Charlie."

"Is this him?" I asked, pulling the photograph of the unknown man from my handbag.

Bernard looked at the photo, then shook his head. "I don't think it can be. I gather Charlie was of African heritage. Dutch, but black. Jazz trumpet player, and an artist too. They often talked about how they missed Charlie's playing when we'd all get together for a drink or two. Seems he used to entertain everyone back in the fifties. I think he died in the late fifties or early sixties. But don't quote me on that."

"It's interesting that the Group lost a member to a drowning," I mused. "Tom Thomson, the Canadian artist, drowned too. Though he wasn't really one of *that* Group of Seven—because they didn't properly form as a group until after his death—he was certainly influential."

"Of course, you are Canadians," replied Bernard. "Yes, Jonas liked the work of Edwin Holgate, who was of the Ten, not Seven, Group. You know what I mean?"

I replied, "He was one of three artists invited to join the original Seven. I have to admit I like Lawren Harris's style the most. We have a print of a piece by him, and one of a Tom Thomson too. We even have a couple of limited-edition prints signed by A.J. Casson himself."

"We do?" asked Bud. "Where?"

"Spare bedroom, with the Brangwyn panels."

Bernard looked surprised. "You must have a large home to accommodate anything by Frank Brangwyn."

I grinned. "Ha! Yes, we have a few small-scale prints of some of the panels he painted that hang in the Brangwyn Hall in Swansea. It's where I'm from originally."

"Jonas went there," said Bernard, surprising both Bud and me.

"When?" asked Bud. Simultaneously, I asked, "Why?"

Bernard smiled easily as Bud and I grinned at each other. "I do not know when exactly; I can't recall. I believe the early seventies," said Bernard. "He traveled a great deal, always following in his beloved Vincent's footsteps. He went to London to see the house where Van Gogh lived."

"87 Hackford Road, just off the Brixton Road in Stockwell," I said. Bernard raised his glass to me. "I used to live close by, and passed it often on my journey to an advertising and PR agency where I worked in Soho, London. It was a sadly dilapidated house back then, and it's in a pretty poor area. I recall it was a local postman who worked out exactly where Vincent van Gogh had once lived. He'd done a lot of research by 1971, and they placed a blue plaque on the house in 1974.

It must have been the seventies when Jonas went there, and, if he was as fanatical as you suggest, most likely in '74, when the address was made known to the public."

"I expect someone with money will buy the house and take it in hand," said Ana. "Everything associated with Vincent is gold. Like sunflowers."

I didn't want to get sidetracked. "There's a thought, Bud. Perhaps I even saw your uncle Jonas on the streets of Swansea and didn't know it," I said wistfully. "Was Jonas a fan of Frank Brangwyn's work, Bernard?"

Our host shrugged again—the action suited what I judged to be a laconic nature. "Although he spoke of his work, and told me he'd been to see the panels of which you speak, I only knew of his great affection for all things Dutch. Maybe he saw something in Brangwyn's work that delighted him. It's grand—even the small pieces. That's what he said about Vincent—his work was huge, even when it was small. Vermeer, Rembrandt, Hals too. These were his idols."

I felt suddenly close to Jonas, and could imagine him admiring the massive panels I'd grown up seeing. "What was Jonas like, Bernard? We're desperate to know."

Bernard relaxed back into his chair. "He was a complicated man, yet lived a simple life. I met him at a concert at the Bimhuis, in 1963. It was almost completely dark, extremely noisy, full of people smoking all sorts of things, and we fell on top of each other at the bar."

"You—drinking? How unusual," said Ana laughing.

"We weren't drunk—then," grinned Bernard, "though we got that way later in the night. He was welcoming. He was with Willem Weenix and Dirk van der Hoeven. By the early hours of the morning we were all like best friends—you know how it goes. We met again a few nights later, by arrangement that time, at a brown café. That's where I met Hannah. She did some modeling for our group, and worked at a bar. I suppose it's not surprising that I was attracted to her. She was a lovely girl, but we were too young. We should not have married. We both realized it wouldn't work, so we moved on. I . . . I moved on by leaving school and didn't return to the Group for a couple of years."

I was interested to hear Bernard's take on the failed marriage, but at least it was clear that Ana knew about Hannah.

"Hannah and Ana, with Loes in the middle," said Ana. "That's funny, I always think."

"So you had an interest in art at that time too?" Bud pressed.

"I was at school studying chemistry. I didn't want to be a chemist, but it was my father's profession, so I followed him. I enjoyed the precision of the processes involved, but I never saw any way I'd ever be able to do anything but be stuck in a laboratory all my life. I wanted to draw, but I knew I didn't have a truly artistic ability, so I am glad I became a draftsman—I was better at that than I would ever have been as a chemist."

"I expect you've worked on some fascinating projects since the seventies," I said. "So much has been built hereabouts since then."

"Indeed," replied Bernard with enthusiasm.

"He worked on the renovation of the Van Gogh Museum, didn't you, and he also worked on the original building that opened in 1973, right?" Ana swelled with pride as she spoke. "This year has been big for the Netherlands—we have a new monarch, and all our best museums and galleries are open again. It is like a spring for the country. We need the tourists, and now they will come again."

"That must have been quite something, to work on the original Van Gogh building back in the day, and then on the more recent changes," said Bud. "I guess Uncle Jonas was jealous of your involvement."

Bernard shook his head. "He was never a jealous man. He was happy for me, and pleased that there would be a Van Gogh Museum. He was a great supporter of the idea. Even before it first opened he applied to work there, and he did so for almost twenty years."

"I can imagine him caressing the paintings at night, when everyone had gone home for the day," I said.

Bernard raised his eyebrows. "I'm not an expert, but Jonas worked security long enough to know how to get around most things. Maybe touching the paintings would be something he would do . . . when no one was looking."

"Was he rule-breaker?" asked Bud.

Bernard gave the question some thought as his wife poured him an inch of champagne. "I think Bernard was a man for whom the normal rules did not apply. He observed those he thought correct, and ignored those he thought wrong. He was a moral man, except when he chose to be immoral. He was an ethical man, except when ethics got in the way of his obsessions. He lived simply, except when he chose to indulge himself."

"A man of contradictions?" I asked. "We are all that."

"True," replied Bernard thoughtfully. "That is what a psychologist would say. What do you do for a living, Cait?"

I grinned. "I'm a psychologist. Well spotted. You remained a draftsman all your career?"

"He still is," said Ana. "He will not retire. Though we have more than enough money to live well, he insists upon choosing projects to work on. Do you still work, Bud?" Bud shook his head. "Then speak to my husband and tell him how good it is to be at leisure."

"I'm not sure about 'at leisure'," replied Bud. "Cait and I moved into a new house—well, a house that is new for us—less than a year ago, so I am rather busy working on that."

"You are traveling now, together. That must be fun," said Ana.

"You're right," said Bud, "it is fun to see new places and people. Do you two travel much?"

Ana snorted. It reminded me of Ebba, and why we were there. "Not enough," she said. Her smile disappeared, just as the sun vanished behind a cloud. The mood in the room shifted perceptibly.

"So far all I can tell my mother is her brother grew up to be a man of contradictions, with an obsession for art, and a few good friends who shared that love with him. Did he ever speak to you about his early life in Sweden, Bernard? Anything at all?" Bud sounded desperate.

Bernard shook his head. "I didn't even know he was Swedish. It never came up. His accent was that of a Dutch man. I had no reason at all to suspect that he was born and raised anywhere but the Netherlands. If he wasn't Dutch, why would he have performed his National Service, his *dienstplicht*, after all? We all tried to get out of it—or at least put it off as long as we could. But they got us in the end. No one would pretend to be Dutch, knowing they'd have to serve. Of course, if he hadn't, they'd never have all met."

I gave myself a moment to let what Bernard had said sink in. Bud looked puzzled.

"Of course," I said, "conscription in the Netherlands didn't stop until—what?—1992 was when they stopped calling men up, I believe. And although it's still on the books—so they can re-enact it whenever they like—the Dutch government ended the whole process four years later. I suppose you served, Bernard?"

The man looked resigned. "We all did. Of course, some studied until they were too old—which was what my father had planned for me. I decided I would rather do it when Hannah and I separated. To get it over with. My father didn't agree. He tried to get me discharged on medical grounds even then. Many people did—and it often worked, especially in the later years. Back in the fifties, sixties, and seventies they used the conscripts for all sorts of projects. Tasks were not purely military, and many conscientious objectors took the option of volunteer service instead."

"You said Jonas wouldn't have met the other members of the Group without having done his service?" I pressed.

Bernard spoke casually. "It's where I believe they all met. Not Greta, of course, because women were never conscripted—and she certainly would have avoided it if they had. But the others? Army buddies."

"You're the first person to mention this, Bernard," said Bud. "I'll be honest and say the notion hadn't occurred to me that my uncle had served with the Dutch military for—what? A couple of years?" Bernard nodded. "Why wouldn't the others we've met have been open about how the Group formed? Were they open about it with you?"

Bernard looked somewhat taken aback by Bud's passion, and sat a little more upright. He looked uncomfortable. "I didn't mean to speak improperly. I think they were all at the same camp, at the same time. They found they all enjoyed art, and kept that link going after they finished their service. To be honest, no, they never spoke of those times. In fact, thinking about it, I recall they were quite . . . secretive is not the word, but they didn't mention it at all. None of those 'didn't we have a great time when we were serving in the army' stories, that sort of thing." Bernard emptied his glass. "That's not normal, when you think about it, is it? All old soldiers have stories, even if they never went to war."

"They do," I agreed. I was trying to do some quick calculations in my head to work out when it was most likely that Jonas and the Group members had been conscripted. 1950-ish? I knew all Dutch men were registered when they were seventeen and could be told to report from age eighteen onwards. Of course, I didn't know when Jonas had "become" Dutch. What I did know was that this was a whole new area of investigation for Bud and me.

"Thanks for that," said Bud quietly. "Do you happen to know where, or when, my uncle served?"

Bernard shook his head. "As I said, it never was discussed in detail, though 1950 was mentioned. I only know what little I do because Jonas told me about their meeting when he was extremely drunk—and I was less so." He flashed a grin at his wife. "It's a night I shall not easily forget. He was crying. I don't know why. It was a hot night, in the summer. Possibly around this time of year. We had been drinking all day, and it was well past midnight. I would say it was in the late seventies. I can't be more accurate than that. Something had reached his heart and made him sad. He wanted to be held, like a child. It was the night he spoke to me about loss. I hadn't felt real loss then—I was too young. No one I loved had died. Jonas talked about loss in a way I couldn't understand. Now that I know he left behind his Swedish family, it makes more sense. I remember he told me he was haunted by someone. I don't think he was clear about who, or why." Bernard shifted in his chair. "Jonas was not without his demons, Bud. His birthmark?" We nodded. "He did a good job of pretending not to notice how people looked at him, but he always knew they did. Sometimes, in bars after a lot of drinking, he would thrust his face into another man's and dare him to take a good look. He could be aggressive about it."

"We've heard about his temper from Pieter van Boxtel," I said, "and we've seen the scar Jonas made on Pieter's face."

Bernard looked puzzled. "Jonas gave Pieter his scar? I never knew that."

The dynamics within the Group of Seven were becoming more interesting by the minute. For a group of people who were supposed to be close friends with a shared passion for art, they were now beginning to look more like a bunch of old army buddies with a fair few secrets. I decided to ask one more key question.

"When you and Jonas were close, did you ever find out how he managed to have enough money to buy the house he lived in—and enough to lend to Hannah for her to buy her bar?"

Bernard sat bolt upright and looked annoyed. "He told me he inherited the house—which cannot be correct. I see that now. I did not know he had given money to Hannah for anything. I thought he allowed her to live in his home cheaply because she ran a good place for him to drink, and to use almost as a second home. It was where he spent most of his days, when he wasn't sleeping or painting. I knew he loaned Willem money to buy his shop, however."

"Is there anything else he told you when you two were alone?" I added, trying to get something useful for Bud.

"Yes. You are making me peel back the years, and I am remembering. On the night I was telling you about earlier—the one when he also told me about his national service—I recall him speaking about the paintings Van Gogh did of the baby Marcelle Roulin. Do you know them?"

I nodded. "He did several."

I dare say my dislike for the paintings showed on my face a little, because Bernard said, "I hope the baby wasn't as ugly as Van Gogh made it look. Jonas only noted it must have been difficult to paint a baby, because they squirm so much when they are held. I couldn't imagine Jonas knowing how it felt to hold a baby at all, and that was the only time he said anything to me about children. It was something like, 'You have to really love a baby to be prepared to do anything with it, including holding it. They are wriggly little creatures, and they grow up to be snot-nosed little tattletales.' Something like that. Not word for word, of course. Then he cried a great deal. I wonder now if he was speaking of your mother. Though the tattle tale thing isn't particularly flattering, I suppose."

Bud didn't respond, so I did. "Thanks, Bernard. Anything is better than nothing. We were hoping you'd be our best chance for insights into Jonas and his life. Willem Weenix's daughter Els told us you were the youngest of the Group, and probably would remember most. We met with Greta van Burken at lunchtime and she wasn't at all helpful. In fact, she declined the two-artist piece Jonas had picked out for her, so we took it back to his studio. It was a rendering of Caravaggio's

Salome with the Head of St. John the Baptist in the style of Botticelli. Quite beautiful." I wondered how he'd react.

"Ha! Great idea for a gift for that woman. Sounds just like her to turn her nose up at a good piece like that. Probably thought it was too much of a novelty to be given wall space," said Bernard. "I don't know why she ever joined the Group, and I could never fathom why anyone put up with her. But I was the last, and the youngest, and when I joined I was always aware of . . . something, some sort of bond they all had that I never really understood. The Group meetings ran out of steam about fifteen years or so after I joined them. Everyone kept in touch, of course, and there were half-hearted get-togethers. Everyone had a family or a career by then, so it was just Jonas, his wonderful talent, and me as a final hanger-on, I suppose. It was fun while it lasted, though. When the Group did meet, we'd all take our painting supplies and sit in a park, or off on a dyke, or even in a bar or facing a restaurant, and sketch, draw, and paint for hours. Peace would reign until the wine or the beer took effect, then we'd pack all our painting kits away and allow ourselves to talk about art instead of making it. If you want to tell your mother about her brother, Bud, tell her he pulled together, and kept together, a group of people who had little in common, that I could see, except a love of art, and he helped them keep that flame alive, and burning in their lives forever. Visiting galleries with a group of people who are knowledgeable about art, and have strong opinions about it, is incredibly stimulating. We did that a great deal too, as well as creating art. You can tell her that. It is not an unimportant thing to have done. I know my life was richer, and still is richer, because of it."

"Thanks, I appreciate that," said Bud with feeling. We could both sense it was time to go, so he added, "I'll just call our driver, who's gone off to the beach. We should leave. We have to see Johannes Akker next."

"He's just down the coast," said Ana. "He is the only one I have met—though Bernard has pointed out Greta van Burken at the

Concertgebouw when we have been there. Johannes has retired. He is much older than Bernard." She smiled indulgently at her husband. "It is the time of year when he has his grandchildren to stay. I expect you'll meet them."

"He's on his way. Five minutes," said Bud, holding up his phone.

"I wonder if I might use your loo before I leave?" I asked. Bud raised his eyebrows, indicating his unceasing surprise at the apparently poor capacity of my bladder, so I ignored him.

"Of course. I will show you," said Ana. For such a large house I was amazed, once again, at how narrow the loo cubicle was, because that's all it could be called. One thing of note within it was a tiny pen and ink drawing in sepia tones hanging on the wall. The frame was at least four times the size of the artwork, so I peered at it, going so far as to put on my specs. It was skillful; it suggested features rather than defining them, and had an unmistakable air about it.

Back at the front door, where the three had gathered I asked, "Is that a genuine Rembrandt in your downstairs loo?" As I spoke, I suspected I'd never have a chance to utter that sentence again.

Bernard smiled. "Jonas told me it was, and I chose to believe him. There's no signature, of course, but Rembrandt rarely signed his sketches or even his finished drawings. The figure resembles one of the women in his etching *Three Beggars at the Door of a House*, I admit that much, but as for if it is truly by the hand of the man himself? Who knows? It is thought that he made thousands of sketches and drawings, and many hundreds are known. But this one? Let us enjoy it for what it is. I believe it is real."

"And Jonas gave it to you. He must have thought highly of you," I said.

Bernard paused, then said, "I think he liked me. I was never a real insider in his Group, yet he treated me with generosity and kindness. I will have a great deal of joy from the paintings he has bequeathed to me. I am sorry I did not see more of him in recent years. I understand he went out less and less, and, of course, I have been busy with my life."

"And work," chimed in Ana, just as I saw Farhad appear at the car.

"Time to leave," I said. "Thanks for your hospitality and your insights into Jonas."

"I truly appreciate it," added Bud.

As we walked toward Farhad, I whispered to Bud, "The Group met in the army? That was news. Bernard was right: he might have been invited into the Group, but there was an inner door that they kept closed to him. I wonder if Johannes will be able to tell us more about this Charlie, or their time in service. We must confront him with our new knowledge."

"You know that's what they call cocaine sometimes? Charlie," said Bud, but I didn't have time to answer because Farhad opened the car door for me.

Tulip Fields Under a Summer Sun

"I WONDER IF IT'S CHANGED much," I said as we hit the road, the air conditioning blasting away the heat that had built up in the stationary car.

"Do you know Noordwijkerhout?" asked Farhad.

"Yes, sort of. I spent a couple of months there one summer peeling bulbs. I was a student at the time and it was a holiday job. Back in the eighties," I replied.

"Some of these places don't change," said Farhad, "but I think you might notice quite a bit of new development there. I hear coastal areas are more popular now. People have bought second homes, or have moved out of the more built-up areas. A lot of people work online now. More women are entering the workforce, and new technologies allow them to be at home to raise their children and work as well. It's an interesting shift in the Dutch economy."

"It was a nice place," I said to Bud and Farhad. "I liked it. It felt both rural and coastal. Lots of bulb fields, of course."

"We'll be there soon enough. If you would like to call ahead again, Mr. Anderson, it should take us about forty-five minutes, at most."

"Thanks, Farhad, I will," said Bud.

True to his word, about forty minutes later we slowed to a crawl as we approached the house as shown on Farhad's GPS. "This should be it," he said, stopping.

"Good system," I said.

"I should hope so," replied Farhad, grinning, "it's the one my girlfriend works on with the car manufacturer. She excels at her job."

"I don't know how long we'll be this time," said Bud. "No beaches here, but I'll call you, okay?"

Once again, Bud and I hauled a pair of paintings toward a front door. This time there was no path and no front garden—the large house had a proper Dutch roof, with tiles coming down to just above the front door, and was right on the street. The bright yellow door opened and we looked down to see a child of about five years of age peering up at us. My spirits fell. I'm not good with kids.

"Is your grandpa home?" asked Bud.

The child swung on the handle, looking blank.

"*Grootvader? Opa?*" I said. The child ran away screaming.

"What did you say to her—him, whatever it was. I couldn't tell, could you?"

"Long blond curls with a green T-shirt and shorts? Could be either. All I said was 'grandfather' a couple of different ways. Not my fault it ran off."

A moment later a gray-haired, bespectacled man, his stooped shoulders covered by a vivid blue cardigan—which seemed completely unnecessary given the warmth of the weather—appeared and smiled nervously. He was so red in the face that he looked as though he needed to be in shirtsleeves, and he was almost as wide around the middle as he was tall. I suddenly realized how few overweight Dutch people we'd met on our trip, and wondered if it was all the cycling that kept them trim.

"Come in, please. My granddaughter Kari called me. You were quicker than we all thought. I am Johannes. My wife, daughter, granddaughters, and their father are in the garden. Would you like to join us for something cool to drink?"

"Thanks, but I suggest we sit in here. There's no need to bother your whole family. In fact, I believe you would prefer things this way. It's you we've come to see and talk to," said Bud.

We all sat, and Bud unwrapped the pictures. Without ceremony, he just plopped the sheets off and there they were. It made a change to the rigmarole we'd been through before. "My Uncle Jonas bequeathed these to you. We are simply delivering them. When we spoke on the phone I asked if there was anything you could share with me about Jonas, because my mother wants to find out about and understand her long lost brother. Have you thought of anything? Was he kind? Good? Interested in anything other than art? Did he have a happy life?"

Johannes Akker looked a bit taken aback by Bud's bluntness, and I was too. It really wasn't like him at all. I'd seen him interview dozens of suspects with equanimity and patience over the years, but now? Bud sounded thoroughly irritated, as though trying to get through something he wanted finished. Fast.

Johannes sat opposite us looking at his portrait, which showed him as his namesake, Vermeer's *Geographer*. Despite his flabby jawline, I could tell he was grinding his teeth. His eyes flitted from the portrait, to Bud, to me, then to the two-artist piece, which was a representation of Van Gogh's *Landscape with a Carriage and Train* in the style of Cezanne.

"I loved him like a brother," he said, almost in tears. "I miss him very much."

This was the first person who'd shown any real emotion about Jonas's death; it was all the more remarkable because it was coming from a man who, apparently, hadn't been Jonas's closest friend, and who'd hardly been mentioned by any of the other Group members. Biting my tongue, I allowed Bud to take the lead, which meant he said nothing.

"I thought he was the most gifted artist I ever met. Just look at this portrait. It is a masterpiece. Every bit as good as the original. Better, because he painted it for me. It is immediately my most precious possession. And this piece? It is a miracle. See how he's mixing styles? He was such a clever man." He dabbed at his eyes with a large pocket handkerchief as the rolls of fat beneath his chin quivered.

For a man who'd spent his life working in the seemingly dry profession of transportation planning and logistics, he seemed pretty highly strung. I studied Bud watching him, certain my husband was up to something.

"Is that it?" snapped Bud. "This is at least more emotion than anyone else has displayed for a dead man they all claim was their friend for years, but you speak of nothing but his talent. What of the man himself? And what of your connection to him? You're not just upset he's dead, Johannes, you're frightened. I can tell. You're a respectable man, a father, a grandfather," continued Bud. "You don't want your family to know the truth about the Group, do you? Has word reached you that I have spent my life in law enforcement, and that Jonas knew it when he asked me to visit you all, distributing paintings as a way to meet each and every one of you?"

Johannes sagged. "Greta telephoned me. She . . . warned me you would be asking about Jonas. She told me I must not say anything."

The man gave himself up to sobbing. It appeared Bud had correctly identified the weakest link in the fence that had been built around the truth by the Group.

"What was your Group's dirty little secret, Johannes? Drugs? Porn? What?"

Johannes looked around in panic. "Please do not shout like this. My family must not hear. They must not know."

"It'll all come out," warned Bud. I'd seen him like this before, using the most forceful part of his persona to intimidate people he felt could be broken. They didn't know he would never cross the line. Poor Johannes Akker didn't know anything about him other than he was a cop, and was sitting just a few feet from his precious family. "Tell me about Charlie," said Bud ominously.

All the blood drained from Johannes Akker's face. He aged considerably in a moment. I knew he was going to come clean. "It was an accident. Honestly it was. He was very drunk. We couldn't believe it had happened again." He looked around and whispered, "He was high on drugs, too. We told him not to go, to stay and sleep it off, but he wouldn't listen. Someone should have gone after him, stopped him, but we didn't. None of us wanted to; we were having fun. We were young, you see? We didn't find out until an hour later. Greta had stayed at the party when he left, because they'd had a huge lovers' quarrel. You might call it a fight, in fact. Eventually she left to go home, and that was when when she found him. She was in a bad state when she came back to get us, and we all went to see if he was really dead, as she had told us. Sadly, there was no question about it. He was limp. His eyes staring. He wasn't injured at all, just dead. He must have overdosed; that's what we all thought at the time, and it's what I still believe happened. It was too late for him, but not for us. We argued about what to do. Jonas said we should call the police, that we couldn't do the same thing again. This time we *had* to involve the authorities, he said. But we voted, and Jonas lost. We were afraid they'd find out about the other time, you see. So we did the same again—we took all the stuff he had in his pockets, anything that could identify him, and pushed him into the water. We knew he would drift. He wouldn't be traced back to us. And afterwards . . . afterwards none of us said a word. Not to each other. Not to anyone." His whole body shuddered with sobs. I could tell one handkerchief wasn't going to be enough.

Bud's eyes glittered with triumph. "What was Charlie's full name? When did this happen, exactly?"

"Charlie de Groot. September 1957. Long ago, but it's like it was yesterday. We were so young. I know Jonas was right. We all always knew he had been. He was right the first time too."

"Tell me more about the first time," pressed Bud.

Johannes Akker looked as though he couldn't take any more, but

Bud leaned forward in his chair—an ordinary chair, in an ordinary sitting room, which felt anything but ordinary.

"All right, I'll tell you," whimpered Johannes. You'd have thought Bud had raised his hand, but all he'd done was lower his voice.

"It was 1950, the first time. And that was an accident too." He bit his lip. "We had been drinking then, also. No drugs that time. We were in the army, you see. The man who died—no, no, he was only a boy—we dared him to keep up with us. He couldn't, so we laughed at him. He stood up and drank down a whole bottle of . . . something evil. A spirit of some sort, I think. Cheap, of course. We didn't know there was anything wrong at first. We thought he was just drunk. Although we'd seen him about at our camp, we didn't really know him, but we all left the bar together in any case—brothers in arms, you understand—and we slept in a field, under the stars. When it was time for us to go back to the camp the next morning, we found he was dead. Pieter, Charlie, Dirk, and I argued with Jonas about it. He said we must be honest about it, but we disagreed. We stripped the body and threw it into a canal. We burned the boy's uniform and went back to our duties. When the lad didn't report back after leave, the officers acted as though he was a deserter. None of us ever said anything. We . . . I never heard if his body was found."

Johannes Akker seemed to have run out of tears. His ruddy complexion was ashen.

"It's what . . . it's what held us together," he added. "All through our time at the camp, and afterwards. We were bound together by it. Forever. When we all got out and returned to our civilian lives, we all felt the need to gather, even though we couldn't talk about it. It was in that way that Jonas brought us all to art. *That* became our reason for meeting up. Whenever we got together it was always as though the dead boy was with us. I . . . I didn't even know his name. He was just another young man in uniform drinking at the same bar as us that night. When Charlie died too, it was as though we were cursed."

"*You* were cursed?" I exploded. "What about the men who died? Especially the nameless boy. What about his family? Thinking he'd walked away from his responsibilities, never to return? What of the 'curse' you all placed upon them? Never knowing what had happened to him." I couldn't help but be angry because Johannes Akker wasn't showing any remorse; he was only sorry for himself, and afraid that what he'd done was about to ruin his comfortable life. I could feel myself heating up from the inside out. I looked over at Bud, who seemed utterly calm, except for his clenched fists.

"And you *all* knew about both deaths? And covered them up?" asked Bud in a frighteningly low voice.

Akker shook his head. "Willem did, because he joined us early on and, although nothing was ever said, I was sure Jonas would have told his best friend what had happened in the army. Not Bernard, though. I don't think anyone ever told him. Greta was the one who found Charlie's body, and she heard us talking about the way we'd disposed of the other one, so we had to tell her all about it. I remember that even though she was very upset that Charlie was dead—despite the falling out they'd had—she made us tell her everything. I never, ever told another soul. Until now." The old man in front of us looked pathetic, but I didn't feel pity for him; I felt pity for the dead boy he'd helped throw in a dyke decades earlier, and the dead man he'd pushed into a canal years after that.

"Thank you," said Bud, and he rose.

I followed suit; I gathered we were leaving.

"I hope you enjoy your pictures," said my husband, and we left.

Outside again, I grabbed Bud's arm.

"I'm so sorry," was all I could manage. "Your poor mother. What a mess—Jonas mixed up in two deaths. That poor, dead boy. We've got to do something, Bud."

"I know," he replied, his eyes steely in the sunlight. "I'm going to make a call before we get back in the car, Cait."

"Your friend 'John' again?"

Bud looked grim. "We've got to get to the bottom of this. It's not something I want to have to hide from my mother for the rest of her life. If Jonas spoke out against what happened, but did nothing, he was complicit." He sighed. "There was me thinking this was all about drugs. This is even worse."

"But we have to know all the facts."

"We do. Whatever it's possible to find out."

"And your contact can help?"

"I believe so. I can at least ask. I saved his life a couple of times, so he owes me. And, no, I can't tell you about it."

I stood at my husband's side while he phoned a man I suspected I'd never meet, and waited while he asked for information that would forever change his life. Our lives. I watched as he listened for a few moments, his face almost a mask. I knew he was being given information, and he didn't like what he was hearing.

Finally hanging up he said, "It's not good, Cait."

"Tell me."

"The medical records show that even if he hadn't fallen, Jonas wouldn't have lived for much longer. He'd been diagnosed with cancer, and had rejected treatment. Back in February of this year he'd been told he had maybe a year to live. That ties in with him approaching Menno with all these elaborate plans."

I could tell the news had come as a shock to Bud. "I'm sorry, my darling. I know this sounds odd, because he's dead anyway, but what you're feeling—the sorrow that he had foreknowledge of his own mortality—that's normal. It's a tough thought to process, but the fall might have saved him from a much more painful end."

Bud sighed and continued. "Jonas's body wasn't checked for toxins, just the usual pharmaceuticals. It showed he had high levels of over-the-counter painkillers in him, but nothing else. His neck was broken, as was one of his legs. There was bruising on his back, and his head had a deep gash on it. As Menno originally told us, it was ruled an accidental death. The medic who did the autopsy has now admitted my uncle's injuries could be interpreted differently. As we know, Jonas was cremated. No samples were retained. No chance to reexamine. We'll never be sure."

"Things might be clearer if we find a motive for someone wanting him dead. Or, if we can be sure there was none, that might allow us to accept his death as accidental," I said quietly.

"Do you think the deaths of Charlie de Groot and the nameless young soldier reached out and touched him now, after all these years? I wonder if the unknown man in all those photos Jonas had, and those portraits he painted, is the young guy who died."

"It can't be. There are photographs of 'our' unknown man at different ages. The soldier who died wouldn't have aged."

Bud's micro-expressions told me his mind was racing, trying to make sense of everything we'd learned—or thought we had.

"Tell you what, Bud, let's have a quiet drive back to the hotel, then a proper conversation. The car's nowhere to discuss this. I'll organize my thoughts, and we can figure out what to do next."

Bud agreed. "I'll call Farhad. I want to get back. Now." He sighed, and pulled out his phone again, shaking his head. "Poor Mom."

A Summer Evening: Hotel Room Interior

THE TRAFFIC WAS MUCH WORSE than Farhad had expected, or we had hoped. It took us almost three hours to get back to the hotel, and Bud and I were both feeling tense and frustrated by the time we tipped the courteous young Englishman and rushed toward our room.

"Let's have room service. I don't care what it is so long as it's got some sort of flavor and there's a beer or two," I announced as we entered our room.

A few minutes later I was at the little desk in the corner making notes. This time they were more cogent and useful. Before too long, Bud and I were sharing slices of pizza; pizza with extra cheese and pepperoni had been my favorite snack when Bud and I worked long into the night on cases back in BC years earlier. The flavor-memory seemed fitting, because I was pretty sure it would help me get a good grip on this case, for that was what it was.

"Shall I start?" I managed between bites. Bud smiled his agreement. "Okay. First of all, I know we've established that everyone has lied to us, and they've also tried to muddy the waters. What I've got here is the best timeline I can come up with. Look." I shoved my papers in front of Bud so he could eat and read at the same time.

1929—Jonas Samuelsson is born in Malmö (in 1933 Ebba Samuelsson is born).

1946—Jonas Samuelsson leaves Malmö.

1947—Jonas de Smet appears in Amsterdam, works at Stedelijk Museum, meets Willem Weenix, sleeps on his floor for two years—query.

1950—Jonas de Smet, Pieter van Boxtel, Dirk van der Hoeven, Johannes Akker, and Charlie de Groot meet during their national service; a young man (unknown to them) dies after a bout of drinking they shared, and they cover up his death; Willem Weenix there too—query.

1951/2—The ex-army buddies form an informal art-lovers' regular gathering for which Willem Weenix begins to steal art supplies to order.

1955—Greta van Burken joins the Group so it becomes Seven; Jonas works as a night watchman at Stedelijk Museum again.

1956—Jonas buys his house.

1957—Charlie de Groot dies; this time all six other members of the Group cover up the man's death.

1962—Willem Weenix establishes his art supply store, with money borrowed from Jonas.

1963—Bernard de Klerk meets Jonas and joins the Group.

1964—Hannah Delaney meets Jonas and the Group, marries Bernard de Klerk.

1964/1965—Hannah and Bernard separate, Hannah moves into Jonas's house, Bernard leaves Amsterdam to do his national service.

1967/1968—Bernard returns to Amsterdam and rejoins the Group.

1970—Jonas loans money to Hannah to buy a brown café.

1974/1975?—Jonas travels to the UK to visit Van Gogh's London house, and Swansea.

1980 onwards—Jonas lives in Amsterdam, continuing as a security guard; Hannah living in his house, he continues to travel to Van Gogh's haunts; as the years pass, the Group gradually drifts apart until only Jonas and Bernard remain close.

1986—Hannah loses her leg in police accident.

1991—Hannah sells her brown café.
2000 onwards—Jonas stops working at galleries and begins to lead city-wide walking tours.
2010—Dirk van der Hoeven dies of heart attack.
Early 2013—Jonas is diagnosed with terminal cancer, and puts elaborate plans in place with Menno van der Hoeven for what should happen after his death.

As I saw Bud's eyes get to the end of the list, I said, "I've noted everything we've been told, but there's at least one major issue here. Willem told us he knew Jonas almost as soon as he arrived in Amsterdam in 1948, so before they would have done their military service. Bernard seemed to believe they'd met there. What do you think? Who should we believe?"

Bud wiped his mouth with a napkin. "My experience suggests that Bernard doesn't know as much as he thinks he does. I'd say we should believe Willem on that one; he and Jonas knew each other before their military service."

"I agree, because the other problem with Bernard's theory is that Willem is a good deal older than all the rest of the Group. Wouldn't he have done his service sometime before Jonas did his?"

Bud gave the matter some thought. "Jonas was born in '29, and we're assuming he did his service when he was twenty-one. Willem is six years his senior, so would have been due to do his service during the war. Maybe that messed things up? I don't know. I reckon Bernard has it all wrong and Willem didn't serve at the same time as the others."

I agreed. "They were turbulent times, and records must have been compromised during the Nazi occupation. That could explain the difference in the ages of the men when they served, and of course we shouldn't assume they were all called up at the same time. If they were each in for a couple of years they might have only all overlapped for a few months."

"I've asked John to look into the records, and to try to find out the identities of any young men who were reported as AWOL or deserters in 1950. I was warned not to hold out too much hope for a quick response. The records for that time have not been digitized. They're all on microfiche."

Despite the seriousness of the topic I couldn't help but smile. "I feel so old. I remember when microfiche was the future."

Bud forced a wry smile. "It's like a different world, isn't it?"

We hugged, and cleared away the detritus from our hurried meal.

"The timeline highlights how little we still know about Jonas," I said, sitting on the edge of the bed. "What we now know is that he knew he was dying, and made plans to call you here to meet all the members of the Group of Seven. Perhaps he always intended them to have their own portraits, or maybe that was just a clever device to make you undertake the visits . . . I don't know. But it's worked. He sent a detective on an assignment, and we have unearthed a secret. Two *accidental* deaths were known about by a group of people who didn't report those deaths to the authorities, against your uncle's wishes."

"You think this is all about Jonas 'outing' the people in the Group who disagreed with him?"

"I understand the psychology of peer pressure. So do you. You've looked at how gangs operate—existing members make belonging look appealing; then, as soon as a person shows an interest, they suck them in and control them by making them undertake some sort of initiation that means the rest of the group immediately has something to hold over them to prevent them from leaving. That's almost what we're seeing here; the death of a man they urged to drink to excess meant most members of what became the Group had something to hold over the others. They bonded because they had to in order to keep themselves safe. Even your uncle, who might have spoken out against their actions initially, but followed through with them all nevertheless."

I paced around the bed and pressed on. "If Willem wasn't in service with the rest of them, it's possible Jonas shared the information with his best friend upon his return to Amsterdam, and then Willem became an 'insider' too. When Charlie died, they *all*, including the new member Greta, resorted to the defense they'd adopted before—clean up the body and disconnect it from the Group. Don't forget—until about the mid-seventies most of the Group had little to lose, but then they began to build careers, families. As each of them had more at risk, so they drifted apart. They didn't need to cling to each other anymore—they'd lived with their secret for so long they all trusted each other to keep it, each of them having as much as the others on the line."

"Except Jonas," said Bud, almost sadly. "He never really had as much to lose as the others, did he? No family. No business. No career. Do you think they feared him most because of that?"

"I think they might have done, which probably contributed to the fact that they all seemed to drift farthest from Jonas, but kept in touch with each other, while Jonas maintained closest contact with Bernard—the one man who knew nothing about the deaths."

"So Bernard says," interrupted Bud. "Are we taking him at his word?"

"Always the cop." I smiled. "I think we do. I read him pretty closely, Bud, and I think he told us what he believed to be the truth about the situation. Which is not to say everything he said is the truth, nor that he told us, or even knows, the full truth. He could have been fed a complete pack of lies by various people over the years. We know they all kept things from him—who's to say they didn't fabricate as well?"

Bud looked annoyed. "Jonas laid a trail of breadcrumbs for me to follow. Do you think that's what the letter hidden in the box meant? That I'd have to make tough decisions about how to act once I found out? His letter said he'd lost sight of what was right and wrong. Covering up two deaths certainly comes under the latter, I'd say."

"Remember what the letter said?" I asked.

Bud smiled. "Not word for word, but I am certain you can recite it. After all, you saw it for all of two minutes. Go on, what did it say?"

I raised a disdainful eyebrow and replied, "It said, 'You who are reading this, I have chosen you because you are of strong moral fiber and an upright person.' You're not named at all. 'You have a task ahead of you that will require you to exercise your judgment, and your sense of right and wrong. I no longer possess this ability. I lost myself many years ago in this respect. I have made decisions that were maybe foolish, but I believe I made them for the right reason.'"

Bud had listened intently. "That could relate to the deaths, certainly."

"You're right, but the next part changed the subject completely. It said, 'Art is the embodiment of culture, history, mankind's societal and moral memories. To destroy it is a sin—if sin exists. I no longer even know that. There is beauty in all art. We must look hard to see it, but it is there. Who are we to judge what is good and what is bad? We can respond to art with our hearts or our heads. I choose to respond with my heart. I have chosen, and I have acted.' For some reason Jonas chose to bring the topic of art into the letter. I suspect he was thinking about what would happen to his works after his death. I reckon this is him begging whoever is reading the letter not to simply destroy his work."

Bud looked thoughtful. "The amount of stuff he had up in that attic? It must have taken him decades to produce it all. Those paintings have been his companions for almost as long as the people they portray, I'd say. It's understandable that he wouldn't want to think of them being dumped somewhere."

"I think he emphasized that when he wrote, 'This has been my life's work.' However, I think he was referring to the cover-ups when he wrote, 'I will be judged by those left behind when I am gone. But you? I charge you with making decisions that mean you will be judged now, while you live. I am sorry I was too weak to do that myself. The journey will be long and will forever change your life. Take care about the paths you choose.' He obviously believed that whoever he'd chosen for this task would do the right thing. It's interesting that he wrote that particular letter before, it seems, he'd chosen you to be that person."

"Do you think the two deaths could be tied up with the fact that Jonas had unaccountable access to large sums of money—possibly all the time, but certainly at critical points in his life? He bought a house, had enough cash on hand to allow Willem to buy a shop and Hannah to buy a café. He traveled extensively. None of this could be expected of a man who probably worked for minimum wage—once that concept was invented—and always for little money. We know he didn't live a lavish life otherwise, but even the lifestyle he had would have demanded more funds than he could have earned."

"Blackmail? Your cop-brain always leaps to crime, eh?"

"Years of practice. And don't 'eh' me." Bud grinned.

"Blackmail's certainly a possibility. Each of the others in the Group had a good source of income—maybe not initially, but certainly as the years passed. And, as we've agreed, he had less to lose than the others. I need to do a bit of digging about on the Internet, but I think I might have an inkling of an alternative idea. If I'm right, it could explain not only how he could afford to travel, but why he did it, too."

"Other than because he felt compelled to make pilgrimages to the places Van Gogh had been?"

"Other than that."

"And you've gone off my idea of drug trafficking?" asked Bud, getting up off his edge of the bed and arching his back.

I'd sat back down, but now I matched his actions. It felt good to stretch. "I am prepared to consider the Group in the way you did—as people with a combined skill set that could prove useful in the smuggling and distribution of illicit substances, but, I have to be honest, I can't say I'd profile any of them as being in the drug business. You?"

"I've cooled on that one too. Clean records all round, as you know, with the exception of Willem, and I've met enough people mixed up with the dope trade over the years to get a feel for them. This lot? I don't think drugs. But accidental, or suspicious, deaths? I hadn't seen that one coming, so maybe I'm wrong about the drugs too. I just don't know any more, Cait. One thing's for sure: I want a face-to-face with Menno van der Hoeven to ask him what he took from Jonas's home that he 'forgot' to mention. I suggest we drop by his office in the morning."

"Before or after we have coffee with Hannah?"

Bud cursed. "I'd forgotten about that. After, I guess. We should deal with her, you're right. Funny old girl, isn't she? She deserves to pick out a painting for herself; then we can decide what to do with the rest of them."

"I wouldn't mind a bit of time to have a good look at them myself, Bud," I added. "I think that, for now, the best thing I can do—*we* can do—is brush our teeth and try to get a full night's rest. If your contact can come up with something—anything—tomorrow, that would help, and I agree we should swing by Menno's office after we've seen Hannah. That's a good plan. Oh no—hang on, it's Sunday tomorrow, so he won't be there."

"I guess it'll have to be Monday, then," said Bud with resignation. "In fact, there's not much we *can* get done tomorrow. Hang on a minute . . . if it's Saturday today, then I promised I'd phone Mom tonight. Good catch, Cait," said Bud heavily, "though I have no idea what to say." His eyes pleaded with me for support.

"Get your head to a place where she won't hear the worry in your voice, then give her the version of the truth she'll want. Say we're seeing lots of Amsterdam, the countryside, and even the coast, that we're enjoying meeting all of Jonas's old friends, and we'll have lots to tell her when we get back."

Bud smiled. "You're much better at telling me how to lie than doing it yourself."

"Trust me. I'm a psychologist." I patted his arm as I headed for the bathroom. "It's exactly what she'll want to hear from her son, and she'll have an easier day because you told her. It's a kindness, not a lie."

The Artist's Home by Daylight

BUD AND I LET OURSELVES into Jonas's house at nine fifteen the next morning. Despite the promise of another warm, cornflower-blue-skied, sunny day, the streets were much quieter than we'd experienced before, and I assumed most people were lingering over their Sunday morning breakfasts. I knew I wished I'd been able to. My sleep patterns were still all over the place, and I'd found myself relatively wide awake and ready to get going much earlier than I'd expected, so Bud and I had agreed to do just that—get going.

Jonas's house smelled even mustier than on previous visits, so the first thing we did was open all the windows on each floor. I wanted to take the time to have a good look, in daylight this time, at all of Jonas's paintings. I knew I'd need Bud's help, so we set about moving pieces around so I could see more of them at once. We organized the works into three main sections, one against each of three walls: the portraits of the unknown man, the two-artist paintings, and the remainder—the slightly altered versions of famous works Jonas had produced. The two-artist collection was by far the biggest. We spread them out against the fourth wall too, allowing me to see them better. It took awhile, and we were both quite warm by the time we'd finished, so we took a breather beside the open window at the back of the house.

Standing there quietly, overlooking the small garden to the rear of Jonas's home—just big enough to accommodate a clothesline shaped like a spider web—and the tiled roofs beyond, I mused, "It's nice here, isn't it? Relatively quiet at the back for an urban home." Bud agreed. "I'm glad we've bought a place to live out in the countryside. I like cities, but I'm happy to just visit."

"So you'd be all right with me selling this place?" said Bud quietly.

"Absolutely."

"Good, because I'm thinking it might be best. I'm not sure I want an international portfolio of rental properties to worry about."

I gave him a friendly punch, then turned my attention to the paintings. "And what about this lot?"

Bud shook his head. "I know in my heart I have to take *some* back to Canada—for Mom, and for me. Us. Let's be honest, these aren't just good, they're amazing. Even I can see that. And, of course, they were painted by my uncle. I know he's not turning out to be an angel, but he's still family. But taking the lot? It's just not practical. Do you think there's anything here you'd like to send off to your sister in Australia?"

The thought hadn't crossed my mind, so I considered it. "I'm not sure, Bud. Art's a funny old thing. For example, there are pieces here I can admire, and even call 'wonderful,' but I wouldn't want to live with them on my walls. Take that Van Gogh over there—the apple blossom one. It's amazing. It's not the same composition as the real thing, but the beauty and technique are, frankly, just as good. That said, I'm not really an 'apple blossom' sort of girl."

Bud hugged me. "Stretching the word 'girl' a bit, eh?"

I shot him down with an expertly aimed eyebrow-arch, then said, "Look, the apple blossom one is sitting beside Jonas's version of *The Dutch Proverbs* by Pieter Breugel the Elder. I admire that one too, but I couldn't live with it. Hang on a mo—is that a Breugel tree I see?"

I crossed the room and pulled out a canvas Bud had placed at the back of the pile. I could hardly believe my eyes. It was *The Hunters in the Snow*, and next to it was the wonderfully grisly *Triumph of Death*.

"I tell you what, Bud. I'd be really happy with both these pieces on our walls at home. The snow scene was another of the prints deigned suitable to be hung on the walls of my old school back in Wales, and

I adore it. It'll also make me smile when I look at it and see the way he's depicted people playing hockey on the farthest frozen pond."

Bud joined me beside the piece and peered at it. "So he did. Yeah, then, okay, that's a keeper. I'll pretend they're the Canucks winning the Stanley Cup."

We both laughed at that one.

"Maybe Jonas cheered for Sweden, like you do sometimes."

Bud looked wistful. "Perhaps."

"Okay, so, if that keeps you happy, and aware of how many hours we've spent talking about what art to hang where at home, why don't we both have another look at these pieces with a serious eye to what use we could make of them back in Canada. We could organize getting them shipped as they are, because the frames are wonderful too."

"Whatever you want. It won't bother me having the one with the hockey around. But that other one?" he gestured toward the corpses and cadavers in *The Triumph of Death*. "That's a bit much to have to face every day. If you hide it somewhere where I never have to see it, then that would be okay. So, yes, I'll pick out a few I like too."

"Great idea—let's do it."

As Bud and I happily pulled canvases forward so we could see everything in turn, we gradually formed a little pile in the middle of the room, leaning up against the legs of the central table. Stepping back to admire our selection I heard a terrible cracking, crunching noise. I looked down to discover that, for the third time, I'd stood on the Seurat/Klimt we'd taken to present to Marlene van der Hoeven.

Bud shook his head. "You just don't like that piece at all, do you? Determined to wreck it. I'd say the job's done now. Pass it to me, and we'll take it down to drop in the trash."

"No, I broke it, I'll dump it," I said, "besides, we'd better get down to Hannah's for coffee, or she'll think we've forgotten her. Let's leave it here for now and ask her about it. She'll know best how to dispose of it. I don't know how the recycling and garbage arrangements work here."

"Sure," said Bud heading for the top of the stairs.

A few minutes later we were at Hannah's door, which opened almost before we'd knocked. Her usually beaming face was a mess. She had a lump that would become a black eye, a split on one side of her lower lip, and she'd been crying. It was a shock to see her looking that way.

"What happened?" I almost shouted.

She tried to smile, but couldn't "Stairs. Fell. Fine," she managed in a thick voice, then she stepped inside to allow us to follow her.

Her sitting room was in disarray. Ashtrays lay about the place full of stubs, and the air was rank; dozens of beer bottles littered every surface, and I spotted a couple of half-empty bottles of Paddy Whisky on the kitchen table. LPs had been taken from their place on the shelves, removed from their covers, and lay on the floor, alongside dozens of others still in their sleeves. Hannah had either smoked and drunk enough to kill a horse since we'd left the previous day, or she'd had people to visit.

My Welsh instincts kicked in and I did what I suspect I'm genetically programmed to do—I headed for the kitchen where I began to organize making a cup of tea, and hunted about for something sweet that the woman could eat. Meanwhile Bud made Hannah sit down, and he opened every window he could reach.

A plate of lemon tarts, which I suspected were left over from our visit, and a pot of tea found their way onto Hannah's lurid coffee table, and, with Bud and me working as a team, it wasn't long before all the bottles and ashtrays were cleared, most of the LPs were back where they belonged, and the place looked a good deal cleaner, with the open windows allowing it to smell much fresher.

Hannah let us do everything. She'd zoned out, fat tears rolling down her face in silence.

Once she had a cup of tea with three sugars in her hand I decided it was time to speak to her.

"So, what happened?" I began. Her immediate reaction was to bawl. Bud handed her tissues, and we waited. Eventually she stopped sobbing long enough to sip her tea, and she even wolfed down a tartlet. I wondered when she'd last eaten; there was no evidence of any food at all in the kitchen.

Finally composed, Hannah said, "I went out after you left yesterday. I was so happy seein' meself in that lovely portrait I t'ought I'd go back to me old café and just, you know, relive a few old memories. I drop in there now and again, and I know some of the young folk what work there now, so I knew they'd look after me, like. And they did. A whole bunch of amateur rugby players from Dublin was in for the weekend for a stag do, and they was having a rare old time of it, to be sure. Said they'd come to Amsterdam for the party 'cos Dublin's full of English blokes doing the same t'ing there every weekend nowadays. They told me they'd been to the Sex Museum, but said they'd avoided the Red Light District. I didn't believe them for one minute, of course, but I played along, you know, as you do. They even bought me me supper, lovely boys. They said they'd walk me back here and I invited them in, of course. The craic was grand. But when they'd gone . . ." she started to cry again ". . . it's gone. They took me lovely picture, so they did. Wicked boys. Looked everywhere I have. It's gone."

My heart went out to the woman. Hannah had an aura about her that made you like her, and made you want to spend time with her. She'd initially struck me as a woman I could trust, and I hated to see her so unhappy. "And you fell down the stairs when?"

Hannah tried to smile again. "First thing this morning. I hadn't strapped me leg back on properly, at some point. Can't remember even takin' it off, but I know it's one of me party tricks, so it is. Might have had one too many." She managed a wink with her good eye. "Them tarts is good," she added, gesturing she'd like another. I passed her the plate, then felt my tummy rumble. I hoped she hadn't heard it. If she had, she didn't react.

"Are you two not havin' tea too?" she said, munching.

Bud and I took a cup each, and we tried to settle; this wasn't the gathering we'd expected.

Fortunately, it only took another ten minutes until it seemed Hannah was feeling quite like her old self again, so Bud and I offered to accompany her up to Jonas's studio right then for her to pick out a piece for herself. "You could choose two, if you like," I added as we set off on our mountaineering expedition. "I'm so sorry your picture has gone, but I know you like the more modern style, so let's see what's there that you fancy."

The Selection of a Piece of Art: Study

GIVEN SHE'D FALLEN DOWN HER own stairs the night before, Hannah Schmidt was surprisingly nimble, for a woman of her age, as she clambered the flights to Jonas's studio ahead of me. In fact, I had a hard time keeping up with her. It was particularly annoying that she wasn't at all out of breath when we assembled in front of Jonas's collection; the ashtrays in her place suggested she smoked a good deal. I'd given up for almost a year, but I was wheezing like an old pair of bellows.

"He's done a lot more since I was last up here," said Hannah.

I decided to call her out on that one. "You gave us the impression you'd never, or only rarely, visited Jonas in his part of the house. You went so far as to say you weren't close. Yet Bernard told us Jonas used to visit your brown café on a pretty regular basis."

Hannah looked me up and down as though I was a leftover plate of cabbage, her nose wrinkling. "And what would he know, I ask you?" she snapped. "I might have been married to the man for a couple of seconds way back when, and he and Jonas might have been as tight as ticks, but he's talking out of his you-know-what. To be sure, Jonas would come to my bar and have the odd free glass or two with me, but that was back in the days when I had the place to offer him such, and that's a long time ago now, so it is."

"That portrait he painted of you suggested that he and you were close, Hannah," I pressed. "The way you were looking him tells me there was a connection."

"Well, now, that's where you're wrong. Never sat for him for that one, I didn't. Plenty of others, many years earlier, when I had the figure and the face for it, as I know I told you. But not that portrait. I didn't t'ink it were particularly flattering in any case. Van Gogh's style didn't lend itself to flattery. Raw his people were, like everything else he put on canvas. Stars, fields, trees, skies—they're all well and good raw. People need humanity painted into 'em. Never any good at that, he weren't. Now, this stuff Jonas did," she said waving toward the piles of two-artist pieces, "this is more like it. Not done in oils, like the one he did of me, of course, but acrylic's all right for this sort of thing. They're hilarious. Very like Jonas to come up with these sorts of ideas. And none of them in clunky old frames, neither." Her face lit up as she added, "You reckon it's all right for me to take a couple?"

Bud smiled his agreement. Clapping her hands with excitement, Hannah moved toward the pile slowly, savoring every second—like a cat approaching a mouse. I couldn't help but smile as I saw her touch pieces with reverence, and move them as gently as though they were made of eggshells. She clearly respected his work, and took her time with her selection.

As Bud and I had done earlier, she pulled several pieces from the collection. In her case she lined them up along the front of the heap, and regarded them with half-closed eyes and a look of rapt concentration. Her hands on her considerable hips, she walked slowly along the line, then looked at Bud and me and said, "It's terrible hard to have to choose. These are all so good."

Hannah's thoughtful strolling had become full-on pacing. She was muttering to herself; shaking her head, she looked at Bud and said, "I can't do it. I can't choose. I'm just a useless old bat. Me head can't cope."

Bud touched her shoulder reassuringly. "You're not useless, Hannah, it's a tough choice. Tell you what, if you want all five, take them. Cait and I would be delighted to know they'll all be enjoyed and loved by someone who knew Jonas, and clearly adores his work."

Hannah stared to cry. "Oh, you're such a lovely, lovely man," she sobbed happily. "I cannot get over how lovely you are. Just like your uncle, to be sure. He was so kind to me, all my life. And now you too." Bud had run out of tissues, so he pulled some paper towels from the roll sitting on Jonas's painting table. Hannah used it to mop her face—avoiding her cuts and bruises.

Finally composing herself, she caught sight of the broken piece lying on the floor. "That would have been a nice one too, if someone hadn't broken it. See how the gold looks like the sunshine?"

I picked up the piece guiltily. "It was the one Jonas earmarked for Marlene van der Hoeven. I managed to break it a bit at her place, then I went and made it even worse when we brought it back here. To be honest, she didn't seem too keen on it, so I thought we'd just pick out another smallish one for her. She seems to have walls full of pictures as it is."

"Strange woman, that Marlene, even if I do say so meself. Always was. Dare say she always will be. Like the character of Countess Aurelia in *The Mad Woman of Chaillot*. Or maybe not; that character railed against alienation and acted to stop it. Marlene was the one who was always alienated from the rest of us. It was as though she had something to hide—something she held close to herself, and only she knew about it."

"The Countess Aurelia oversaw a mock trial, then led the men planning to redevelop her home to their deaths," I mused. "Having met Marlene, she doesn't strike me as the nemesis type."

"Never can tell with them nut-jobs," said Hannah with finality.

I fiddled with the edge of Marlene's broken picture as we spoke, and was horrified to discover the whole skin of the gold leaf Jonas had applied was beginning to peel off. Of course, I couldn't resist picking at it and, by the time Bud had gathered up the larger pieces Hannah was taking, and they had begun to make their way down the staircase, I had pulled off a good four or five square inches of Jonas's work. I rolled the metallic substance into a little ball, then noticed the thick, milky coating I'd spotted when I'd first damaged the painting was beneath the entire piece, and, through it, I thought I could make out the shape of a horse pulling a cart. Jonas must have reused canvases as Bud had suggested.

I'd missed my chance to ask Hannah's advice about disposing of it, so I plopped it back onto the floor and picked up the last of Hannah's pieces. It was pretty lightweight, largely because it had no frame, save the wooden box-like structure it shared with all the others of its type. I managed to turn it at an angle so it didn't hit the walls or trap my fingers as I made my way downstairs—extremely carefully. It was a relief to see the daylight as Hannah held open both front doors, allowing me to leave Jonas's and enter hers.

"Just put them over there," she announced airily, indicating the wall with the record collection. "I'll place them later. Don't suppose you'd fancy knocking in a few nails for me, would you, young man?" she asked Bud playfully.

Bud bowed graciously. "I'd be happy to, Hannah. I can't promise when, because Cait and I are going to take some time for ourselves today. We're going to walk the city, take in the sights, and even visit a gallery. I know we're both looking forward to a long, leisurely lunch. Can you suggest anywhere?"

"Somewhere good for lunch? In Amsterdam? On a Sunday? What do you want to eat? What do you want to see when you're eating? There's a lot of tourist places, and some better local places."

"Does the brown café you used to own do lunches?" I asked.

Hannah beamed. "Good bread, good cheese, good beers, good anyt'ing you want to eat or drink, in fact. It's plain and simple, though it's not got what most people would call a view, so you'd sit inside if you know what's good for you. You should go. It'll be grand. I'll write down all the details, and if you've got a map I'll put an *x* on it for you. I'll even phone them up and tell them to keep you a table."

I felt a bit embarrassed, and realized I'd walked Bud into a plan he might not have wanted to follow through. "No need to do that, Hannah, but I'll take the details. If we're close by, we'll check it out."

"If you're going to cover the Museumplein, you'll be close enough," replied Hannah.

Armed with a map, with an afternoon ahead of us to do as we pleased, Bud and I headed off into the now-busy streets to join the throngs of tourists. I felt a lightness in my step, and enjoyed the touch of the sun on my skin. I was already excited about visiting the Van Gogh Museum, which we'd agreed over our second cup of coffee that morning was what we'd do. I was finally going to be able to gaze at real Van Goghs rather than Jonas's interpretations.

Pictures in a Museum

I'M NOT AT ALL KEEN on the idea of a bucket list. It smacks of mortality and tends to lead people to do things with a different attitude than if they'd just planned a nice holiday. But I get it, psychologically speaking. It's like knowing what you'd do if you won the lottery, or stopping in front of the windows that have photos of homes you could never afford . . . unless you'd won the lottery. It's all about dreams. We humans like to dream about "what ifs." In many ways it's healthy, in that we each of us need, and indeed have, an inner life. But sometimes, when people are doing what they've dreamed of doing for a long time, it can turn them into selfish little monsters, as Bud and I discovered in the line as we shuffled our way toward the ticket desk at the Van Gogh Museum. It was busy, with more people wanting to enter than could be rapidly accommodated by the ticket sellers. They were doing the best they could, but that didn't stop people from moaning, annoyingly loudly, about how long the process was taking, and that they had less than two hours to "do" the whole place.

As we stood there I thought we should have booked ahead, online, but I didn't want to say anything, because we hadn't really known when we'd be able to get there, so I kept my mouth shut and shuffled along with everyone else.

I picked up, from snippets of excited conversations taking place about us, that there was some talk about a new Van Gogh having been discovered by the museum. It made me wonder about French barns and back rooms of bars, where a penniless artist might have exchanged what would now be seen as a masterpiece for a meal or a night on a straw bed during his wanderings. I wondered how Vincent, the man, would have felt about seeing his work displayed in such a fine place, and treated with such reverence. Art—it's not a field where just beauty is in the eye of the beholder; that's where the value lies, too.

Soon we were able to leave the lined-up throng to join the milling-about throng and stand, in awe, in front of the work of the man who probably produced more world-famous pieces of art in a few short years than most artists had done, or ever would do, in a lifetime. I'd been to the museum before it had been updated and modernized, and I liked the way the place had changed. It had been starkly white—almost sterile—on my last visit; now colors saturated the walls, and they'd made some laudably sympathetic choices. I liked the feeling of the place, and was glad the climate controls made the building cool and not at all humid. I wished the hordes away in my mind's eye, and allowed myself to sink into the art. Bud and I didn't talk much, and we managed—with a fair amount of patience and head-bobbing—to see everything.

A couple of hours later, with feet so sore I almost wished they'd drop off, we visited the little shop with a plan to buy a few prints for our walls back home. We weren't alone, and it only took a few minutes for us both to decide we needed to leave the chaos. Before we tried to head out, I caught a chunk of conversation between two of the women behind the cash registers; they were nattering about the news stories, which we'd missed, from that morning, and were gushing about the idea that there really was a new Van Gogh piece, and it had found its way to the gallery. They discussed how the resident experts had arrived at the place even before they had that morning—on a Sunday—and had all pored over the newly discovered piece. It seemed they were preparing for some tests to be carried out, but were arranging a press conference for that very evening, with a view to making a big announcement. It lifted my spirits to know that even people who worked at the place every day still loved, admired, and were excited by the man's work.

Bud had overheard the women gossiping too and commented,

"So they reckon they've found an undiscovered one of his paintings? How can that happen?"

"It can do, especially with an artist who was as much of a wanderer as Van Gogh. They've had a piece here for a couple of years that was bought as a real one, then declared fake by this very museum back in the early nineties, but a couple of years ago they decided they'd take another look at it. They haven't pronounced yet, so I am guessing they must be very certain of this one if they're going to appear on TV to talk about it. Unless they're just going to say they'll think about this one before they say yea or nay."

"That's probably better than constantly changing their minds."

"Technology changes. Different experts have different opinions."

"Smoke and mirrors, and hubris, if you ask me," said Bud with finality.

Outside we discovered the air wasn't as fresh as it had been in the museum. Indeed, the hazy cloud cover was making the atmosphere heavy, so we decided we'd head straight to Hannah's old café for some much-needed refreshment. The walk across the open green space of the Museumplein was a good way to stretch our legs, and it was fun to cross the canal bridge, enjoy the slightly cooler air that came up from the water, then head down a little street toward the unknown. The Marie Café was exactly where Hannah had said it would be, although we might have missed it if we hadn't been looking for it; for all intents and purposes it was a narrow-fronted house. Only a small sign—and the bustle of people around it—signified anything out of the ordinary. Inside, it was like another world.

Dark wood covered the walls, floors, and beamed ceiling, where the wood was etched with deep carvings. So many bodies were packed into a small space that it was difficult to move, and there were little tables around the outer edges, allowing for folks to stand in the rest of the space. It was a bit of a zoo, and I wondered about the choice we'd made. I was already imagining the freshness of a cold beer sliding down my throat, so we wriggled our way to the bar, which sported a forest of beer taps. I grabbed a beer list and was dazzled; there were over 150 to choose from, ranging from the pretty standard Amstel, Hoegaarden, and Heineken, to wonderful brands like Kwak and Brugse Zot. It seemed they specialized in Dutch and Belgian brews. I wasn't up to making a difficult choice, so I shouted out, "Two Hoegaarden whites," at the nearest barman.

I was taken aback when he said, "Are you Bud and Cait?" We nodded. He jerked his head toward a narrow staircase. "Go up, there's a table for you. Order up there," then he turned his attention to a tall young woman with the hair and profile of an Afghan Hound.

Bud and I struggled through the sea of warm bodies to the stairs, then up them. "If this place was built in 1643 as it says outside, it seems the Dutch have always preferred their staircases like this—narrow and steep," said Bud once we'd reached the top.

The babble of the downstairs bar reached us a little, but we found ourselves in an oasis—albeit a brown one. About two-thirds the size of the lower floor, this upper level was full of tables, with no standing room. A young girl came from behind the bar to greet us and showed us to the only empty table in the place. Curious looks followed our progress. I wondered how privileged we were, and suspected it was a rarity for two obvious tourists to be seated where we were, which was by far the best table in the place, at a window, in the quietest corner.

I ordered our beers again, and Bud and I finally settled. It was a treat. Surrounded by history, our heads full of art, we were about to have a lovely lunch in a unique setting.

Our chatter was all about what we'd seen at the museum, and our surroundings. Bud chose a steak with fries, while I opted for a quiche that had the most tender pastry I'd ever tasted and a filling of smoked ham, several cheeses, and light, moist, mousse-like egg. The fries that accompanied it were perfect—thin, crisp, fluffy, and served with mayonnaise. Bud almost inhaled his thinly sliced steak, with perfect cross-hatched grill-marks, and happily dunked his fries in the mayonnaise like a local. The beer slipped down, and soon we began to relax our shoulders, and even laugh. It was as though everything we'd experienced since our arrival concerning Jonas was fading into the background, and we were able to be just us, with no mysteries to solve, no family death to come to terms with, and no possibility of police intervention in anything we were doing.

It didn't last, of course. We'd both finished our food and were just contemplating trying a third different beer each, when Bud's phone rang, and we were snapped back to reality.

My heart sank as his face clouded. He didn't say much, which meant it wasn't good news. My smiling, carefree husband had disappeared by the time he put his phone away, and grim-faced Bud, the retired law enforcer, was looking at me.

"Go on then, tell me," I said.

"Willem Weenix's shop was broken into in the early hours of this morning. His daughter called the cops when she heard the disturbance below her bedroom. They got there pretty quickly, and, although some damage was done, only a cash box was taken. The event led to a medical emergency for Willem, and he was rushed to the hospital. He died before dawn. Heart. Too much for him on top of the stroke he'd had. My contact was informed because of the digging he'd been doing into Willem. Word's come down through him that the daughter wants to see us. Her father told her something before he died that he wanted us to know. My guy says there's going to be a big get-together at Willem's place tomorrow. Sounds like a gathering of what's left of the Group of Seven. We're invited. He'd like to be invited too."

I reached across the table and took Bud's hands in mine. "That's sad. I liked the twinkle in Willem's eyes."

"It's a great shame, certainly," replied Bud gloomily, "but there's more."

"Go on."

"His daughter told the people who answered her emergency call she thought someone had come to kill her father. My guy said the report was that she was terrified when she phoned and was screaming 'They've come to kill my father because of the paintings.' He's passing this on to me because he's curious—deeply curious—about exactly how what we're up to might be linked to a break-in that led, albeit indirectly, to a death. I think we should have a sit-down with him this evening, and take him through everything."

I leaned in. "What's his real name? Your secret squirrel contact, 'John.'"

"John Silver. And before you ask, yes, he's really quite tall. So no jokes. He's heard them all before."

I grinned. "John Silver? And he's tall? Oh, come off it."

"I kid you not."

"Okay then, 'Long' John Silver it is. Where will we meet him, and when?"

"Our hotel, 7:00 PM."

I looked at my watch. "It's gone three now—we should head back. I could do with freshening up, and I wouldn't mind a bit of quiet time to do some thinking about all this—before we do the talking. You okay with that?"

Bud smiled warmly. "Let me settle up, and we'll make a move. It'll take a while to walk back in any case." He waved his arm toward the girl behind the bar who shot over to us. "Could we have the check, please?"

"No."

"Pardon?"

"There is no check. You were here as Hannah's friends, so you are here as our guests. It has been our pleasure."

Bud and I blustered a bit, but there was no arguing with her, so we left as graciously as we could, leaving a good tip behind us, and banking some wonderful memories.

Dream Time: A Study in Silence

BY THE TIME WE GOT back to the hotel the heat was like a rubbery wet blanket that we couldn't throw off. My head was beginning to throb—a sure sign of a thunderstorm approaching—and all I wanted to do was have a cool shower. Bud and I took turns using the bathroom, and we both ended up sitting on the bed wearing waffled white robes, with our feet up, and the air conditioning on full blast.

"There's something we're missing, Cait," said Bud. "I know we've uncovered a reason for the Group forming and having to stick together, but there's more. I know it, you know it, but I can't put my finger on it."

"Yes. I know I've learned things I can't put together the right way. There's something on the edge of my consciousness, but I can't grasp it. What I'd like to do is use my wakeful dreaming technique. I think it could help. Can you bear with me while I do that—you know it can take me quite some time."

Bud sat up and said, "Of course I can put up with it—all you do is sit there, or lie there, completely silent, and think. It's hardly much for me to put up with. Do you think it might help?"

"I really do. I need to allow everything I've experienced since we got here to swirl about in my mind, then settle into its own patterns. I need to not think about it—so I might look like I'm thinking about it, but wakeful dreaming is almost anti-thinking. It's the process of allowing perceptions to tell me their own story without my interpreting anything."

Bud shook his head. "I still don't get it. I don't get how *not* thinking about something helps."

"It's like when you can't remember someone's name when you meet them, then it comes back to you later when you're *not* thinking about it. Our brains work in strange ways, Bud, and I know you know that."

"Yours does," mugged Bud.

"Thank you. I'll remind you of that after I've given this all some non-thought and have new, fresh insights. Come on, move over and give me some room."

Bud wriggled away a little and I settled my body into a comfy position, then closed my eyes and began to conjure nothingness.

I hear laughing—loud belly laughs. I look up and see a figure that is both Hannah and Willem all at once. Her body, his face, then her face and his body, then her face then the body of *The Laughing Cavalier*—but this is a real body, and it's shaking with mirth. Its arm points at me as it covers its face with its other hand, then it pulls off its face, and Jonas is grinning at me. I look away. Jonas/Hannah/Willem is pointing to something behind me. I turn to see Hannah running away, her long brown hair blowing in the wind. She twirls as she runs, joyfully dragging her hands along the tops of the swaying ears of corn that wave about her. She is young and old; she is beautiful, but crying that she is ugly. I hear the Beatles singing "Eleanor Rigby." She melts to become an extremely ugly baby who offers me a plate of cookies and says, "They're special" in a deep voice that turns into a howl of agony. The baby drops the plate, runs away from me, and bounces down a ladder-like flight of stairs that is suddenly gaping below us. The baby rolls, unharmed, and starts to giggle. "You'll never catch me," it calls in a Swedish accent. It lands on a pile of white, waxy corpses. They are dripping with water and weeds. The baby is gone. The bodies are gone, but I know they were Jonas, Willem, Charlie, Dirk, and the young soldier—a mass of limbs, but no faces.

I look up, because the gaping hole is still there and I don't like how it makes me feel. Above me, sitting in a chariot pulled by flying peacocks, is Greta van Burken. She's waving a giant hat pin that transforms into a giant paintbrush and is shouting to the birds to fly higher, fly faster, because she is late for an appointment. Suddenly a figure swoops down; it's Jonas, his face burning with a purple flame, his eyes glowing like coals. He pulls Greta out of her chariot and takes her seat. She plummets into the darkness below me. He takes her paintbrush and touches the peacocks with it. They transform into pigs, and start snuffling their noses in the ground next to me, snorting and smelling of the barnyard.

Marty joins them. His tail is wagging, and he's sniffing the pigs rather than the ground. He looks up at me, begging for a treat, but I show him my empty hands. From nowhere he drops a sparkling crystal at my feet, smiling. His head turns. Someone is calling him, though I cannot hear anything. He's anxious to leave me, but first he puts his paw into my hand. I see it's not his paw at all, but a box made of pure gold that's glittering in the sunlight, which I cannot see. I open the box, but it's empty; weighs nothing in my hand. The gold falls away and I see that the box is made of butterfly wings, which shimmer and gleam with myriad colors. The box disintegrates in my hand, and I feel cross that I've been so clumsy.

"Come, come," shouts a voice. I look around and see a row of men, hundreds of them in a line, all wearing clothes covered in paint. Jonas runs along the line and touches each head. As he makes contact with them, each one explodes into a shower of colored powder, until the air is all used up and all that is left is color. Through the colors a figure is approaching. As it draws closer, I realize it is the man I have seen in Jonas's photographs and portraits. The Unknown Man. He is smiling a broad smile. He comes close to my ear and I know he's about to whisper his name, but he's gone. What remains is the smell and heat of a thousand flashbulbs. I try to see him through the colors, but all I can see are rows and rows of perfect tulips, waving in a non-existent breeze.

Jonas is right in front of me again. His face is so close to mine that I reach out to touch his birthmark. The purple stain starts to peel off his face. I panic, and try to press it back on again, but there's nothing to press against—he's dissolved, and in his place is a little girl, crying, holding a doll with a purple face, and asking for her mommy. I reach down to comfort her, but she throws the doll at my head, screaming that she'll never forgive me. I turn toward the sound of a bell ringing in the distance. It's a church bell, mournful and discomforting. A coffin appears. It's being carried by Johannes, Pieter, Dirk, Jonas. A man I somehow know is Charlie leads the party. He is at the front, playing a trumpet, which sounds like a bell. The casket passes me. Jonas turns to me as he walks by and says, "I dream the paintings—they come to me in dreams, like this." As the funeral procession moves away, I see that Jonas has grown antlers, which he swats off his head onto the ground. Just before they disappear into the darkness, the lid of the coffin lifts and Mona Lisa sits up smiling and waving. "I'm off on my travels," she shouts happily. "I hate Paris," she adds, then lies down in the coffin again.

An alarm bell rings. Its loud, frantic peals are all around me. I clap my hands to my ears. My head hurts. Menno appears and the noise stops. He is holding a glass jar. Inside it is a book. "I have it now, it is safe," he says, handing me the jar. The glass of the jar breaks in my hands and the book flies away like a bird, screaming like a crow as it goes. It's a terrible sound—it's the sound of real human misery, grown men and children wailing of loss.

"Cait, Cait, you're crying. Come on, Wife, come out of it."

I opened my eyes and took some tissues from Bud. "How long?" I asked.

"Almost an hour. I kept a close eye on you but, if your face was anything to go by, you were 'seeing' some pretty unpleasant, or at least puzzling, things. You okay? I worry about you when you do this, you know."

I sat up. "I'm fine. I saw a lot, and quite a few things make more sense now. In fact, I'm really glad we're going to be talking to your John Silver, because I think he can be of real use to us tomorrow, and we can be to him. I've been looking forward to meeting him—this man whose life you saved."

Bud smiled gently. "He's a good man. I think you'll like him. I do."

"Is he Dutch?"

Bud shook his head. "English, I believe. We never discussed it. I was here on a fact-finding mission, not for social chatter."

"How on earth did you end up in situations where his life was at risk, twice, on a 'fact-finding' mission?" I was puzzled, and somewhat alarmed.

Bud hugged me to his side. "So much always depends on the sort of facts you're trying to find. That's all behind me now, and I am free to wallow in married bliss, and leave those days of gang logistics, hierarchies, and hit lists behind."

I hugged him back. I didn't like the sound of "hit lists," and was glad he was in my arms, not chasing drug dealers, or gunrunners, around the back streets of Amsterdam.

"I'd like us to take your guy over to Jonas's place this evening. If we're meeting him here, let's not hang about too long—let's get over to the studio and show him what's there."

Bud sighed. "I guess I'm gonna have to wait for you to tell me what you've come up with until you tell him, right?"

"Yep—I need to get ready to go. Look at the time."

Bud did, then I flew into hyperactive mode—we only had fifteen minutes to get down to reception to meet the mysterious Mr. Silver. I could hardly wait.

An Agent of the Law: A Portrait in Shadows

I EASILY SPOTTED JOHN SILVER in the lobby of our hotel. Leaning against a dimly lit wall, he looked like an ordinary tourist whose height seemed to disappear, so innocuous was his manner of dress and general appearance. If I'd been profiling him across a room, I might have guessed at his being a doctor, a veterinarian, or an academic. He had a professional air, but no swagger. A middle-aged man with wire-rimmed specs, not much gray hair, khaki pants, a blue open-necked shirt, and shoes that, being of woven leather, marked him out as at least European, not North American. As we approached him, I noted his body type was neither skinny nor heavyset. This was a man who worked hard to not stand out anywhere.

"A pleasure to meet you, Cait," he said with a voice that was mid-range in pitch and level. A polite handshake followed. He grasped Bud's extended hand with both of his, and I noticed a genuine warmth in the men's greeting of each other.

"Been a few years," said Bud. "You haven't changed a bit." He slapped John on the back.

"Neither have you, except you've dropped a few pounds," replied the man, smiling.

Bud patted his tummy. "Fewer late-night meals on the go. Now I'm home to eat properly, not just shoving stuff into my face whenever I can."

"Not easy, you're right. Want to talk here, or . . . ?"

"We thought we'd take you to my uncle's studio. It's private. And

Cait wants to show you—well, she won't tell me what, so I'll let her surprise us both when we get there."

John looked me up and down. "Must be interesting being married to the psychologist who courts controversy. Professor Cait Morgan is well spoken of in certain circles." He bowed his head toward me.

Feeling quite proud, I replied, "Thank you. Of course, until this trip I had never heard of you, and Bud only told me of your existence a little while ago. If we head off to Jonas's house, you two can catch up along the way, and we can all pat each other on the back when I've done some explaining. How about that—business first, then pleasure?"

"A woman after my own heart," smiled John Silver as we made our way to the doors.

"She can't have yours, she's already got mine," quipped Bud, who had a spring in his step that I hadn't seen in several years. It did my heart good to see him with a colleague again—I knew he missed his friends from the force a great deal, but he hadn't wanted to mix with them at all since his retirement. He felt he'd let everyone down by leaving, but we'd both known it was the right thing for him to do.

When we got to Jonas's, Hannah opened her door before we could get in. I hugged her warm, round shoulders and thanked her for making all the arrangements for our luncheon. As Bud and John went upstairs, I allowed the aging woman to bathe in my enthusiasm for the café that had once been hers, and praised her choice of such a beautiful, historic place. Despite her split lip, she managed to beam as I spoke, and I, once again, warmed to her.

"I've not quite made up me mind where I want all those pictures hung yet, so tell your man he's off the hook for tonight," she said, laughing at her own little pun.

We swapped phone numbers so she could get in touch with me directly when she was ready, then I labored up the stairs to the attic, ready for what I knew would be some interesting conversations.

The room was still bright enough for us to not need to light the candles, but, when I finally arrived, I could see that Bud had removed the bricks from the wall and was showing John the place where the box had been hidden.

"Cait spotted it," he was saying with pride, "but it makes me think Menno van der Hoeven wasn't as honest as he could have been with us. I think he neglected to pass on a vital piece of information that I believe my uncle would have wanted me to have—otherwise, without that lucky break, we'd never have found the box. And I'm pretty sure Jonas meant us to. Ah, Cait, there you are. Come on, let's get this done."

There was only one chair, plus the tatty chaise, in the room, so I sat on the wide window ledge. It wasn't terribly comfy, but it meant I could look down at Bud and John and study their faces as I spoke, whereas I was in silhouette. I noticed that John tried to angle his seat to get a better look at me, but I hoped it wouldn't work. I needed this man, who still carried some sort of badge, to do what I asked, and I felt that a position of psychological superiority might help me convince him to do so.

"Let me start by telling you I know almost nothing about you, John, which I am sure is how you and Bud would like it to remain. I have deduced you're in active service, probably working for an international agency, or at least liaising with one or more of them. You must somehow be connected with international crime in some way. Thanks for getting us the information about the medical records pertaining to the deaths of Dirk van der Hoeven, Jonas de Smet, and now Willem Weenix. Did you manage to find out anything more about the death of Charlie—or Charles—de Groot?"

John glanced at Bud with a knowing smirk. "All business, this one. Good choice, Bud." I heard Bud's sharp intake of breath.

I don't like being spoken of as an object, and decided to nip this "old boys" thing in the bud. "We chose each other, John. On first meeting, you struck me as someone who would understand that. But is it your upbringing in the countryside of the West Midlands, your attendance at public school, or your military service that's given you this idea that women are happy to be spoken of as something to be picked off a shelf by a man at will?"

Seconds of silence passed. John sat more upright on the shabby chaise. "You've accurately read my accent, and the changes it underwent, as well as my general bearing, Cait," he said. There was an edge to his voice that hadn't existed earlier. "I've read your papers on victim profiling. They've proved useful in certain quarters. I know Bud's retired, but we're always on the lookout for people who might want to . . . spread their wings, shall we say?"

My body wanted to stand, but I told it to remain seated. "So this is a job interview for a position in which I have no interest?" I kept my voice as level as I could manage.

"Doors close, windows open," John replied. Bud shifted uneasily in his chair. "I understand there are some departmental changes afoot at your place of employment. And you have no tenure."

"Universities are prone to such realignments," I said. "I trust my qualifications, published works, and teaching record will stand me in good stead."

"Maybe they will," was his patronizing reply.

Bud's eyes darted between John and me. I could tell things weren't going quite as he'd planned or hoped. "We should return to the matter in hand. If we're going to be prepared for the gathering at the art supply store tomorrow, we'd better focus," he suggested.

John beamed at Bud and allowed the warmth to reenter his voice. "You're right, of course, Bud. So, where do we start? With the recent accidental deaths, or with those from previous decades?"

"Charlie de Groot. Did he die of an overdose, as we've been led to believe, or . . . ?" Bud left the alternatives unspoken.

John's jaw tightened. "Sorry, Bud. Not an overdose. He was stuffed to the gills with all sorts of mood-changing substances, and he suffered severe head injuries, but neither of those things killed him. The head injuries were all post-mortem and likely the result of him banging along the sides of the canals for a day or so before they hauled his body out of the water. There was no water in his lungs, so he was definitely dead before he went into the water. What killed him was a series of sharp-trauma injuries in and around his heart, made by an unidentified, and certainly not discovered, long, very thin object. They opened a file on the case, but never got anywhere. It seems Charlie de Groot was quite a sociable fellow—and most of those he mixed with were about as talkative as an abomination of Trappist monks."

Bud looked puzzled. I stepped up. "An 'abomination' is the collective noun for monks. It refers to the older 'an abominable sight of monks,' and possibly began in the sixteenth century during the dissolution of the monasteries under Henry VIII."

John stared, round-eyed, for a second or two, then continued. "As you say. What it all boils down to is that the cops were overwhelmed with brief, uninformative statements. The case is still, technically, open. I hate to say it, but your uncle played a part in a cover-up of a murder."

Bud and I exchanged a horrified look. "That's one of the things I was afraid of," said Bud. "That Charlie's death wasn't because of an overdose, or that one or both of the 'bodies' Jonas helped dispose of wasn't dead, and he and his cronies ended up unwittingly killing someone. It's a real risk when people don't call the cops and try to hide things. Thanks, John. It's terrible news, but I guess it helps, in a way, to know at least that much of the truth." The men exchanged a significant look. I stood and lit the candles, because the light of the day had all but gone.

"Yes, thanks, John," I said, retaking my perch. "Have you had any luck regarding a young soldier who 'deserted' in 1950 yet?"

"Not yet. I'll keep you informed."

"Thanks," said Bud quietly.

"If there's nothing more we can do about that part of the mystery, should we move on to these paintings?" I asked.

"The paintings?" said Bud sounding puzzled.

"Bud, you've seen and heard everything I have, and I know you both have a good deal more knowledge than I do about smuggling rings. Let me show you something you might not have fully appreciated."

I walked across the attic to the spot where the broken Seurat/Klimt picture lay, mangled and forlorn. Both men joined me. I picked up the piece, turned it over, pulled the back of the box frame away from the broken edging, and held the entire structure up to the flame, so the candlelight could dance through the canvas.

Both men let out a little sound of surprise, and I knew from that moment on that John Silver would likely do as I asked of him, without too many questions. It was an excellent feeling.

A Gathering of Old Friends and Colleagues

WILLEM WEENIX'S DAUGHTER ELS HAD asked us to arrive at the family's store at 11:00 AM. It had been a late night for all of us. John Silver had taken on the most impressive and onerous workload. Having now met the man, I had no doubt he would have completed his tasks.

Neither Bud nor I had packed clothes for our Amsterdam trip that were suitable for a memorial gathering, so we picked out what looked least jolly and headed off to the shop.

We were early. The glass door of the store was boarded over—a result of the break-in, no doubt—and a sign had been placed in one of the windows telling potential customers the shop would not reopen until further notice. Curtains had been closed behind the items in the window. Els and Ebba greeted us quietly, with three kisses each. They both looked drawn.

A semi-circle of chairs had been arranged facing the staircase at the back of the shop, and the alcove beneath it. Els had placed *The Laughing Cavalier* portrait of her father there, draped with black cloth. It made for an imposing sight.

Gradually the others arrived. Each was greeted by the grieving women and took a seat in the mournful space. Any conversation was muted, and old friends greeted each other warmly, but with sorrowful faces.

Greta van Burken was late, which I'd expected. All the other people at the memorial, even Bud and I had elected to wear somber clothing, but Greta presented herself in the sort of outfit that suggested she was off to a garden party; her wide-brimmed straw hat was decorated with sunflowers. On this occasion her hat pin sported a large, ceramic cornflower on its end. She was even wearing lace gloves, suggesting to me that she didn't want to touch anything or anyone, which I suspected she would feel to be beneath her.

Red-eyed, Els and Ebba stood on either side of Willem's portrait. Els fingered a damp handkerchief, and her daughter's loving glances toward her mother showed concern and her own grief at the loss of her grandfather.

"Where's Willem? Willem should be here. He's such a good dancer. I hope he comes soon." Everyone turned to look at Marlene as she leapt from her seat and began to fuss.

Menno answered his mother weakly, "Mama, Willem is dead; that's why we're all here. To remember him."

Marlene van der Hoeven stood still and took in her surroundings for what I suspected was the first time. "Of course he is," she said. "Look, there he is, smiling," she pointed at the painting. "I'll miss him so much," she added, then began to cry, her son's comforting arms around her, guiding her back to her seat.

Els also began to sob. "We'll all miss him, and that's why I wanted you all to be here, together, so we could acknowledge that. And . . ." she paused and looked at her daughter, seeking support, it seemed, ". . . because I wanted to tell you all something. Before he died, my father told me some terrible secrets. Secrets that involve you. Secrets he'd kept to himself almost his whole life. Secrets that frightened him."

Els had everyone's attention. I watched the faces in the room; a few looked more than a little apprehensive. Johannes Akker's wife began to cry, stroking her husband's arm. They knew what was coming.

"My father told me about the cover-up of the death of a young man with whom most of you served in the army, and he also helped to conceal the fact that one of your group, Charlie de Groot, died in suspicious circumstances."

Menno van der Hoeven leapt to his feet. "No one say anything. Not a word. Anything you say could get you into trouble—and not just because you are in a room with a retired police officer." He stared at Bud, his face red. "I am a lawyer. I can speak to you alone about this matter. I understand what the law in the Netherlands says about possible crimes of the past. Do not speak. I say Willem lied. Say no more."

Els looked shocked. "Menno, how can you say this? My father would not lie about this, not when he knew he was close to death."

Consoling his mother, who looked utterly confused, Menno replied, "I have said what I will say. That is the end of it. I advise no one to respond to what you have announced."

I watched everyone's reactions. My gaze fell upon Bud. We exchanged a look that conveyed a great deal of understanding and dread, and I stood, ready to play my part in what we both knew was about to unfold.

Abstract: Resolved

THE SINGLE ELECTRIC FAN ELS had set up in the corner of the shop provided nothing in the way of refreshment—it was doing little but moving heavy, hot air around the place, and it thrummed annoyingly. I noticed the creaking of old chairs as people turned to look at me with surprise.

"I think you might all want to take Menno's advice," I began, "and stick to it while I speak. Els, Ebba, you might want to sit down. I'm afraid what you found out about Willem isn't the last discovery you'll make about him, and this might not be what you want to hear right now, but it's high time *everything* came out into the open."

I walked to the front of our little gathering, and stood with my back to the painting of Willem Weenix as *The Laughing Cavalier*. I gave myself a moment to take in the scene before me, and mentally pictured what John Silver would be doing at Jonas's house at that moment. It would all be over in a matter of hours—for Bud and me, at least. For everyone else it was the belated arrival at the end of a journey upon which they had all agreed to travel together, knowing it might come to this.

"When Bud and I arrived in Amsterdam," I began, "we knew we were following the wishes of his late, and only recently 'discovered,' uncle, Jonas Samuelsson, or, as you knew him, Jonas de Smet. We came here because Jonas wanted it that way. We did his bidding, and we have, for the most part, I believe, fulfilled his wishes. I'd like to tell you about him. The real Jonas, that is. He was the eldest son of Bud's grandparents, a big brother to Bud's mother. He was born at a time when Europe was about to be torn apart by war. He had a noticeable birthmark on his face. I believe these circumstances led to his growing up with a specific sense of right and wrong. His character was molded by an overbearing father, frustration at being subjugated at home, and being bullied by his peers because of his appearance. On top of all this, his young life was terrorized by the Nazis, who shaped the world in which he lived during his most formative years. Jonas found his escape in the art he discovered in the pages of the illustrated volumes his young sister recalled as being his constant companions. By the time he arrived in Amsterdam and began to live his life here, Jonas's temperament was uneven. He was given to violent outbursts, often as a result of having drunk too much; he was a solitary as well as social drinker, so those outbursts might have been quite frequent. In his own way, he was controlling—as witnessed by the fact that so many of you followed his lead toward art. Even Bud and I followed his detailed instructions after his death. He probably traded on how his disfigurement made people feel differently about him than if he hadn't had it; sympathy, curiosity, revulsion, and guilt can lead to a complex set of responses when it comes to personal relationships."

"Jonas was a complicated man," said Bernard softly. "Though I'm not sure he was as you portray him."

"He had a vicious temper on him," said Pieter. "I should know. He scarred me for life in one of his outbursts."

"Indeed he did," I said. "I realize you might not want to respond when I put certain facts to you, but you should at least listen. In 1950, Jonas was serving his conscription service with you, Johannes, and Pieter, as well as the late Charlie de Groot and Dirk van der Hoeven. A riotous bout of drinking led to the death of a young soldier, who, as a group, you decided to strip and dump in a canal, escaping any difficult questions that might have been asked by either the military or civilian police."

Only Ana and Bernard de Klerk reacted, with a sharp intake of breath each. Their eyes wide with astonishment, they looked aghast at both men.

"I have been told Jonas spoke out against this course of action at the time, but was voted down. It's understandable that you panicked and reacted too quickly to a situation you weren't able to properly judge, given the amount of drinking you had done, and your general youth and inexperience. But the fact remains: you did what you did, and, somewhere, a family never knew what happened to that young man. Bud has put wheels in motion that will hopefully reveal the man's identity, and establish whether his remains were ever found. It might take time, and it would be a good deal faster if we knew his name." I paused, but no one volunteered any information.

"Upon returning to Amsterdam after his service, I believe Jonas shared this story with his best friend, Willem Weenix, and six men were bonded by the knowledge of the death of another. Under the direction of Jonas, they struggled to make lives for themselves in post-war Holland, each in their own field, and Jonas used his passion for art to bring the Group together at regular intervals. Maybe you all really enjoyed the art to begin with, but Jonas used his force of character to keep you together as the years passed; he held the moral high ground, giving him leverage over you all. When you two became lovers, Greta, Jonas invited you to join the Group. Then, when Charlie de Groot was found dead in the street, and none of you wanted to be connected to a probable drug overdose, you were all forever further bound by your involvement in disguising a death that was at best suspicious."

"You do not know what you are speaking of," said Greta haughtily. Johannes Akker sobbed aloud. Greta turned to him and sneered, "Weakling. Control yourself."

"It's too late for him to do that," I said. Greta guessed what I meant, and the color drained from her face.

"Youth leads to folly," she said.

"Not always," I replied, "and in any case, when Charlie died you were all old enough to be aware of what you were doing. A few years later, the 'gap' in the Group of Seven was filled by Bernard, who brought new spirit to the art-loving activities of the Group. As more years passed, careers and families were built and developed. You drifted apart, but the threads that always held you together were your complicity in hiding the deaths of two men."

I waited for a couple of seconds. I sensed a certain relief in the room, which was what I'd expected. I looked over at Bud, who had his phone in his hand. The lighted screen told me he'd just read a text. His grim expression drove me forward.

"Jonas had set out our instructions in great detail and entrusted them to Menno, son of his late good friend, Dirk van der Hoeven." I bowed my head in acknowledgment of the lawyer, and he returned my action. "About six months ago, Jonas was diagnosed with terminal cancer. He declined treatment and began to set his affairs in order. Hannah, you mentioned he was clearing out his home during that time, and I think that's understandable. Menno, he came to you with various packages, and instructions for you to follow upon his death. The medical examination of his remains suggests it truly was a fall that killed him, but we will never know exactly why he stumbled at the top of a flight of stairs he'd used thousands of times. However, given the facts at our disposal, I think it's safe to say his was an accidental death. But that's not what Marlene thought, was it Menno? Your mother said she thought both her husband and Jonas were killed by people who were trying to get their hands on 'paintings,' something you said yourself when you called the emergency services the other night, when this shop was broken into, Els."

"Well, of course that's what I said. I thought someone was breaking in to steal the paintings here," said Els sharply.

"But you don't have any paintings here. Only the ones Bud and I brought from Jonas's home. Unless you have a collection of old masters on the walls in your living quarters upstairs?"

"We have some excellent pieces up there," snapped the grieving woman. "My father was a collector of sorts. I assumed that was what anyone breaking in would be trying to steal, because who would want to steal a selection of prints or our stock of brushes, paints, and canvases?"

"Exactly," I replied. "No one *would* want them. But they might want the cash you're likely to keep on the premises at the end of a busy weekend at the height of the tourist season, and this store isn't exactly modern when it comes to security measures, is it? The glass at the front provided an easy point of entry, and the thieves hoped to get away with a cash box."

The distraught woman looked surprised. "That's exactly what they took, though how they knew where we kept it—under the stairs—is a mystery."

"Not much of one, Els. That glass front door that they broke allows anyone to peer inside and see what you do with the cash at the end of the day. Being overwhelmed by your father's heart attack means you probably haven't thought too much about the robbery. Let's not make more of it than it was: a common smash and grab. Unfortunately, your father's heart couldn't stand the stress. We're all terribly sorry for your loss, Els, Ebba. Sometimes bad things happen to good people, and you are two innocents whose lives have been forever changed by the actions of criminally minded strangers." The mother and daughter exchanged mournful glances.

"Unfortunately, others here will find their lives impacted by the actions of those they love and thought they knew. You see, the big question in my mind was, 'Why did a group of adults collude to hide the death of their good friend?' It's puzzling. It's not beyond reason to understand the half-baked actions of a few irresponsible, drunken army lads, but for six mature men and women to roll the body of a man with whom they'd had a close relationship over years into the canal? Why would *you* do that? The answer had to be that you didn't want to come into contact with the police because of Charlie's death, which you thought was due to his taking too many drugs. I reasoned that it might have been because you'd been enjoying a night when you'd indulged in illegal narcotics too, and didn't want that known, but then I had to consider that it might be something more. And that's where Bud's experience came into play."

All eyes turned toward Bud, who shifted uncomfortably on his seat for a moment, then returned peoples' curious looks with a professional air.

I pushed on. "Els mentioned that her father wasn't keen on the cops, and Greta, you were kind enough to share your disdain for my husband's profession in a particularly personal way. Thank you for that, because your reaction was instrumental in helping me get to the bottom of all of this." It was Greta's turn to be on the receiving end of dagger-looks.

"Bud knows cops often experience a generally negative public reaction to their doing their job. In this instance I allowed my inner profiler to work through the reasons that might be beyond the natural desire to not have a fledgling career blighted by a drug bust. Bud's last post, before he retired, allowed him to gain a deep understanding of how drug-dealing organizations work across global markets, and he spoke of how your Group of Seven was amply supplied with people in the sorts of positions and professions that would help in that type of undertaking."

"A bit of use in the privacy of our own homes isn't the same as being international drugrunners," said Pieter loftily. "There's no proof that any of us have done anything like that."

I looked directly at the man who'd challenged me. "I agree. No proof at all. And even when one considers that we have a group made up of Pieter the money man, Johannes the transport man, Greta the greaser of political and police hands, and two marvelous channels for importing, exporting, and distributing the goods—this very store, and your father's antiques' business, Menno—neither Bud nor I could peg *any* of you as drug traffickers."

"Good," snapped Greta. "We are not."

"I know," I replied. "But you *are* a ring of international stolen and forged art smugglers. And we've got you all for that. Thanks to Jonas and Johannes."

"I didn't say anything," said Johannes to his friends, quaking. His wife looked at him with disbelief.

"Shut up," snapped Menno. "I told you all, shut up!" His voice was much higher than usual, the apples of his cheeks pink.

The electric fan hummed and whirred. I could hear the tocking of what must have been an extremely large, old clock somewhere. I waited, then pounced.

"My work as a profiler means I make decisions based upon observations, experience, and the best theories and hypotheses available. It's my job to look, to see, to understand, to infer, and then, whenever possible, test my theories. A long time ago, I decided to put my skills to work on victims rather than perpetrators. I consider how their life has been lived, and in what ways that life might have intersected with whoever caused them to become a victim in the first place. I turned those processes toward the investigation Jonas de Smet sent us to carry out: a journey to reveal his co-conspirators and bring them to justice. I believe when he discovered he was dying he took the tumultuous emotion he'd held inside him throughout his life and turned it, spitefully, upon all of you. His actions have brought you into the spotlight of the law, and there's no cover-up possible. There is no escape."

Els leaned forward in her chair. "Cait, I don't know what all this is about—but we never, ever moved stolen art through this store. I would have known about it. My father was very old; even before his stroke, I was running the place. I have done so for the better part of fifteen years. And I was on the spot for a long time before that; I've worked here since I was in my teens. I had nothing to do with stolen art. Ever." I knew she was speaking the truth, and the expression on her face bore testament to that.

"You're right. This place hasn't been used to shift merchandise for quite some time. I believe it was in the early days, back in the fifties, when all this started, and I'm afraid your father was deeply involved then, and for many years afterwards. When he opened this store in the early sixties it was to provide a legitimate business through which illicit deals could flow. By the mid-nineties, Jonas was a one-man, hands-on operator, no longer needing to use this store; walking tours allowed for the exchange of items in the street in plain sight. Once Jonas left his security jobs in the museums, he operated out in the open—quite literally."

Els's puzzled "What?" and her daughter's equally confused "Grandfather used to deal in stolen art?" led me onward.

"Els, you mentioned your father had been questioned when forged paintings turned up at flea markets and so forth. It's a reasonable assumption that a man who sells art supplies knows artists of all sorts—some of whom might not be squeaky clean. Amsterdam has always been a city of art. Galleries and museums have finally started to get their act together when it comes to security systems. Art is frequently stolen around the world. Sometimes it's as simple as a person taking a piece off a wall and walking out with it under their arm; it happens with amazing regularity, especially when pieces are displayed in commercial properties—like hotels or even corporate headquarters. The pieces might be ransomed, be returned, disappear, or be found. World-famous paintings have been stolen and have then turned up in public lavatories, outside police stations, or inside getaway cars. It's quite a phenomenon. For example, right here, in Amsterdam, in December 2002, two thieves used a ladder to climb to the roof and break into the Van Gogh Museum. In a few minutes they managed to steal two paintings, *View of the Sea at Scheveningen* and *Congregation Leaving the Reformed Church in Nuenen*, valued at $30 million. Those paintings have never been recovered—and that's just the tip of the iceberg. In 1991, two armed thieves spent forty-five minutes in the very same museum—the one where Jonas had worked for many years—selecting twenty pieces, and then left them all, inexplicably, in their getaway car. Those pieces now hang in the gallery, and Bud and I were fortunate enough to see most of them when we visited yesterday."

"We all live here. We know about these incidents. What's your point?" asked Els impatiently.

I stood aside, allowing everyone to see Willem's portrait. "Splendid, isn't it? Almost as good as the original? Of course the face is changed, and yes, Jonas has signed it. But this, and the other works Bud and I have had a chance to examine, tell us Jonas's skills were certainly equal to producing expert forgeries. I put it to you now that over the past several decades, the Group of Seven worked to orchestrate the theft of many pieces around the world, sometimes selling them on, sometimes holding them for ransom, and sometimes simply using their theft as an opportunity to sell fakes to avid buyers happy to believe they have the real painting while a fake hangs on the wall of a museum."

Ebba raised her hand. "I'm sorry to disagree, but I must. This cannot happen. I work in restoration, which means I have also studied attribution and the examination of works of art. When a painting is attributed to an artist, it is only done when it's been accepted as authentic by an entire group of experts. That's especially the case when something's been outside the controlled environment of a gallery or a museum. When pieces are recovered, they are reassessed by the experts who already know them well; they test the pigments, the canvas, the paints. They are rarely fooled."

All eyes turned to me. "This raises two issues, as you correctly identified, Ebba. The first is attribution—the agreement by the art community that a piece is definitely the work of a certain artist. The second—the assessment of the age of a piece—can help with that process. The scientific tests of which you speak can only prove a piece isn't a modern fake. Although some key tests have existed for decades, many of them required the use of quite large samples, so those tests weren't often used. However, they were sophisticated enough to prove that Han van Meegeren painted fakes in 1947. You yourself told me one of his most famous was a version of this very piece, *The Laughing Cavalier*, which has disappeared."

"You cannot be saying this is a Van Meegeren?" cried Ebba.

"No, I'm not saying that, but I am saying a young man—a talented artist like Jonas—arriving in Amsterdam in 1947, when a world-class forger was a national hero, could have seen a way to make some money. He might have plied his trade at local flea markets, selling good fakes, building up income as he spent little, sleeping on Willem's floor for years."

"There's a leap from that to forming an international art-smuggling ring," said Willem Weenix's granddaughter angrily.

"You're right. However, I am suggesting the operation began in earnest back in the early fifties, when the Group first formed, but before Greta joined. Dirk van der Hoeven was a fledgling importer and exporter of antiques, who could have acquired original, poor-quality works executed on the right age of canvas needed for the fakes. Pigments mixed from original compounds, and glazes that looked just like the real thing, could be sourced by your grandfather, through his art-supply connections. By then, it was common knowledge that

Van Meegeren had cooked his canvases in an oven to age them, and his techniques were more than adequate, if used by the right artist, to fool even avid collectors. I believe, as the years passed, Johannes's expertise in logistics planning, Pieter's ability to hide the money being made, and eventually Greta's family connections all played their part. It was a well-formed group—fit for purpose. The purpose being the enjoyment of art, yes, but not in the way you have all portrayed."

"Is she saying my Dirk was a bad man?" asked Marlene vaguely.

"Be quiet, Mama," snapped Menno. "She's talking nothing but rubbish. Everyone knows you cannot fool the experts."

A general sense of unease was growing. "Ah, but you don't always have to. Sometimes you only have to fool the questionable collectors who are prepared to pay huge sums for works of art. And, if you understand their psychology well enough, they can be pretty easy to hoodwink. They are people whose desire to own a piece is so intense, not only will they pay almost anything, but they will also keep it just for themselves, never allowing anyone else to see it. Special rooms are built, and huge safes are installed, just so the owner can enjoy their very own priceless masterpiece. Would a passionate collector scrape the paint off a Van Gogh to check that it's real when that very piece has been 'stolen to order' and then 'recovered' by the police? No. Their hubris means they *know* they have the real piece, and the great unwashed public is paying to shuffle past an excellent fake. Jonas had ample opportunity to study the real pieces when he worked in the museums and galleries here. His work could have convinced many collectors that way."

Once again Ebba raised her voice. "You can always tell a fake. There's always something that gives it away. Just a simple X-ray would show enough to give cause for concern, and it wouldn't damage the painting at all. Most well-known pieces have at least been studied this way and are known about, so you'd have to replicate everything under the paint too."

"I agree, but where are those 'known X-rays' kept? In the secure offices of the museums where Jonas was a guard. And don't forget, sometimes collectors are also happy to buy a 'newly discovered' piece too—one that has never been studied, x-rayed, or pored over by anyone. It's thought there are hundreds of lost Rembrandt sketches, for example. Who's to say if Van Gogh's comments in his letters to his brother that refer to 'several studies' of a certain subject mean just the three we know of so far, or ten more that might be adorning the walls of various homes in the regions where he lived. Jonas travelled the world, following in his idol's footsteps. He could have 'found' works in many places. He'd have intimate knowledge about locations, and all he had to do was magic up a couple of undiscovered canvases upon his return to his attic. I am guessing you all heard about the excitement at the Van Gogh Museum yesterday morning when a 'new Van Gogh' was delivered to their front doorstep? We're able to tell you the piece everyone is in such a furor about is a portrait of Hannah, painted by Jonas. He didn't sign it, but you only have to look at it to see that it's Hannah."

"My picture," said Hannah gleefully. "They've found my picture? How did it get there?"

"I expect there's an Irish rugby player or two who could answer that one for you, Hannah," I replied. "I believe your guests from the other night thought it would be a great prank—little realizing what they were about to unleash in terms of an art-world frenzy."

"Will they give it back to me?" asked Hannah hopefully.

"I should think they'd be only too glad to give it back. We'll help you out."

"So you're saying the Group helped Jonas to fake paintings, and sell them to people who thought they were buying stolen, or newly discovered, works of art?" pressed Els. "My father did this?"

"Yes."

"I don't know as much as my daughter does, but wouldn't even these greedy people get experts to look at what they were buying?"

"Indeed they would. Of course, they'd be using the services of only those few who were prepared to authenticate such illegal purchases, but even the world's best can be taken in. Indeed, Van Meegeren proved that, didn't he? Let's think about it for a moment. Who are these people who say 'Yes, this is a Van Gogh,' or 'Yes, this is a Vermeer?' Men—and they usually are men, sorry Ebba—who have studied, examined, and built their reputations upon verifying dozens of other pieces by the same artists. There were, and still are, no exams to pass, and there are no definitive qualifications for the job; those who verify art, even today, have only their reputations, built over years, to hold up as proof of their abilities. The very people who said 'Yes, it is by x' are the ones who could never, ever afford to change their opinion in the light of new techniques to 'No, it's not by x.' Remember the kerfuffle when the 'experts' changed their minds about the authenticity of a Van Gogh at the museum? Entire careers were called into question."

The people in the room I knew to be involved were all looking decidedly anxious. Even the innocent were beginning to understand that my points held weight.

"And the Group did this over many years?" asked Els weakly.

"I believe so. It was of particular interest to me that Bernard mentioned that Jonas visited at least England and Wales around 1974. That year, nineteen paintings, including works by Vermeer, were stolen from the Beit collection at Russborough House, just outside Dublin. It was a well-publicized theft, and the world breathed a sigh of relief when all the works were found, safe and sound, in a cottage in County Cork less than two weeks later. The same place was robbed again in 1986 and 2001. It seems some people never learn."

"I can see what you mean," said Ebba grudgingly. "You don't

have to go on. I understand that a scam could have worked in the way you describe."

I answered gently, "Thank you. Having got away with it for so long, and knowing he was dying, Jonas decided to blow the whistle on the art world, and you." I allowed my gaze to sweep the room. "He even wrote a book about it all, and brought Bud into the picture."

"There's a book about all this? Our names will be published?" squealed Johannes.

"Not if Menno has anything to do with it," I replied. "You took Jonas's laptop with the manuscript on it when you visited his home after his death, didn't you? Had he asked you to arrange for publication—not thinking you'd read his words before you followed his wishes? I know you went to his home. I know you removed a laptop. Did the content of his book terrify you? Show you the man your late father had really been? Did it set you off on a frenzy of activity, trying to ensure he hadn't secreted any copies of his words anywhere in his home?" I watched the lawyer carefully as I spoke to him.

He feigned nonchalance. "Jonas left me instructions to destroy his laptop, and to get rid of any copies of the book he had made. I simply did as my client requested."

"Oh, I see. You're going with that, are you? Jonas had a change of heart and asked you to clean up after him? His fridge was empty, I'll give you that, and he might well have instructed you to clear out his rubbish and so forth. I'm guessing he did *not* tell you to get rid of the manuscript, nor to read the instructions he'd written on a card pinned to his bedroom wall, giving the details of something he'd hidden. You saw the note, couldn't resist, followed the details, and discovered a box hidden in the wall of his attic, didn't you?" Menno shifted in his seat. "We saw evidence that someone had removed the bricks before we happened upon them. When we found it, it was obvious the box was meant for Bud. Jonas would have left some instructions for him about it."

"How do you know it was meant for Bud? It was just an empty box."

"And you'd only know that if you'd found it and opened it." Menno's eyes flashed with annoyance as I spoke, telling me my assumptions were correct. "So, what did you hope to find in Jonas's secret hiding place?"

Menno slumped. "I did not know. I read the note he pinned to his wall for Bud and decided to find out for myself. How did you find it? I realized when you arrived I'd forgotten to replace the instructions. They were in my coat pocket."

"A trick of the light, Menno—just a trick of the light. Like so much of this case, it was all about things not being what they seemed. An empty box with a false bottom that could only be opened by a key too big for the keyhole. A letter written in red ink, made to look like blood, confessing to bad judgment and poor choices. That on top of too many letters, clues, hints, and requests. Too much complexity—all hiding a simple truth. Jonas's travels were a cover for smuggling fake art to buyers, and to allow him to demonstrably be on the spot when art thefts were undertaken—a little 'convincer' for any buyers who wanted to be even more sure he really had arranged for works to be stolen to order for them. For quite some time the Group managed to do that job well, because, as I said, all you need to be able to successfully run such a scam is an astonishingly good artist and a group of people who could provide supplies, grease palms, smooth travel plans—oh, and a chemist. That's where you came in, wasn't it, Bernard?"

"Bernard is a draftsman," said his smiling wife confidently, "not a chemist."

"He studied chemistry at university before he offered himself up for conscription, as you know," I replied with equal confidence. "It was only after his service that he began his training as a draftsman. He'd been a member of the Group when he was still planning on following his father's footsteps to become a chemist. When he returned to Amsterdam after his military service, he was an even more popular addition because the times were changing. The sixties saw the beginning of much more widespread chemical analysis of art, and that's where Bernard's background came in handy; if curious and insistent buyers wanted tests done, Bernard's superior chemical compounds and the canvases supplied by Dirk allowed for at least age tests to turn out well."

Bernard blanched. Ana stared at him as though for the first time.

"You've all lived very well off it, haven't you? I was puzzled by how Jonas had enough money to be able to afford his own house and studio. How could he loan Willem the funds to buy this store—or should I say supply shop? And when Hannah was well established as the manager of a brown café, why not lend her the money to buy it outright? It gave Jonas a public place where he could easily agree to meet buyers, people who would carry out robberies, and even sellers of art that had already been stolen. In bars, one is used to seeing people coming and going carrying unusual packages. Jonas was the artist without whom none of it could work. He was the one who held the moral high ground over you all. When a new type of science came along, and you all had good, solid careers that could explain away your income levels, you all began to spend. Houses, genuine and expensive artworks, good clothes, family holidays, even second homes—they could all be accounted for because of your careers. I expect you did an excellent job of hiding it for people, Pieter, using your accountancy skills. Jonas was the only one who spent the income early on, and that was only to set up the system, which allowed the ring to work effectively. No one has mentioned it, but I wouldn't be surprised if he had a hand in setting up your father's business as well, Menno."

"He did," said Marlene, taking everyone by surprise. "Jonas gave Dirk the money for our wedding, our house, and the business. Dirk didn't like it. But Jonas said he would tell if we didn't do what he said. He made Dirk take the money, like he made Dirk marry me.

He was a wonderful dancer, but Dirk never loved me, and he hated you, Menno."

Menno turned to his mother. "Don't say that, Mama. He loved me, and he loved you. He was your husband, my father. Why wouldn't he love us? I told you, don't say *anything*."

"He wasn't your father. We just said he was," said Marlene placidly. Menno's mouth fell open.

"Was it Marlene that you and Jonas fought over, Pieter? Was she the woman you 'wronged?'" I asked, knowing the answer.

Pieter stared hard at Menno, his mouth wide open too. He sagged. "I never knew," he said quietly. "No one said anything."

"Dirk was a good man," said Marlene, smiling. "He took me and the baby on. You didn't. You dumped me, Pieter. I loved it when I danced with Dirk." She closed her eyes and began to hum.

Menno buried his face in his hands, shaking his head. "You're saying Pieter's my father? I can't take it," he said quietly.

"I'm afraid you have to, Menno," I said. "You made a choice to remove items from Jonas's house that could have incriminated the man you always believed to be your father in covering up the deaths of two men. You let it slip that Jonas was writing a book. You tried to cover up by suggesting it was a book about art—but I believe it was about a group of people with a secret or two."

Greta van Burken stood up. "I have listened enough. Nothing has anything to do with me. I am leaving." She sneered at me. "You are horrible and think you are so clever. You have no idea who I am. I am above this. This will not touch me. Go back to wherever you came from, and stay there. I leave now."

"Stop where you are, Greta," snarled a no-longer-sobbing Johannes. "You're not getting away with it. You're the one who made it all run more smoothly. A signature here, a blind eye turned there—your contacts allowed Jonas to work where he wanted, for as long as he needed to. He could plan how to steal the pieces, take the time to study them to be able to make the copies we could sell, and even gain access to any records, or photographs and X-rays, that could also be 'amended.' If I'm going down, you're coming too."

"And there you have it," I observed. "Exactly the attitude Jonas had when he found out he was dying. He knew it was over for him. And he wanted all of you to suffer. He also double-crossed each of you out of a great deal of money. There are many more valuable works in his attic, disguised more ironically."

"There's nothing there but his obvious copies, some of his portraits all with the same face in them, and those double-artist things," said Menno. "I looked."

"And there's the irony. You've all looked, but you haven't seen. He bequeathed each of you one of those inventive two-artist pieces, alongside your portraits. I must say his sense of humor hit the mark with his choice of pieces every time. Even more so because each of those wonderful, if thickly painted, acrylic works of art is hiding a secret. If you peel back the acrylic, there's a covering of masking fluid, then, beneath that, a masterpiece. Yours might be a sketch by Rembrandt, a small portrait by Hals, or . . . who knows? The art fraud squad has been clearing out Jonas's attic for the last hour. They've also been executing search warrants on all your homes to collect the stolen pieces Bud and I unwittingly distributed to you, and to search for other obvious 'missing' artworks. I know for a fact that I saw a lovely painting that looks exactly like Vermeer's *The Concert* on the wall of your sitting room, Marlene."

Marlene smiled at me. "The one with the women and the piano and that big man's back?" she asked. I agreed. "Jonas said he painted it for Dirk. I don't like it. I thought I might take it down and put up the nice picture of my lovely man instead. Would you like it? It's not very . . . colorful."

"Thanks, Marlene, but I think it will be gone when you get home. It was stolen from the Isabella Stewart Gardner Museum in Boston in 1990, and has never been seen since. I'm sure the experts will have fun deciding if what you have is a genuine Vermeer, or a genuine Jonas."

"That's fine. I didn't like it anyway," said Marlene.

"So he had pots of money all this time? And he was covering over masterpieces up in his attic?" asked Hannah. "And he used my brown café to do his dirty business, all the time pretendin' to be me friend?" She sounded hurt. "Blackheart! I lied for him, you know?"

"Yes, I know," I replied. "You tried to convince me you hardly knew Jonas, but you knew him very well, didn't you?" Hannah looked sheepish. "All his very expensive, if old, clothes neatly laundered and pressed, and you with a washing machine and a clothesline? You did all that for him, didn't you?" The woman made brief eye contact with me, then looked away. "I suppose you were grateful to him because he created fake paperwork so you could change your name, and live as a Dutch citizen, owning your café and living life as you chose, on your terms, without needing a man to support you."

Hannah looked tearful. "I did that," she said hoarsely. "And when I lost me leg, he begged me to keep the place on longer than I wanted to. That's why he did it, in't it? And there was me thinkin' he was doin' it because he thought it would be good for me to have an interest." She shook her head sadly. "It's true what they say. You never know a person."

"You don't," said Els quietly. "I'm sorry about your grandfather, my darling Ebba, and all of this. I'm sure it doesn't feel like it right now, but it's best for the truth to come out." She pulled her daughter close to her and wept quietly.

Greta had remained standing, and I noticed she was eyeing the door. "No point running, Greta," I said. "The police are outside, waiting for you all. They are keen to interview each one of you. This time, there's no way out. And by the way—just for you Greta—they'd like to talk to you about the death of Charles de Groot. You told your friends you'd found him dead in the street, and suggested an overdose. They accepted what you said, and helped you cover up what they believed to be a tragic, but accidental, death. But it turns out Charlie died of stab wounds to the heart. Wounds made with a long, very thin spiked instrument—rather like the hat pins I understand you've always favored. It should be an interesting time for you, explaining how the violent end of an affair with a man—witnessed by so many of your friends—coincided with the end of his life."

The only sounds in the room were of the fan droning, quiet sobbing, and my heart pounding. It was done at last.

A Summer Afternoon on the Canal

BUD AND I WATCHED THE cooling waters of the canal churn in the wake of our tourist boat, and held hands as the breeze tousled our hair.

"Hannah seemed pleased at the idea she'll be moving to a new apartment," I said to Bud.

Bud agreed. "She did. I'm happy about that at least. It's going to take a long time for the teams to work out exactly where all the profits of the ring went, but I'm thinking the properties are bound to be taken into consideration, so I don't know what they'll decide about the money Hannah made from selling the café. Not for me to guess, but we'll keep an eye on her, make sure she's taken care of somehow."

"Investigating organized crime's not my thing, as you know, but I understand it can take years. Then attribution and restitution teams get involved, too. It could go on . . . well, it might never all be resolved, I suppose."

Bud smiled. "I've cooperated in every way I can. I've handed control of everything Uncle Jonas owned to the authorities. I've even given them his ashes. There's no more I can do, so let's not worry about it, Cait. However, I still have one question," said Bud, holding me close as the boat slid beneath yet another bridge. "The guy in those photographs and portraits. He wasn't the young soldier who died, so do you have any idea who he was—or is?"

"There's an app for that," I grinned. "Come on, look straight into my phone's camera." I snapped a photograph of my husband, pressed a few buttons, then held the screen for him to see.

He looked puzzled. "That's not me, is it? It sort of looks like me, but not."

I pressed a few more buttons and showed him a second picture.

He looked even more puzzled. "Again—not quite me."

I looked at both photos and agreed with him. "You know how I hate seeing photos of myself?"

"Yeah, yeah, you're always going to lose twenty pounds, I know," grinned Bud.

I shrugged. "Well, yes, there's that, but not liking photos of oneself is really quite normal. The person we see in a photo is not the person we know, because our reflection is always reversed. A face in a photograph isn't reversed—and our brains have a bit of a problem dealing with that. But this?" I held up my screen. "This is an app that takes each half of your face in turn, then duplicates and reverses it; one shot shows you with the left half of your face, twice, the other shot with the right half of your face, twice. Each side of a face differs quite markedly from the other, and it's fascinating to see what happens when you make a whole face from a double-version of each of the two halves. Like you said, they both look a little like you, but not quite. That's what these photos are." I took the photo of the unknown man from my handbag.

I held it so Bud could see it. "Your uncle used a similar photographic technique to replicate the side of his face that was unblemished, giving him this vision of himself. He repeated the process over the years and, once he knew what he might have looked like without his birthmark, he painted that face obsessively into portrait after portrait. Didn't you notice there wasn't one single self-portrait of him as he really was? This was his vision of the person he could never be. His unblemished self."

"Maybe he should have worked harder to come up with a lifestyle that didn't involve so many moral blemishes, then," said Bud. "This is a mess, and I have no idea what I'm going to tell Mom."

"If you tell her the truth I don't think she'd be hurt or surprised," I said. "She didn't have a terribly high opinion of him. Remember she kept telling us he was bad? It looks like her childish judgment was spot on—maybe his birthmark really did contribute to forming the sort of person we saw him to be, by his actions, in later life. I have to say I also believe the choices he made were what led him along the particular road he chose, rather than just an accident of genetics, because not everyone with an obvious or unusual blemish ends up a crook. However, I think your mom would be quite happy to be proved right in her assessment of her brother. She likes to be right almost as much as I do."

Bud smiled wryly. "Dad has said, more than once, that you're a lot like Mom."

I gave it some thought. "No, I don't see it. Anyway, what's the alternative? Lie to her? Forever? That's a slippery path to tread. And we would both feel the injustice of it too keenly. I really think it has to be the truth, Bud. All of it. And we have the box for her too, don't forget that."

"The box?"

"The one Jonas hid in the wall. John Silver cleared it so we could take it back to Canada with us. I'm betting the letter *s* carved into its lid is for 'Samuelsson.' It's the sort of thing your grandmother might have used to hide any pieces of good jewelry. If it *is* what Jonas took when he left Sweden, it could have financed his journey to Amsterdam."

Bud sighed. "You're probably right. You usually are."

I hugged him. Tight.

Acknowledgments

THERE ARE SO MANY PEOPLE who have shared their love and knowledge of the Netherlands with me, and have shared time with me there too, that it's impossible to mention them all by name, but some must be thanked! To Roy—that was a long time in a tent. To Hans and Els—thanks for welcoming me into your home, and for sharing your love and intimate knowledge of Amsterdam so many times, over so many years, with such true friendship. To Emma and Menno—thanks for showing me different parts of the Netherlands, for letting me be in your lives over so many years, and for allowing me to use your names. To Loes (and remembering Lennert)—thanks for all your encouragement. Thanks, too, to everyone I've ever dragged around a gallery or museum; to have people share my love of art is to have people share my love of life.

Thanks to the person possessed of particular expertise in this field, to whom I promised anonymity, for sharing your insights into the "business" world of art. Your secrets are safe (-ish) with me.

My family has been as supportive as ever; my mother and sister listen to endless hours of storytelling, I'm not sure how my husband puts up with me sometimes, and I'm glad the dogs are happy to play when I need a break, while remaining at my feet while I type.

Thanks to you for choosing to read this book. I'm grateful to all the reviewers, booksellers, and librarians who have helped you find my work. The TouchWood Editions team has, once again, been stellar, and I'm always aware of all the "invisible" people behind the scenes, like printers, distributors, and the salesforce, who ultimately play pivotal roles in this book being where it is now—in your hands.

Welsh Canadian mystery author CATHY ACE is the creator of the Cait Morgan Mysteries, which include *The Corpse with the Silver Tongue, The Corpse with the Golden Nose, The Corpse with the Emerald Thumb, The Corpse with the Platinum Hair, The Corpse with the Sapphire Eyes,* and *The Corpse with the Diamond Hand.* Born, raised, and educated in Wales, Cathy enjoyed a successful career in marketing and training across Europe before immigrating to Vancouver, Canada, where she taught in MBA and undergraduate marketing programs at various universities. Her eclectic tastes in art, music, food, and drink have been developed during her decades of extensive travel, which she continues whenever possible. Now a full-time author, Cathy's short stories have appeared in multiple anthologies, as well as on BBC Radio 4. In 2015 she won the Bony Blithe Award for Best Canadian Light Mystery (for *The Corpse with the Platinum Hair*). She and her husband are keen gardeners who enjoy being helped out around their acreage by their green-pawed Labradors. Cathy is also the author of the WISE Enquiries Agency Mysteries. Cathy's website can be found at cathyace.com.